Ursus Major

URSUS MAJOR

by Roberta Smoodin

Alfred A. Knopf   *New York*   1980

Library of Congress Cataloging in Publication Data
Smoodin, Roberta [date]   Ursus Major.
I.   Title.
PZ4.S6642Ur   [PS3569.M647]   813'.5'4   79–22743
ISBN 0–394–50973–0

For Eric and my mother

Part One

The bear dances on the bar top with bear abandon, an animal wish to be liked, and an artist's lack of self-consciousness. Wearing a red and yellow striped clown flounce of some stiff material around his neck and shackles on his hands and feet, the bear dances the Frug, the Swim, the Freddy, the Mashed Potato, the Jerk, the Monkey, the Shuffle, and even a little of the Twist (which might strike him as a trifle too passé, because he swings his bulky body low into a sinuous Twist and comes up in an arm-waving Monkey or Swim, the Twisting no more than a bridge, a connecting part of the continuing dance: this is a sixties bear, a bear rooted in the musical tradition of the English invasion of mop-haired groups, of Chubby Checker, and of the Beach Boys, a bear unwilling to learn the new dances which frequently demand a partner). He is the only bear Ray and Joy own, and they make so little on him that they can't consider obtaining a partner, causing him to be stuck in his own particular time warp, dancing on bar tops for indifferent patrons, for dimes and nickels and all the gin and tonics Joy and Ray can drink, for stories of lost love as poignant to the bear as his lost dances, as all lost arts like illuminating manuscripts or writing operas, as winding streets lost in some new city and never found again when streetlights wane and some unknown section of town dawns upon Ray and Joy and the bear sleeping in the back of their orange Ford van. Ray played drums and Joy rode a motorcycle before they found the bear and began their unending tour, avocations they were pleased to give up in deference to the bear's greater artistic merits and to the changing of the decade, which left them feeling empty and uncertain.

A woozy drunk sitting at the bar picks at the fuzzy hair on the bear's left foot as the bear strains upward on his toes in a hip-shimmying, rope-climbing movement; the drunk seeks to make eye contact with the bear as he pulls the bear's foot hair, but the bear's neck and back arch, his brown and black eyes close, he is Dancing. Drunks are always trying to determine whether this is indeed the genuine article or only a man in a bear suit (drunks having a passion for two things: liquor and reality, the latter of which they can feel tangibly slipping away from them much as one can watch a train receding from view in a station, a loved one's hand growing smaller, smaller as it continues to wave from a train car window, the more they succumb to the charms of the former, a relationship they perceive with scientific interest and seek to pursue further in other aspects of life—the identity of a dancing bear, for example), usually by pulling on some portion of him, his hair, an ear, his black, moist nose.

"We better get him out of here," Ray murmurs, and he and Joy begin to collect the quarters, dimes, nickels scattered over the bar top, and to down the remainders of their drinks. Then Ray leaps upon the bar next to the bear and attaches a red leather leash to his clown collar. The bear stands almost motionless upon his back legs for a moment, quivering so slightly that the ringing jingling of his shackles seems the sound of faraway stars vibrating messages to one another through the empty velvet void of space; then he slumps over into his all-fours position, losing all grace of movement, his large hips jutting up and out behind his slimmer chest, his square legs leading like table supports into his bulky body.

"Thank you very much," Ray says, bowing, though none of the bar patrons looks up at him or seems to notice the bear

anymore. Even the woozy drunk, whose previous investiga-
tions into the truths of animal nature had overwhelmed the
rest of his conscious meanderings, stares down into his amber
glass as if the future lies there, revealed in glorious liquid
pessimism.

"Better get him some ice cream fast," Joy says over her
right shoulder. "He's going to be pissed." Ray follows Joy,
leading the bear by the long red leash. The bear lumbers like
a cartoon bear, raising first one side of his body, two legs,
front and back, in tandem, then setting it down with a clump,
batting and smashing the frail wooden chairs which sit empty
around the bolted-down tables of the bar, then raising the
other and lowering it, a symmetrical motion which makes his
rear end seem mounted on a spring, more amusing than
wanton. He shits on the floor of the bar just before reaching
the door. In the dim light and fetid, smoky air, the surprise
might wait for hours before discovery, but animals, unlike
people, do not feel compelled to see the outcomes of their
jokes, relish the means rather than the end, and for this are
thought to be simple.

Outside, in the dim green neon light of the bar's flickering sign, the COME BACK INN, the COME BACK INN, the COME
BACK INN, the bear stands up once more and looks at Joy and
Ray. Joy appears to be depressed, her long brown hair slightly
greasy, her face gray from road and bar grime between the
ghoulish green flashes of the sign. Ray's face seems made of
stone, of wood, of anything inanimate, unfeeling, but not of
flesh, especially in the late night city light, probably from
years of drinking and drugs, of drumming under hot lights,
the acid of his own sweat drowning the humanity out of his
face, though once he becomes aware of the bear's scrutiny he
smiles and rubs his hands together and does a little dance,
some soft-shoe routine from one of the movies of his childhood.

"Oh boy, ice cream," Ray says to the bear. "Wouldn't you
love an ice cream cone right now, big fella?" Ray wears
opulent turquoise rings on six of his ten fingers, fading Levi
pants and jacket, a wrinkled gingham cowboy shirt with pearl

snaps instead of buttons, and carries a cigarette tucked behind each ear; the bear continues to scrutinize him until Joy pulls on the leash, grabs Ray's arm, and leads both of them in the direction of their van parked down the street by an expired parking meter.

Joy starts the engine up while Ray swivels in the passenger seat to look at the bear, sprawled out on the mattress that covers the whole back of the van.

"What flavor do you want tonight, big fella? French vanilla? Remember that stupid dude who bought you some blueberry cheesecake ice cream, that real ugly purple stuff, trying to woo you away from us? Some kinda offer he made you. But you weren't uppity then like you are now."

"Lay off him, Ray," Joy warns as the bear unhooks his red and yellow clown collar, removes the false shackles from his legs. "The bear does the best he can. Now turn around and help me look for an ice cream place. These goddamned one-way streets'll drive me crazy." Ray continues to stare at the bear, however, leaning over the back of the van's front seat to watch the bear struggling with the last of his phony iron anklets. The bear puts his costume into a small wooden chest hidden under the mattress, his face inscrutable (one of the two choices when it comes to animal facial expressions, unfortunately for the bear: he can either look inscrutable, the bland stuffed-animal look which some interpret as stupid, some as cunning, some as winsome, or he can look fierce, which allows no time for interpretation because it clears the room so fast). Then he advances upon Ray while Ray continues to stare and Joy runs a red light through a deserted intersection as she watches the whole scene in the rearview mirror.

"Why don't you get a ringmaster's hat? A whip? A chair? White tie and tails? I'm sick of these gigs," the bear says, his face so close to Ray's that Ray smells the slightly sour, desirous breath of the hungry carnivore. "We're not an act. There's me, and there's you, and there's them, and I dance and you pick up the coins and buy me ice cream cones. Now that ain't no act."

"Baskin-Robbins," Joy says, "and just in time, with you guys getting it on like a couple of grubby capitalists."

"Whooooo," the bear roars, his customary ice cream roar for when he can almost feel the cold cold goop numbing the back of his tongue, the sweetness tickling his bear palate, the chocolate chips or raisins or pralines sticking in his jagged, pointy teeth, taste the brown-sugar richness of the cone.

"Now, what ya want?" Ray asks the bear over the top of the van's front seat.

"A double chocolate fudge," the bear says, "unless this is the month for bittersweet chocolate."

"I'll wait with the bear," Joy says. "Get me a cone of peach with some sprinkles, and don't take a lick until I get it."

"Right right right," Ray says as he jumps from the van. The bear and Joy watch as he steps into the cool white fluorescence of the shop, an atmosphere like gaseous ice cream, and speaks a few words to the girl in the pink striped pinafore. The bear begins to drool on the front seat Ray has vacated; Joy plays the radio loud, a station with a sixties format of Rolling Stones hits, the Righteous Brothers, the Supremes, even some Beatles. She and the bear hum along, considerably cheered by the music and by the sight of Ray dealing with the outer world with aplomb, already on his way across the midnight sidewalk with his hands full of ice cream cones, many-colored like faraway stars, like women's ear baubles, like a bouquet of new spring flowers being offered to the bear to make peace between them once more.

After ice cream, they decide to go looking for another bar in which the bear can dance.

"We haven't even made tomorrow's gas money," Joy says, looking at the red arrow on the gas gauge slowly lapping toward the big black E like a thirsty tongue. The bear already danced all day on the sidewalks and corners, in the brown-grassed parks and faded kiddie lands, in the polished shopping malls where myriad bear images reflected in the glass and chrome and in front of the blazing-signed supermarkets with the huge green and blue and yellow letters singing out the bargains inside, the circus banners, the dedicated women with high hair pushing their steel baby carriages filled with meat. The people of this city seem blasé, unconcerned, pass by the bear in crowds without looking up from newspapers; they also give little money for the bear's dancing, lots of dimes and expired bus tokens and theater ticket stubs. The bear's ecstasy and grace matter little among these people, and he winds up getting irritated, frustrated, and making huge demands upon Joy and Ray, quarts of exotic ice cream, double chocolate shakes, even a banana split. Most of the day's take has been spent keeping the bear pacified, and after that last bar, he's ready to make the break, to get out on the highway with his hairy bear thumb in the air. Joy knows this, can feel his disgruntlement, and wonders at Ray's callous attitude; after all, what would they do without the bear?

"Maybe the big fella ought to expand his act. I mean, specialization's become a thing of the past. These days, everyone's expanding and broadening. A renaissance bear, you know what I mean?" Ray says. "We could get him some boxing gloves and purple satin trunks and let him take on guys who think they're tough. People would pay to see that."

The bear's mouth twists on his face, revealing the long yellow points of his teeth. "I won't fight," the bear says, "and I won't play any more gigs tonight. You guys hustle your own gas money. I'm going to sleep."

Joy pulls the van over to the curb, then looks at Ray with contempt, her eyes narrowed to wolf slits, her mouth tight. "All right. I'm sick of this bickering. The bear deserves to get some rest. We'll have to try to dig up money somewhere," she says as Ray fiddles with the pearly snaps on his cowboy pockets, making them play a little staccato tune, a drum roll on his chest. Joy reaches under the dashboard behind the steering wheel and finds the little chamois-cloth purse from which she extracts one long yellow cigarette looking like a sickly bear tooth. She lights it, takes a couple of deep drags while the thing quivers in her mouth like a trumpet or trombone vibrating loud, clear notes (the bear can nearly hear the

high, clean tone of it, the plaintive wailing, the bliss, being a
bear tuned into the cosmic music of marijuana, a bear who
has seen *Easy Rider* in drive-ins with Joy and Ray, from the
last row where vans can park without obstructing other
viewers, where dope smokers can sit on top of their vans and
puff perfect light brown clouds up into the heavens, clouds
that sometimes create prismatic effects, building rainbows in
the air above the vans until the whole back row looks like
some unfinished Peter Max canvas waiting to become a Coca-
Cola commercial).

"Come here," Joys says to the bear, and he does. She puts
her hands on either side of his head, right below his alert
round ears, then places her whole mouth over the bear's big
black nose, and exhales until her body seems to contract, to
lose mass like a deflating balloon. She drags on the joint, then
repeats the artificial respiration procedure on the bear's nose
again and again. The bear's lungs begin to sing a high-pitched
song of contentment, and his tongue lolls out of one side of his
mouth. "Now you try to get some sleep," Joy says. "Ray and
I'll hustle up some money for tomorrow, we haven't worked
as hard as you today. Just don't get silly and decide to take a
walk or anything. You know the law. We'll see you later."
Ray scowls as he opens the van door, but Joy's look of warning
keeps him from needling the bear. They lock the van doors,
pull on them to make sure no one can get in, then stroll off
down the silver sidewalk, stingy and pale auras surrounding
them in the flickering night light of stars and street lamps
and drape-shrouded glows from mysterious apartments above.

The bear, left by himself, thinks about vague concepts
that come to him in the shapes of other beasts: dignity appears in the undergrowth of his slightly stoned brain as a doe
with downcast eyes, ambition springs from ear to ear in the
form of a sharp-toothed jackrabbit, artistic achievement soars
like a golden eagle, the sad state of animal kind, leashed and
enslaved, appears to him as a small, coiffured poodle dog.
His dreams and ideas, so bound by the parameters of nature,
reach bear heights because of his civilized state, because of

his wide travels and his knowledge of the Dance; in the con-
text of a national park, with tourists driving through to show
their children the bears, where a bear's zenith of achievement
might be pressing his nose against a Volkswagen's windshield
to create unknown comic effect for a family from Iowa, the
same animals would flit across a bear's movie-screen consciousness, but only as possible meals.

He lies down in the back of the van, stretching arms and
legs across the mattress as he would never dare do when he
has to share the space with Joy and Ray: then he is relegated
to the bottom, where he must curl up pitifully, often getting
poked in the eyes and ears by their toes. A vague melancholy
comes over him despite the luxury of aloneness. (Or because
of it? Like a wan Chihuahua left behind in the back seat of
the Pontiac while mama goes into the supermarket to buy
her itsy baby hamburger? Like a pampered Siamese boarded
at the kennel in a private room with a bath while the folks
are off in Hawaii? The bear would shudder at such analogies,
summon up inarticulate bear curses in the form of growls and
moans and shake hairy fists at his captivity, at Ray's setting
concrete face, at Joy's dank tresses.) He begins to whine without recognizing the sound of his own voice, knowing it only as
some sad part of his sadder universe, the cries escaping his
mouth like lost souls flying ghostlike into the night. Finally,
the music of his despair puts him to sleep, the midnight void
of bear dreamlessness.

The bear awakens to Joy and Ray getting into the van.
Though they make every effort to be quiet, they jingle like
the arrival of Christmas, their pockets heavy from the coins
they've collected. Ray and Joy are masters of the spare change,
able to look so down and out, so faded and wan, so much the
ghosts of the decade past that people will give away their
long-saved Kennedy half-dollars in order to avoid thinking
about what they were doing, and with whom, on December
31, 1969, the last New Year's Eve. In the middle of the night
they look especially tragic and ethereal, and theatergoers,
movie patrons, nouveaux riches waiting for red-coated valets

to fetch their Mercedes-Benzes from stacked-up parking lots, pay Joy and Ray off as readily as they pay their shrinks, and with as much gusto and good feeling: it's like paying their pasts to dry up, to disappear, to crawl into a hole and die, and they feel cleansed and healthy as Joy and Ray, greenish and gaunt in the street light, float down the street away from them, loaded down with their pirated silver.

"Whoooooo," the bear says in confusion, hoping to scare away any strange interlopers; then, realizing Joy and Ray have returned, he stretches by pushing his rear end up into the air, his chest down against the mattress, and ambles over on all fours to meet them and see if they've brought him anything, a chocolate soda, an ice cream sandwich, an Eskimo Pie.

"Hey, big fella," Ray says, holding out his hands in greeting, showing their emptiness. The bear's ears fall back against his head in disappointment. "We got a gig for you. Tomorrow night. Now go to sleep so you'll be fresh."

"Dancing?" the bear asks, sitting up on his haunches and shimmying his shoulders; his thick arms begin to snake through the air in exaggerated dance motions, his head begins to weave figure eights above his shoulders in anticipation. He's already forgotten all about ice cream.

"Sort of," Ray answers, then snatches one of the cigarettes from behind his ear and pats the many pockets on his body for a book of matches. The one he finds in the right pearl-buttoned shirt pocket comes up empty, a matchbook looking like a mouth of snaggle teeth, a wayward smile from a lifetime gumdrop chewer. The other shirt pocket yields a shiny gold matchbook from Don Pedro's, and the bear remembers California, sun and ocean, dancing in the woody, plant-filled bar with a sombrero on his head and maracas in his hands as blond women sipped Margaritas and men in lightweight business suits, Hawaiian shirts, French-cut T's threw him quarters and bits of the happy-hour snacks the bar offered patrons: tiny hot dogs wrapped in cheese, oysters on the half shell, miniature tacos. In California, the bear felt nearly human, and could walk with Joy and Ray free from the red leather leash because no policeman wanted to ticket a free-floating bear there. Blimps with neon signs on their sides hung in the air like friendly cumulus clouds, light planes crashed onto freeways and school playgrounds, women went without brassieres: the air was full of far more interesting things than six-foot-tall brown bears. People nearly bumped into him on the sidewalks because their heads were always turned to the sky, looking for UFO's or airplanes writing above the beach TAN WITH COPPERTONE.

"Don't worry about tomorrow," Ray says as he drags on his ear-dented cigarette. "It's in the bag." The bear looks at Joy, who has remained silent throughout the arrival conversation, but her face, three-quarters turned away from him and glowing like metal in the streetlight, reveals nothing. He curls up at the far end of the mattress and, a little later, feels Joy's and Ray's toes tickling his fur as they seek his hairy body for warmth: their feet are always cold, and always rest on him throughout the night.

In the morning, the bear awakes first and quietly begins to dress for the day, putting his sham shackles on arms and legs, fastening his stiff red and yellow clown collar around his furry neck. Ray takes his face out of the lumpy pillow he sleeps on and looks at the bear through the red filter of haze that covers his eyes.

"You can dress up if you want, big fella, but you don't have to work today. We're taking the day off. We'll do anything you feel like doing, it's your day."

"We can go to the zoo," Joy says as she awakens, stretching out her slender arms, her fists tight at the end of them: the bear thinks of flesh-colored ice cream cones, perhaps the flavor would be toffee, or butterscotch.

"Whoooooo," the bear says. He loves to go to zoos. Not only for the ice cream, though that's part of it. All over are ice cream vendors, men in white with small refrigerated carts in front of them, sometimes gaily striped umbrellas over them

proclaiming FUDGSICLES or FROZEN BANANAS or CHOCOLATE, VA-
NILLA, STRAWBERRY. Nickels and dimes and quarters disappear
from Joy's and Ray's pockets at the zoo, because the bear demands a constant stream of ice cream delights; he forgets his
usual manners in the excitement, and sometimes devours
whole ice cream sandwiches or Eskimo Pies in a single bite,
saliva dripping from his long bear teeth as he opens his
mouth, his pink tongue flickering once and then disappearing
like a captive cobra.

More than eating ice cream, though, he loves to see the
animals. In all of them, the majesty and the enslavement, the
regal bearing behind bars, seem to him to be worthy of study,
a kind of bear group-therapy. He studies them in the best
way he can: by his responses to them, the hair-trigger movements of his body which surprise even him, the instant crouch
when he sees the big cats, the alert ears at the sight of the
small mammals, the stock-stillness in the reptile house. He
learns about himself and his own bondage through zoos, because he's never had a life in the wilds, has grown up an
artiste, a dancing bear, without a childhood in the country,
without a doting mama bear to teach him how to fish for
salmon in a rocky river or to build a cave home to sleep in
through the winter. All he has is Joy and Ray, who taught him
how to enjoy marijuana, how to disregard the slights of
drunks, how to walk with the red leather leash leading him.
The posturings and ear quiverings inspired by a visit to the
zoo amaze him and make him feel powerful and free, if only
in some nearly unknown vestige of his bear psyche (the missing link, the small, shriveled primitive ancestral bear inside
him, the non-Dancing animal).

At the zoo (Joy and Ray pay the regular adult ticket price
for the bear, who then slips neatly through the turnstile without arousing guard suspicions) Ray looks zealous, as if with
some mission in mind: he seeks out the large plastic maps
with the YOU ARE HERE orange arrows which point out the
various attractions, lion and tiger country, the aviary, the
monkey house, the great apes, and then speaks quietly with a

guard while Joy stays with the bear a few feet away. Ray points, crosses his arms, then points in a different direction while the guard calmly explains the most direct route to something.

"You've been flimflammed. I want you to know I was against this whole thing," Joy says in a low voice, though Ray would never have heard because of his concentration on the careful instructions of the zoo guard. The bear stands very still, his senses alert, as if a mountain lion were about to spring on him from a high tree branch, as if some barely perceptible sound of peril might be audible, but only children's high-pitched voices in an impressionistic chorus of oohs and ahs fill the air which tickles the hair on the bear's ears.

"This way," Ray says, his rigid face showing great animation, a constant motion of the eyeballs, a small stretching of the mouth which is his smile. He leads them past many animal areas outside of which people cling to the barred railings like so many flies sticking to a screen door on a hot summer day, children poking their heads through the lower parts of the bars, adults holding children on their shoulders for a better look, adolescents leaning over the bars as far as they can, trying to pet the tigers, feed the monkeys, steal the prairie dogs, or show off for their girl friends. Some teenagers even teeter on the railings like high-wire artists, walking on their toes with their arms churning for balance, trying to make their ways to a better vantage point, to a point where their lives will be in greater danger, thereby proving their heroism. Ray takes them into the hinterlands of the zoo where the crowds thin, away from the most popular animals. Giant tortoises lie lazily in the sun, each blinking one eye or the other when an adventurous child tries to climb on his scaly back, and nervous antelopes hide out among the trees, peeking small shining brown muzzles out to check for safety before running for a brief drink of water. The bear, still ice cream-less and dissatisfied with this trip to the zoo, follows Ray at top speed until he sees where they are heading. Then he comes to an abrupt stop, sending Ray skidding on the concrete like an out of control car as the red leather leash snaps between them. Joy shakes her head from side to side, causing her wispy hair to fly into her eyes and cover her cheeks.

Ahead lie the bears, sitting languorously on their rumps in the sun or swimming in the moats with the most lackadaisical strokes barely propelling them through the water. Their eyes, glazed and stupid, stare out over the heads of the few people watching them, out at the clouds in the pale blue sky of afternoon, trancelike. They seem to be hardly alive lumps of ratty fur. Ray drags the bear up to the railing, skid marks left on concrete by the bear's recalcitrant feet, then ties the red leather leash around a bar so he can lean over to observe one of the swimming bears. Joy stands to one side, several feet away from both of them and, like the bears in the zoo, seems involved in her own special Buddhistic negation of the real world.

Then a previously invisible door in the imitation cave which forms a part of the bears' dwelling opens, and a blue-suited zookeeper sticks his upper body out into bear country. His face, covered by a screened mask, looks insectlike and, to the children gathered near the railings, quite humorous. They laugh and point, and interest in the bear cage heightens immediately. The masked zookeeper turns toward his audience at the railing and nods his head as he doffs his cap once; the bears watch this performance as well, a keenness coming into their eyes, an alertness of expression on the tightening mouths which have, before, been slack and drooling. All bear heads turn to the masked man. With a theatrical crinkling of paper, the zookeeper opens a blue and white gingham-check package of commercial white bread. At this, the bears in the cage snap to attention like well-trained soldiers hearing reveille: they stand up on their hind legs, the swimming bears lumber out of the moat and, shaking themselves off on their dry brothers, also stand up, and a low, humming growl comes from them in unison.

"Dinnertime," the zookeeper calls out, though his voice, from behind the mask, sounds less than human, almost as if it has been previously recorded and played and replayed many times over. He pulls one piece of squishy, light-catching white bread from the package, another cue to the bears. All the standing bears begin to clap their front paws together in simulation of a first-night audience at a new hit play: they clap and utter guttural sounds, whining requests, as the zoo-keeper flourishes the swaying piece of white bread in the air like an explorer claiming a new territory for his beloved monarch. The bears clap and clap, and finally the zookeeper responds to this ovation by throwing the piece of white bread to the nearest bear, then another to the next, another, another, until all the bears are using their long-clawed paws to shred white bread, and their chewing makes a sticky, spongy sound. The people standing pressed against the railings applaud, the zookeeper doffs his cap once more, then disappears, leaving an invisible door closed behind him and a couple of still-hungry bears halfheartedly clapping for an encore.

"Well?" Ray says to the bear. But the bear stares dumbly at his comrades, who now resume their lazy animal antics, though two of them engage in a brief shoving match over a scrap of bread they simultaneously spy. The bread ends up falling into the moat as the two skirmish, so they slap each other in friendship and both dive in, playmates once more and uninterested in the soggy, gluey leftover.

"He thought you should see some other bears before tonight," Joy says. "We know you usually like to avoid the bears when we go to the zoo. I told him that last night. But maybe this was for the best."

"Sure," Ray says. The bear, despair creeping over him in the vision of a moonless night, a hoard of ravenous ants on the march, a mother puma protecting her offspring, allows himself to be led meekly out of the zoo without noticing a single ice cream man, without tasting a single bite of the cool sweet goo which on every other zoo trip so gladdened his hot bear tongue.

He doesn't speak to Joy or Ray for the rest of the day, remains aloof, indifferent, a bear apart from their everyday life. After sunset, Joy drives the van to a semi-industrial part of town, the area where tiny, run-down diners mix with open fields and factories, oil-drilling machines and trucking centers, grubby men lounging on fire hydrants, on unpainted bus-stop benches, on half-torn-down brick walls with no obvious meaning to the property around them, walls dividing nothing from nothing, walls meant to support the bony rear ends of the out-of-work men who enjoy watching the big rigs tooling in and out of the yards, who enjoy the rhythmic monotony of the oil pumping because it matches the rhythmic monotony of their own lives. One of the small buildings, slightly less run down than those around it, has yellow lights proclaiming it the TAP 'N' CAP, and this lighted sign is highlighted by black circles painted on the beige exterior of the building, some of them with rounded windows also painted in to give them a cartoon sense of depth: champagne bubbles, or a stylized conception of beer foam, or perhaps the merry carbonation in all-American Coca-Cola. The Tap 'n' Cap sign does not seem to float in lighter-than-air spirits, however; Joy turns to give the bear a doleful look before she opens her van door, and Ray pretends the bear doesn't exist.

The bear follows Joy and Ray through a ghost town of a bar, small and rickety and empty except for a thin, nervous-looking bartender wearing a soiled white shirt and dark blue sunglasses. Ray gives him a hand-to-forehead salute, and the man makes a nearly imperceptible nod toward a door hidden away in the gloom of a musty corner. Joy and Ray slip through the barely opened door without causing a sound, but at the sight of the bear, dim visions swirling before his still-adjusting eyes which have trouble with depth, with people and things more than ten feet away from him (an animal's world is immediate in terms of memory and vision: only nearby-ness attracts his attention, because of physical limitation and a basic lack of belief in anything that doesn't smell dangerous or edible), a crowd of raucous men begin to howl and hoot and stamp their feet. The bear cowers by the door, but as Joy and Ray begin to disappear into the visual soup that the rest of the room seems to be to the bear, he follows them until he finds himself in the middle of the large room, faced with one corner of a regulation-size prize-fighting ring.

"Get up there," Ray orders in a low, mean voice. The bear rolls one front leg and one back leg up and over the ropes and near-somersaults onto the resiny mat, looking more like a hairy football with legs than like a heavyweight contender. He squats down in his corner and watches while the bartender, now coughing so hard that his glasses shake off his nose to reveal red and yellow eyes leaking viscous tears onto his cheeks, first reaches into one pants pocket for a handkerchief into which he blows his nose, then into another for a thick packet of money. The latter he hands to Ray, who forces his wooden mouth into a gracious smile. Joy whispers something, but Ray shakes his head and seems to thank the thin man more than necessary, which sends him on his way holding his handkerchief, stained the same color as his grimy shirt, to his fleshless mouth. The crowd once more begins to stamp and holler for action; the bear turns to face them and sees only dark figures in shades of sepia, the dirt and gloom and deceptive size of the room adding to his depression and feeling of impending doom.

Simultaneously the dirty, grumbling men light up cigarettes, cigars, joints, and the smoke and sulphuric fumes hang around their heads for an instant and then rise like a yellowed mushroom cloud. The bear stands in his corner of the ring backed up into the ropes. As the newly created smog begins to rise and dissipate, another creature climbs into the ring across from the bear, a mammoth figure in the gloom resembling the Creature from the Black Lagoon creeping out of his fen to grab a blonde in a bikini, a creature who shines electric green in the smoke and who causes the bear to lift paws to his head in despair because the ever present music in his head whenever he performs has for once stopped playing. The layer of smoke hits the ceiling, bounces back a little like a flat basketball, then sticks a foot from the top, and the bear sees his opponent. The creature in the electric green satin fighter's robe is another bear: a huge muscular beast, about six feet six inches tall, wearing a leather and chain muzzle which clamps his hideous mouth shut, circles his black nose in metal, then climbs up his face to form a mask revealing beady onyx eyes and alert round ears. Beneath his official robe he wears tight-fitting trunks, also green satin edged in white. He faces each side of the ring, turning counterclockwise like a professional, showing his grim visage to all the excited fans, then showing them his back, a vast shining green sea on which is written, in white satin letters, BEAR BODKIN. Bear Bodkin is a huge, glowering seventies bear, a bear always looking over his shoulder, a bear alone among owner and trainers and fans, as isolated as a seventies President, a bear with no music to dance to, a bear who has never been in love. Ray and Joy murmur to one another as they stand behind the bear's corner, but their words are lost in the heightened mumblings of the bloodthirsty crowd. The bear tries hard to remember the melody of "Jumpin' Jack Flash," but nothing comes to him. Bear Bodkin walks to the center of the ring and lifts his gargantuan front legs up to quiet the audience. A moment of silence, and all the orange-burning cigarette tips in the room turn toward the bear. Joy and Ray push at his ankles through the ropes, and the bear lumbers forward to the center of the ring, walking as if on board a sinking ship in a typhoon, as if airsick and on his way to the claustrophobic lavatory in the back of a jet, as if into deepest nightmare sleep.

As the bear reaches his confrontation with Bear Bodkin in the center of the ring, a small man in a yellow and green Hawaiian shirt leaps between the creatures and holds his hands in the air. In a machine-whine voice, the man says: "We want a clean fight here, no clawing, no below the belt. There will be one five-minute round. To win, one bear must pin the other bear's shoulders to the mat, and hold him for the count of ten. When the bell rings, come out fighting." Bear Bodkin hops up and down snorting, wriggles his arms until the shining green robe falls away from his massive shoulders, and retreats to his corner like the king of bears. The bear slinks to his corner with his head drooping onto his chest so that he looks deformed, a cartoon caricature of bear-ness at its most stupid and lazy, the shiftless Disney bear of Uncle Remus and the tar baby, the bear who should be wearing a flowered straw hillbilly hat and speaking in country stutters. As he approaches his corner, he sees Ray counting many green bills, new clean money; Joy watches the fives and tens passing before her eyes as one watches a magician preparing to perform a card trick. The crowd, quieted for the prefight announcement, begin to yell and whistle and hiss and boo once more, to stamp their feet and clap their hands while all the extra smoking, burning limbs hang menacingly in their mouths. The bear shuffles his feet in rhythmless, animal manner, and lets his arms hang limp and loose at his sides, while Bear Bodkin puts on a magnificent shadowboxing show at the other end of the ring. The smart money is clearly on Bear Bodkin, the favorite, the front-runner, the flashy pretty boy. The bear feels like a patsy.

Dong, and Bear Bodkin comes out smoking. In the center of the ring before the bear knows what to do, Bodkin raises his arms to shoulder height and waves them in the air like two baseball bats aching to hit horsehide; he plants his feet like a hairy colossus and waits, growling with a contained, fierce intensity through the leather and chrome of his muzzle. The bear takes one last and desperate look at Joy and Ray, who are eating steaming, drippy hot dogs with excesses of mustard and ketchup and holding frost-silvery mugs of frothy beer; realizing no reprieve will come, he steps to the center of the ring.

Immediately Bodkin leaps upon him, grabbing him around his middle in an attempt to flatten the bear and end the fight with a quick KO. The bear loses his footing more from the overpowering stench of Bodkin than from the tenacity of the hold: Bodkin stinks of wild animal, of crusted saliva and blood and other bodily emanations. His fur, pressed up into the bear's nose, seems the tangible representation of all fetid odors, including a faintly sulphurous, burned hair smell which, as the bear sees from close up, comes from many perfect and round cigar burns which have been inflicted upon Bodkin's body, hardly denting his skin but taking out swatches of fur as a power lawn mower might. The crowd stands, roars, waves burning objects in the air which look like fireflies on a foggy night. The bear's feet scrape and shuffle on the resiny mat and finally forget how to stand, and his whole weight hangs upon Bodkin's muscular front legs. Papers begin to fly into the ring, shaped like primitive airplanes and hats and rocks: when Bodkin swipes at one with an upraised paw, growling hideously at the crowd, the bear swivels his shoulders in a gesture reminiscent of an early shimmy and escapes to the mat, rolling and feinting and somersaulting to one end of the ring as the crowd's stamping and clapping become rhythmic, a steady and hard four-four beat, a rock and roll beat on a facile drum solo, the beginning of some ersatz Motown single in 1967 with girl singers trying to sound like Martha and the Vandellas singing about lost love: the bear *hears* it. He rolls his head back on his neck, shrouds his glazy eyes in furry bear eyelids, and feels his feet begin to move in a slow Mashed Potato, his heels twitching out and in, his knees swaying slightly; his paws come up to waist height and begin to snake around his cumbersome bear hips. He is dancing. Bear Bodkin comes toward him in a wrestling stance, a learned high/low arm arrangement and aggressive pelvis approach, hoping to throw him off balance, and for an instant, it appears that the bear won't see his opponent, that a private tape recording of a sixties radio station, B. Mitchell Reed playing the top forty in the bear's head, will swallow him up with help from Bodkin's half-nelson. The crowd gasps, becomes silent, remains standing and puffing and waving ten-dollar bills in the air like a boy scout signal corps. As Bodkin's gigantic bear arms begin to encircle the bear's shoulders (a love grip more than an assault, to judge from the bear's beatific expression, his languorous and sensually swaying body), the bear lifts a snaking right arm into a Swim and slips under the embrace of his bigger opponent, followed with a perfect left-handed Swim which drags his circling hips behind, and escapes with glorious grace to the other side of the ring.

Bodkin spins around, amazed. His ferocious half-nelson assault never fails, and this limp-wristed sissy has cruised right out from under it, and now appears to be climbing an imaginary vine while his feet move in time to his swinging hands at the opposite end of the mat. Rage flows from his muzzled, slavering mouth down to his grasping, working paws and pumping legs, and he leaps upon the bear in renewed fury. No finesse is left in his approach: only an animal desire for conquest, destruction of an apparently weaker, less-deserving-to-live animal enters his inscrutable bear mind, and he sees visions of helpless baby rabbits in their warrens, of gimpy-legged moose left behind by the herd, of exhausted salmon huffing and writhing against an upstream rock. Bodkin is ready for the kill.

But as Bodkin circles, the bear dances away, the most brilliant dance of his illustrious and unique career. He does the Monkey in place to taunt Bodkin, then Twists away in a wicked imitation of Groucho Marx, complete with shimmying hands and flat feet. When Bodkin cuts across the mat in a vain attempt to swoop, the bear struts away with his head loose on his neck, his nose in the air, his shoulders gyrating like ball bearings. The crowd picks up the rhythmic clapping, and the bear begins a suggestive Jerk, jutting his bear behind out at Bodkin's contorted features. Bodkin's black and beady bear eyes strain against the leather muzzle, about to pop out or break into a sweat.

"Get down!" Ray yells, and makes high hooting noises.

With time running out and his reputation on the line, Bodkin becomes frantic. He makes great dives for the bear, ending up stretched full length on the canvas or hanging from the ropes like wet laundry, while the bear always escapes with complete grace in his gyrating frenzy. Bodkin seems exhausted. In a move of complete audacity, the bear steps into the very center of the mat and goes into one of his favorite combinations, a Stomp for the lower half of his body, a Swim/Monkey combo for his arms, a heavenward attitude for his ecstatic face. Bodkin lunges for his feet, and a great gasp echoes through the smoky room: all on the side of the bear now, the last thing the crowd wants is to see the spell broken, to see the bear transformed once more into a zoo-type buffoon rather than a *danseur* (taking folk art from the masses being an unwise move in the best of times, a disaster in times of crisis). But in a dazzling basketball lay-up move that defies gravity and all other natural laws, the bear twinkles his toes and rises from the mat on perfect point, reaches for the sky, swivels his hips for the ultimate time as the bell rings and applause and yells and whistles of praise call for an encore. Someone throws a rose onto the mat.

The bear makes a graceful bow, his ears nearly sweeping the mat, and hunkers to a corner where he climbs over the ropes and walks toward a door, disappearing into the people and smoke and flying hands and floating five- and ten-dollar bills and whistles zooming like arrows through the heavy yellow air. Stomping and clapping continues, together with the sound of quarters and dimes hitting the prone form of Bear Bodkin, sometimes a soft thunk when the coins hit leather or knotted fur, every so often a tiny *ping* when an adept marksman bounces one off the chains of Bodkin's muzzle. Bodkin seems to sleep in the center of the ring, despite the shower of coins, looking like a large, hairy, six-and-a-half-foot-tall baby, his outsized head resting on his curled-up front legs, his body forming a mountain range behind: the animal's ability to relax amid chaos, to turn docile after ferocity, to sleep away trouble and illness and pain (the lack of an evil, always functioning subconscious mind, a Freudian might say, the ability to escape into the void which so terrifies humans; if Freud had owned a bear, his theories might have been drastically altered). A chant of "Encore" begins, though no dance can be performed after that dance of betrayal and escape, of the transcendentalism of art, and no one notices that the bear has opened the door leading to the alley out back of the Tap 'n' Cap, has stepped through it without a backward glance and, once outside, has sneaked to the van and removed from it the small wooden chest which holds his few belongings. After tucking the chest under his left arm, he flees into the gleaming fog of the night, slipping into it as anonymously as a bear can, turning sideways to aid his disappearance, cutting and zigzagging like a first-rate basketball player on a fast break, finally vanishing into the steamy neon yellows and greens that light the fog like *Twilight Zone* Christmas tree lights.

The crowd begins to disperse when no encore appears and when Bodkin shows no signs of storming around like King Kong in annoyance at these irritating silver missiles flying at him. As the room clears, Joy and Ray search for the bear, looking in the corners of the fight room, in the front room which houses the deserted bar, and finally on the sidewalk outside, looking up and down the street, squinting into the glittery mirror-world of the fog. They stand, stunned and still, on the sidewalk, letting the crowd coming out of the Tap 'n' Cap jostle them and push them, already unable to remember exactly what his face looked like, what his ice cream wail sounded like, the bear as dim a memory as 1965 and seemingly as far away, and they start to walk to the van without a word. A final group of three men, each holding a cigar used like a saber to give importance to his excited speech as they recreate the fight, comes out of the bar.

"The way he just about flew through the air, leaving that other big bastard hanging out to dry," one says.

"Never seen anything so quick in my life. Not even Ali when he was Cassius Clay and still had the footwork," another says.

"What a bear," the third says.

Joy and Ray take a final look before they get into the van, but it is useless, like looking for an invisible bear, a bear existing in myth rather than deed, a bear hanging in the stars as

some bears do, or on flags in California, or in the mountains
of Washington State where the natives whisper "Sasquatch."
Ray lights one of the cigarettes he keeps behind his ear, and
Joy follows the signs that say HIGHWAY, the too-real highway
stealing away into the silver midnight of moonless, bearless
times.

The bear sits on one of the padded benches in the garishly lit main terminal of Dulles Airport; four in the morning, and tired airline clerks play with the buttons on their minicomputer terminals, neaten stacks of circulars and pamphlets printed in the selected colors of their airline (they wear these colors as well, as if they were representatives of a horse racing stable, but at four in the morning the flying, fluttering silks begin to look a trifle rumpled as ties are loosened, blouses unbuttoned for comfort, shoes removed behind the counter), and eye the few people who wait for planes with unwavering suspicion: airports, bastions of modern technology and the cleanliness always connected with it during the day, at night become as seedy as bus stations and train stations, something to do with the nature of fluorescent lights untempered by the sun, and also with the nature of those who choose to travel by dark, in the grand old vampire tradition of capes pulled up tight under their noses, preferring invisibility, seeking to avoid the nervous, drunken camaraderie of daytime flights crammed with businessmen in vested suits and other socially acceptable types, secretaries, families, visitors to long-lost relatives. Late at night, the airport seems to be a stopping-off point for those on their way to Morocco, Guyana, the Indies, rather than such mundane points of arrival as Detroit and Cleveland, by virtue of the colors and accents of those waiting for planes. Dark-skinned people lounge uneasily in corners with rumpled flight bags and pouches clutched under their arms, traveling alone rather than in the usual daytime pairs. Spanish-speaking people, talking in the quick, sharp sounds of the Cuban dialect or the more languorous Mexican version, stand closer to the counters, hoping to hear the first announcement of "flight now ready for boarding," less cool about their eagerness for escape than the lone black men and aware of their difficulties in deciphering the English-spoken flight numbers (which can be remedied, they hope, by proximity to the source of the voice of authority, and by assembling in groups, thereby having more fingers to count on, more linguistic ability, a genuine case of parts being worth more together than their theoretical whole might indicate). Add to these a few Oriental people, as silent and alone as the black men and women but without the support of comforting corners, always upright, straight-backed, and with a line of vision indicating that they see nothing of what lies in front of them, a vision transcending place and time and bodily existence, consciousness abiding, perhaps, at the firm base of the spine. Everyone blinks a lot, a combination of the white white light and the various staying-awake and going-to-sleep drugs (more justified at this hour: flying loaded during the day, in the warm golden sunlight with jaunty and cheerful stewardesses, carefully pressed gentlemen in the seats next to yours, could be thought of as sinful; flying loaded at four in the morning seems to be a necessity, a method of self-protection, an added ingredient to the cloak of invisibility, the hard-eyed look of despair incognito behind sunglasses). The bear feels right at home with this shifting, drifting bunch, and watches with a feeling of warmth usually reserved for a meeting with one's own species in a silent, clean-smelling glade which is neither's territory, a neutral place where alliance becomes possible, as these down-and-outs get on planes for Miami and New Orleans and Atlanta and Chicago; has been watching, in fact, for a couple of hours with no thought of moving on and no thought of sleep. Twice, he has been asked for a light.

At first, the bear felt hopeless and lost when the last ride he hitched let him off at Dulles Airport in the middle of the night; right outside of Washington, D.C., the Virginia landscape turns rural, with forests glittering organically in the moonlight, glimpses of deer, chucks, rabbits at the side of the highway (and a vast population of skunks, squirrels, and rabbits squashed in the middle of the road, screamingly illuminated for a startling moment by headlights, then flattened by car after car, the highway crowded with the masses of small earthbound ghosts attached by the animal homing instinct to the scene of their quick demise), which frightened the bear. As an urban bear, the country makes him uncomfortable. Humans never perceive the many threats whispered in clean country air, the smells of carnivorous beasts, of poisonous plants, of territorial markers not to be ignored. Actually, the bear has never been alone before, in the city or in the country, so every act seems freighted with new import, seems significant and dangerous. As the memory of Joy and Ray recedes into the gloomy forest night of his bear brain (animal memories being as quick as animal reflexes, recorded and forgotten, designed to save the owner's life in a moment of need and not to be cumbersome brain baggage otherwise: no bear Proust ever to emerge, no bear memoirs but these, ghost-written by necessity), the bear's new freedom seems frighteningly complete, his recent nomadic existence seems to have always been. He spun and blinked and waved and applauded while standing on the highways trying to flag down rides, and wondered (an image of deer running for their lives, bounding over streams, over lightning-downed logs, over their own dead brothers) how he had made it that far. Finding a tribe of wayward wanderers and a warm place to sit gladdens him, allows him to be still and unwary, lets him breathe in the familiar smells of the late night, the stale cigarette smoke hanging near the ceiling and around the fluorescent lights in small yellowish clouds, the perfume and sweat of night women, the hair grease, the starch in cheap new clothes, the ammonia of wet baby diapers, the crisp and pungent smell of anticipation, a smell only humans emit, the smell that warns animals away in the woods, that causes ducks to fly in a boomerang formation in the sky to avoid a clumsily constructed blind, that causes rabbits to stand statue-still, their noses wiggling, before a speedy disappearance in a flurry of dust and flying fur and waving ears, an insult to even an inexperienced hunter.

With no real warning, the humming and pounding of airplane engines becoming a constant, an unrecognized annoyance like too much punctuation in an essay, a group of gigantic men stumbles through the terminal, their legs still bending and bowing from too much time spent in the air: all of them as tall or taller than the bear, most of them as dark or darker than he, all of them walking with the slouching shoulders, the scuffling feet, the near-humorous guise of exhaustion and stupidity that in men characterizes jet lag, in bears everyday existence. There must be fifteen of them, most carrying small vinyl bags with a snarling dog logo decaled on the side, and the warmth the bear previously felt for his fellow night travelers nearly consumes his being. He rises and pushes his way into the center of the group of giants, assuming their stance, their posture, which for him is natural and right, an enormous wave of belonging to a real bear family sweeping him, and shuffles out into the cold Virginia night with them only to find they are already dispersing as he revels in his glow, some getting into waiting cars, some filing into battered graveyard-shift cabs; they gently push him out of the way as they make for their cars or steer him toward one cab or another, until he sees his chances for lasting friendship begin to wane as the jostling decreases. With fine animal instincts he grabs his opportunity and lunges torpedolike and smooth into a cab that already holds three of the giants, two in the back seat and one in the front, and closes the door behind him. The giants nod their massive heads, one of them raises a large black hand and points out the windshield by the driver's nose, and the cab speeds off into the night as the bear, suffused with good feeling, prepares to take a nap.

"You one of the new boys?" one of the giants asks; the bear, already halfway into a snooze, hardly realizes he is being spoken to.

"A rookie," the giant in the front seat says. "He's one of the rookies. He doesn't know any better."

"Well, look here, boy," the giant next to the bear says, poking him in the arm with a huge bony elbow, waking the bear into sharp-eared alertness. "Coach don't have much of a sense of humor. He likes to see us dress sharp when we come home, even in the middle of the night. You hear what I'm saying?"

"Yeah," the front-seat giant says. "Just 'cause we lose doesn't mean we don't have any pride." He punches the roof of the cab with a quickly upraised fist; the others giggle anomalous, high-pitched laughs which seem to emanate from their nostrils and teeth rather than from their relaxed, muscular bodies (else how could such tinkly sounds come from the mouths of giants?).

As the taxi drives on, charting a crazy parabolic course around animal bodies in the road, stalled cars with steam billowing from their calliopic insides, cars skidding on the phosphorescent green rain-slick surface, and aggressive middle-of-the-night hitchhikers stepping out into the street with hands raised more in threat than in supplication, the bear examines his new traveling companions. A flash of oncoming headlight or streetlight or sizzling flare like a cartoon stick of dynamite illuminates sparkling details invisible in the rural darkness: the small golden earring like a star in the ear of the brown giant closest to him in the back seat; the grayish insides of the other back-seat giant's hands, gigantic and looking more like complex maps of the waterways of Mars than like human appendages; and the long white fingernails of the same giant's hands, flat and shining as semiprecious gems, lace agate, or quartz. The giant in the front seat remains mysterious, the darkest figure of the three, his head and shoulders given a vague aura when cars pass in the oncoming lanes,

a nimbus too pale to be spiritual, too faint to be sinister: perhaps one of those cases of the physical world giving its characters a hint of things to come much as characters in novels
are presented with symbols, images, foreshadowings as sign-
posts by which to direct their lives (and, like characters in fiction, the bear fails to interpret, though no handwringing will
catch up with him later in the story, no thick remorse or
twentieth-century guilt: bears, in fiction and in real life, wear
interpretive skins only in the eyes of doting humans who see
reflected in brown animal eyes their own questionings of the
elusive nature of the universe. The bear sees only the gossamer halo surrounding the giant as it becomes engraved
upon his retina and shot laserlike back into the recesses of the
bear brain, files it away as a trait of the front-seat giant the
same as the earring and the hands, and promptly forgets that
it ever existed).

"Man, my stop's first, and I hope my old lady is waiting
up," the giant with the earring says, shaking his hips against
the bear and the other giant and beating a thumping tattoo
upon the cab roof as the driver pulls his shoulders in against
his neck and clutches the steering wheel a little tighter.

"All *right*," the other back-seat giant says. "Hey, Big, you
going all the way into the city as usual? Then you know I'm
second, and you get stuck for the tab again unless this closed-
mouth rookie's gonna fight you for it."

"Where you going, baby?" Big, the front-seat giant, asks.
The bear makes an elaborate bear shrug, wrinkling his fur
into folds in unlikely places where humans never suspect
bears have bones and cartilage. In the eerie, sporadic light,
his face appears almost sad. "I know how it is when you're a
new boy," Big says, "when you get to know all the motels close
in to the stadium 'cause you're afraid if you stay anywhere
else you'll never find your way to that nice warm bench by
game time. Hell, that speed's just starting to go, and I'm much
too old to feel tired when chances are I might never wake up
from one of those full-court press dreams. You can come with

me, boy. Got a nice couch in my living room turns into a bed, and I'll even drive you to practice tomorrow. Man, but I'm tired."

"Thanks," the bear says as the cab stops to let the Earring out.

"Lay-tah," the Earring says, swinging his flight bag with the snarling dog out after him: illuminated in silver for a moment, the club logo strikes fear into the bear, who, unaware of the forest nature of professional sports, the rules of the wild run rampant, the elbows in stomachs and fingers in eyes and near-nude men running as if from raging fires in dry chaparral, quickly resumes the feelings of goodwill and belonging that have characterized his whole relationship with the giants and, as far as he foresees (probably into the next five seconds or so), will likely continue forever (another common animal notion of timelessness: since they cannot plan for even the next ten minutes, "forever" takes on a whole new shape, that of a balloon about to bounce off a cactus, perhaps, or of a day-old golden butterfly).

Hands gets out, and then the cab enters the city. The bear immediately begins to salivate, for on the horizon he sees, illuminated as if in a dream, many white-frosted wedding cakes in various huge sizes, one two stories tall, one long and flat and rectangular, one spectacularly domed though without the requisite bride and groom atop. Baroque squiggles of decoration, Grecian columns with white flowering bottoms and tops, trellises and cupolas and smooth-frosted stairways big enough for the bear to dance up as he eats are strikingly lit by gigantic spots, the kind usually reserved for the largest egos on Las Vegas stages but here pure, clean, like candied rays of summer sun. Having worked a few weddings in his dancing career (though no concrete memories remain with him, only the ability to recognize a wedding cake when he sees one, even if it's two stories tall), the bear begins to feel excited, and his feet start a slow shuffle which causes the remaining giant's head to roll on his neck as he catches the beat, giving him a shimmying yellow aura in the deep night, growing suddenly at one extended end, then shrinking at another, then globbing out into the rhythm of the dance at yet another like a thriving galaxy in the void of space. The bear once more feels deep love for this giant who seems to be an ideal dancing partner, an unhairy brother, and in an unparalleled lucid moment he almost sees the spotlighted symbolism of this ride through wedding-cake land as a host of pairs of various forest creatures which seem to emerge from the brush and shrubbery of his tangled bear brain in startling, pleasant symmetry.

"Hey, man, you like to dance?" Big asks, but his voice sounds dreamy, demanding no response. "All basketball players can dance. Ballet if they wanted to. They can cut, they can leap, they can run like gazelles across that floor and they can soft-step it like some spatted-up hoofer finessing the wax finish on the wood to death. We got the longest legs this side of giraffes, and arms like gorillas. Just watch us in slow motion on the six o'clock news. We beautiful, baby, gravity don't mean nothing to us. Making those shots from half-court while the clock ticks out might bring in the dollars and the fans, but the players who last, the fifteen-year men like me, we get paid for grace. Our hook shots are geometry lessons, our bank shots get named by color men, our legs become instantly recognizable to the dumbest fan by the collection of bandages and tapes and scars we grow like barnacles on some old sunken hull of a ghost ship. That's what's worth aiming for, not the between-the-legs dribble that trips you up half the time, or the low percentage twenty-footer from the corner. Take a lesson, man: we're dancers, big long skinny jazz men, and nothing else."

"Where'd you get a name like Big?" the bear asks: used to the mundane regularity and meaninglessness of human names, the bear appreciates the forthright descriptiveness of this one, the only truly possible name for the front-seat giant.

"You'll get a name too, just wait," Big says. "My mama called me Sonny because I was her only boy, four girls all older than me and most of them disappeared from the city with one man or another before I was grown. By the time I was fourteen, I reached six feet six and showed no signs of stopping, so I got called Big Sonny and left alone by the gangs. That caught right on in basketball, where Big's the easiest nickname to remember. For a few years I was Big Sonny, the only one in the league. Then they called me Big Son for a few seasons. Then Big S, that's even what they had printed on my jersey when I joined this lousy expansion team. Finally it was just Big, almost like my name shrunk as I grew, a life of its own. There've been Big O's, Big Bills, even Big Lous. But I'm the only Big."

The cab drives on in silence, past more wedding-cake monuments, a snaking stories-high needle with ruby eyes and thrilling spirals of light around it, a brown glassine river like so much cautious molasses and over it twisting, many-leveled bridges of mausoleum white. The bear, intoxicated by the sight of the giant white edibles spanned by concrete and maple syrup, fails to notice the ruins of a previous banquet hidden out of the gleaming spotlights: in the dark, crumbling buildings deteriorate by the minute, filling neighborhoods with the sound of constant rain as plaster and bits of brick and wood ceaselessly fall to the sooty sidewalks. As if in fear of staying indoors longer than necessary to avoid the impending apocalyptic crunch when the last beam is chomped through by a horde of termites and ceilings crash and walls fold in like a movie version of a great and perilous earthquake, inhabitants of the dark half of the city fill the streets, blending into the night with their midnight skins, slouching and hanging out and leaning and shooting and knifing and calling and hooting and buying and selling, doing all the things folks in the other parts of town, the parts caught in the snowflaky extremities of one or another of the spotlights, do indoors, in private.

"My hometown," Big says in disgust as the cab traverses the dangerous dark streets with chorus lines of hot-pantsed, thigh-booted black women with long straightened hair, arms outstretched in near unison, right legs extended in invitation, but the bear (in a great leap of selective vision) sees only the

next illuminated wedding cake up ahead, like a desert traveler seeing only the faraway emerald green of oasis when
the brilliant hallucinatory golds of the sand stretch around
him, catch in his eyelashes, stick to his tongue. Also, the bear's
poor eyesight makes the dark parts of the city blend into a
foggy mass full of darker, floating shapes, some massive, some
small and dense, but certainly nothing to vie with the bakery
splendor of the white-lit monuments decorating the city's
landscape.

Big lives in the section of the city that has street lamps,
with bureaucrats and lawyers and directors of programs and
people with varying levels of security clearance: in the up-
wardly mobile dichotomous world of dark and light, rich
and poor, sports has made Big socially acceptable, and though
success didn't change his skin, it could improve the depth of
his night vision and chances of surviving a midnight moonlight stroll. A range of dollhouses stands pushed together and
freshly painted to make the most of historical space, almost
all details in miniature: delicate gratings on windows, tiny
fences, welcome-mat lawns, little steps leading to the door-
ways, fastidious small houses in varying colonial styles, some
in New Orleans bordello style, some in Virginia plantation
style, some New England captain's houses, all skinny and
hunched, connected like anomalous Siamese twins, each not
knowing where the other came from. When the cab pulls up
in front of Big's New Orleans French Quarter style house, perfectly manicured as a poodle with pink bows in its ears, the
bear feels a spreading discomfort similar to that a gathering
of rain clouds brings to an arthritis sufferer: the bear has
never known people to live in such antiseptic surroundings,
his experience has always been with the seamy, the sullied,
the unrestored old, with things smelling of decades of cigarette smoke, of whitewash turned gray and beige and brown
and charcoal, with black-bagged eyes and torn pants knees.
This place smells new, the streetlights aren't even old enough
to have collected decomposing moth bodies inside the glass
fixtures, and even at this hour cheery warm rooms uncurtained

in neighboring houses crazily reveal scenes straight out of television commercials, couples sipping wine together in front of fireplaces, mothers dutifully serving Campbell's soup from gleaming brass tureens to redheaded freckle-faced children, women with heads piled high with suds grasping plush robes around their bodies as they rush to answer ringing telephones. The bear (with a reluctance to deal with the new, the different, the unknown aroma which makes his nostrils quiver in amazement, the high-pitched dissonant chord of irregularity which makes his ears flap and ache) hesitates, and reluctantly leaves the cab when Big nears his bright blue front door and begins searching his snarling-dog flight bag for his keys. Camaraderie overcomes powerful natural aversion, and the bear ambles on all fours after Big as the front door swings open: Big appears to falter or stagger suddenly, to sway like a skyscraper in an earthquake, and when the bear reaches his side his eyes look like the eyes of Easter Island sculptures, lidded heavy with stone. Big turns on no lights in his home. Without a word he opens a sofa for the bear to sleep on, then disappears into another room, behind a closed door, through which the bear can discern none of the usual human preparations for sleep, almost as if Big has climbed into a waiting coffin filled with his native earth. These considerations actually don't enter the bear's strained consciousness at this moment, however: finding himself faced with overwhelming luxury in the form of his own bed in a room which he shares with no other beings, separated from his newfound brother by only a thin wooden door, he clambers onto the sofa and instantly falls asleep, the void of bear dreamlessness seeming softly illumined, almost opalescent, unthreatening as a void can be.

Years of sleep, eons of sleep, the bear's body comfy enough for a winter's hibernation, and when he awakens he expects bright-colored tulips to have sprouted outside the house's windows, the lawn to be dew-spattered, with each blade of grass reflecting tiny prisms, perfect spring rainbows; instead still another gray winter day, the air outside thick with near-frozen humidity like smoky sheet glass.

"Aw, man," Big says as he comes out of the bedroom and sees the bear curled up into a furry brown basketball in the center of the sofa bed. "Aren't you up and out of the silly getup yet? We got practice this afternoon, in case you've forgotten. You're gonna get a penalty laid on your ass that could be half your year's salary." Big walks to a huge walnut outgrowth of one wall that looks like the control panel of the Pentagon's computer facility, clicks a single black switch, and fills the room with bass-heavy music, pounding and nerve-vibrating. The bear's toes begin to twitch, and he sits up straight and stares through the waving, pulsating air of the room at nothing as his dancing muscles begin to adjust to a condition similar to an astronaut's introduction to weight-lessness, to stretch and contract in readiness. Curtis Mayfield's high, thin falsetto strikes him like a bolt of lightning, sending him flying into the center of the room with arms and legs in manic disarray, windmilling and rotating and flailing like a man falling off the top of the Empire State Building or a man just finished collecting a right hook from One-Punch Teofilo Stevenson. The voice whips him into shape and calls him to saluting attention, forces his heels to start pounding the ground in beat, causes his freshly stilled arms to start Swimming through the bouncing sound waves like a surfer seeking a still point from which he can catch that elusive twelve-footer. His knees rise and fall, his shoulders rhythmically court his ears in a sinuous mating dance, he swoops Twisting and spiraling down and comes out of it into free-form movement touched with madness, with the electricity that moments before propelled him into the Dance. Big watches the spontaneous performance, amazed.

"Hey, if you play like you dance, we got a chance of making the playoffs," Big says. "How come I haven't seen you around before?"

The bear considers this question: he hasn't wondered where Big has been during the course of his own previous existence. Being a much-traveled bear, a bear used to the limelight, a performer and wanderer and hairy gypsy of the first order with only the haziest memories of his myriad gigs, one-night stands, strange sleeping places, his life can be seen as highly analogous to that of the lifetime professional basketball player, and therefore the bear is equally deserving of asking such a question. Of course, all this occurs to the bear as a briefly shining light, a glimmer, a shooting star poignantly illuminating the forest night sky with its question-mark path. Then he answers, "I don't know."

"Well, no matter. I was just about to offer you some morning speed, but I can see you don't need it. You young players. Hell, you're probably a vegetarian, and I bet you do yoga an hour a day. Shouldn't look down on old players who need outside stim-u-lation. My muscles are like old rubber bands by now, and I don't let the coach see that I gotta wear glasses for reading the newspaper. When I get sent in off the bench, I can feel my joints grinding away like brakes that need relining, sometimes my legs and arms feel as brittle as tree trunks. It's all pain now, the physical part of the game. That's why old players tend to get into religion, to read philosophy though they never paid any attention in school past the fourth grade. We become downright spiritual, and game time at the arena is our church. A little reverie was never hurt by speed, man. The humming in your ears starts to sound like Gregorian chants, and your heart feels big with the presence. The young guys may be quick, but they ain't got the spirit."

"I've hung out with worse than you," the bear says, still swaying to the music.

"Grew up bad, huh?"

"Sure," the bear answers.

"C'mon," Big says, and puts his arm around the bear's shoulders. "Let's get down to practice. I can feel that religion in my veins already, and it's a sin to waste it."

In daylight, the city looks far less inspiring: what were wedding cakes at night become dead gray concrete during the day, and hordes of men and women, each couple surrounded by a miasmic buffer zone of multisized children, fill the steps and walkways that last night were tiers of cake, climb on the statues, blunder into the streets in efforts to find good camera angles or in actual mistaken identity, the dark asphalt of pavement being similar enough to the paler color of monument to fool some of the more backward tourists. If the bear were a human, he would have felt as if he'd just awakened from a disconcerting dream of an unknown place; as it is, he rubs his eyes and stares in uncomfortable disbelief at what was previously a vision of delectable edibles. Inversely, the poor parts of town grow lighter with day, lose the anarchic blackness of the abyss which makes all things possible once the sun goes down. They too look like ordinary gray city during the daytime, dirty and teeming, though a sense of warfare in the recent past also pervades, buildings that look bombed-out, grenaded, jagged holes in walls, windows exploded, fences broken down, stores boarded up. And the people walk quickly, with nervous movements of the head, watching their unguarded rears as well as their fronts, scanning the skies using their flat, open hands to shield vulnerable eyes. The bear feels the weight of daytime urban reality settling upon him like a gruesome storm cloud, and has a hazy epiphany: this is why previous owners never took him out much during the day, why his life has been a nighttime life, dancing in the cool, transparent night air in which light could be magic, could play tricks with the very nature of things, change sad to happy, gray to sparkling white. Anyone with sense avoids sunlight in the city, because it kills romance much as it kills vampires, causes it to disintegrate into dust, as cruel a death (because it is so much more banal) as the old sharpened wooden stake through the heart.

Just outside the city Big pulls his car into a great deserted ghost town of a parking lot which, with its symmetrical white lines everywhere, huge yellow arrows and land-dividing marks, looks like a complex landing pad for an armada of invading spacecraft. The area up ahead appears to the bear to be a

gigantic beehive, one of his favorite natural images, and his
instinctual affinity for basketball players and the game itself
swells again and erases the gloomy picture the city presented
on the ride over. In all the open space Big's face becomes
transformed, and he skids his hot little car over white and
yellow lines, crisscrossing them with black rubber from his
tires, turning lanes into imagined obstacle courses, and finally
careening into a parking place right up next to the arena
between two equally sharp and shiny small foreign cars.

"Gotta get the blood flowing before I go in or some
rookie'll nail me for sure, and then I'll have to elbow him
good to keep my pride," Big says as he gets out of the car,
unfolding his body as a musician lovingly unfolds his prize
accordion. "With my nonorganic spirituality, once that
adrenaline starts, it breaks the sound barrier." The bear
quickly slams his door and hunkers off to follow Big, who
already strides over to a door in the huge beehive and begins
to make loud hooting noises which the bear recognizes to be
announcements of his bravery, an audible territorial marker
any forest inhabitant or creature with the forest somewhere
in his genes would know.

Hallways lead in every direction inside the beehive,
curving so that they give the impression of infinity; doors as
large as the portals through which our nightmares take us
look like the monuments of the city, man-made dinosaurs too
immense to be part of present-day real life. Everything seems
to exist on a scale separate from that of everyday reality,
water fountains blooming from walls at the bear's chest
height, ceilings far enough away from his mouth to suggest
echoing possibilities. These possibilities become fact in the
mammoth locker room which looks like it's made of old
battleships: metal lines every wall, deep gray and shineless,
punctuated by tacks and rivets and screws holding it together
in a random pattern like notes in contemporary dissonant
music. Every footstep reverberates tinnily, the slamming of a
locker makes a noise that shoots past the bear's ear like a
whizzing Apache arrow, one of Big's whoops takes off into the

stratosphere until it reaches inaudible dog-whistle pitch and disintegrates against the ceiling in a formation similar to a mushroom cloud. The bear sits on a metal bench while Big exchanges his street clothes for a silver and white scanty outfit of shorts and sleeveless T-shirt, his high-heeled leather boots for pure white gym shoes with silver stripes like wings down their sides. Big looks at the bear, disheartened.

"Where *is* your uniform, boy? I swear you the dumbest rookie this team's had in its three years of life, and being an expansion team, we've had some real prizewinners in the brain department." The bear looks at Big with usual bear expressionlessness which Big interprets as bewilderment and chagrin, something about a sadness in the eyes, a slight fluttering of the ears.

"All right," Big says, "put these on." He grabs a small shining mass of material from the bottom of his locker and tosses it at the bear. When the bear disentangles his muzzle from the stuff, he straightens it on the bench beside himself and sees it is another pair of silver and white shorts exactly like Big's. "Ain't got no extra shirt. But it ain't my fault if they hoot at you, chump. At least you'll be decent."

At the end of one of the snaking hallways the bear has his first glimpse of the heart of the arena: on the gleaming, wood-grain basketball floor, a dozen giants leap and spin and crouch and whirl and twinkle their toes and dazzle with their shots in a random arrangement worthy of the best modern choreographers. Both the bear and Big stop to admire the flying kaleidoscopic beauty. High above the court, hanging above even the scoreboard, a monumental banner flutters in the air conditioning. Decorated at one end with the snarling silver dog logo, the banner reads, in letters standing so slanted they look like they got caught in the sudden backfire of a jet engine: HOME OF THE VIRGINIA WOLVES.

"Hey, look what's with Big," one of the giants who's just thrown a wild pass into the seats says, beginning a chorus of clapping, whistling, and high-pitched hollering.

"Where'd you get the bear, man?" another yells.

"Looks like a hardship case to me," from another.

"Gotta shave if you wanna join this team, bro'," another says.

Big realizes he's got to do some fast figuring, his brain hurtling down rusty tracks like the speeding Superchief on its way to Albuquerque, his fingers drumming on his naked thighs in exasperation.

"Something tells me this cat ain't no rookie," he says aloud; the bear glances up at him adoringly as the rest of the team gathers around the two of them, fingering the bear's fur, looking for zippers or buttons, pulling up his lip to look at his long yellow teeth, laughing in high-pitched cackles and low moaning giggles. Everyone has new respect for Big: bringing a bear to practice is the best joke the team has ever seen played.

At the side of the court a huge man who has been sitting with his face in his hands while the others have been gamboling on the court rises slowly from his seat, as if in intense metaphysical pain. Unlike the others, he wears rumpled street clothes, and his body has a sense of the past about it. A large, tragic head sits atop massive shoulders, but the chest thickens past the bounds of musculature, the stomach bulges against pants waistband, thighs look soft as a package of white bread, and calves fail to spring when he demonstrates to a player what was wrong with a shot, bringing him down flatfooted and heavy and feeling a million years old. The coach was once a fine basketball player on a championship team and is now a professional worrier. Saddled with a turkey expansion team made up of rejects and cocky rookies, signed to an overgenerous contract, he finds himself trapped in a moral dilemma: how much money are your ulcers worth, what pays for the heartbreak of losing for a man who's always won, do six figures compensate for crucifixion by local sportswriters and booing fans who figure they can do better with your gang of goons and outlaws and spastics? Coach Mahoney sticks his hands deep into his pants pockets and walks over to where his team gathers to see what all the fuss is about.

"Outta my way," he growls as he slaps at his players, his big red hands and octopus-tentacle fingers clearing a path for his corpulent body much as they magically used to evanesce rival one-on-one defenses, leaving a hole just big enough for lithe young Mahoney and the bouncing ball that obeyed his every command. When he gets to the center and sees the only member of the squad he trusts, Big, with a bear in the team trunks, he drags one of his huge hands over his face as if attempting to erase the mug he's been given and start over from scratch, pushing his mouth grotesquely to one side, flattening his nose, bunching fat up on his chin. When he finishes, he closes his eyes for a few seconds before he speaks: "Is dis your idea of a joke? 'Cause if dis is your idea of a joke, man, I ain't laughin'."

"Sign him up, man," Big says. "If this cat can play basketball like he can dance, he'll save this team."

"Dis 'cat's' a bear, Big, man, maybe you need glasses on your old eyes, dis 'cat' belongs in da circus, all dis 'cat' can do wid a basketball is balance it on his nose and den ask for pennies. Take him back to da zoo you stole him from so we can get some practice," Coach Mahoney says, rubbing his mouth as he talks so only one of every three or four words comes out intelligible.

"Tell him how you dance, baby," Big says, throwing his long dark arm around the bear's shoulders once more. The coach rubs his eyes with gigantic swollen hands like boxing gloves.

"I've danced professionally for a few years now. All kinds of gigs. I've never played basketball, though," the bear says, trying to sound humble and worthy of Big's friendship.

After a moment of team silence, the coach scratches his head. "All right. I begin to see da possibilities, I'm not so dim. Let's see what your protégé can do, man. We'll have a scrimmage. Bear, you play wid Big."

"Wait a minute, bro'," the Earring says. "I don't get paid no million bucks a year to play with some bear."

"Yeah, and when are we ever gonna get another chance to

see a bear play? This ain't no entertainment just for you, coach. We wanna see too," another one of the players says. The bear begins to feel like the selected prey of a pack of ravenous wolves, itching under the weight of Big's heavy protective arm.

"Let the bear go one-on-one," someone at the outside of the circle that formed around the bear yells, and the cry is picked up.

"Yeah, one-on-one."

"Who'll take on the bear?"

"I'll play the bear to twenty."

"I'll whip the bear with my right hand tied behind my back."

Mahoney sticks his hands under his arms and squeezes his eyes shut tight. "You guys kill me. Dis team is just a bunch of playground hot dogs."

"My bear can take on any of these chumps one-on-one," Big says. "Pick your man, coach."

"Okay. Okay. We'll play to twelve, and no fancy shit. Da bear gets first out. After dat, loser's outs. Barnett, you take him. And if you get hurt, I swear I'll murder you wid my own hands." From the throng of giants, one moves in next to the coach in the inner circle. The bear recognizes him to be Hands from the previous night; indeed, even among these other men with prodigious hands he stands out. His hands are massive by any measure, looking like the huge impassive stone hands that sit on the larger stone thighs of the dead immortal kings at Abu Simbel, fine stylized hands with none of Rodin's grotesqueness, none of the oversized masculine knuckles and giant rounded fingertips, more like the boyish, reposing monsters tourists to Florence marvel at on Michelangelo's sweet-faced "David." Barnett smiles at the bear in recognition.

"I remember thinkin' last night, he be the craziest-lookin' rookie I ever seen," Barnett says. "And, man, I been to college."

"Barnett," the coach says, sneering and grimacing at the same time in an attitude formed over years of suffering and turmoil, of having the fat on his face creep up into his eyes and down toward his neck in a human example of the properties of expanding mass and gravity. "I don't wanna take advantage of your fine and sensitive nature. Now, it doesn't say anywhere in your contract dat I can tell you to go one-on-one wid a bear, and I'm aware of dat. Just so dis doesn't turn up on da front page of da sports section as another example of what a Hun I am, I'm asking you to do dis as a favor to me, and to show dese other goofs what da quality of mercy is all about."

Barnett salaams to the coach, and someone in the crowd yells, "All right." A ball flies from nowhere into the hands of Big, who holds it aloft as if it is the Olympic torch or a symbol with equal depth and meaning for these men with fire in their limbs, a signed check with a vast collection of zeros after a lone numeral, perhaps.

"This is your big chance, baby," Big says to the bear as he hands him the icon, the symbol, the leather-and-sweat-smelling basketball. "Take his hat, man."

"Give it to him, Barnett," someone yells.

"Come on, children," Mahoney says, waving his arms like a preacher exhorting his flock in hymn. "Come sit down over here wid da old man and watch da animal act. Dis is being taken out of all your paychecks as a lack of effort at practice, and dat *is* written into your contracts. All of you except Barnett, of course. And da bear, if we sign him."

The bear walks to the sideline, holding the basketball clumsily between his two furry hands, not yet daring to attempt a dribble. Barnett does a couple of stretches and bends, then assumes the defender's crouch just inside the court, his knees slightly bent to camouflage his true, awe-inspiring height, his arms raised to above his head, his face intense and frightening in a manner totally detached from the aggression of animals, a cool precision in the stare, a set of the mouth that marks a professional in any field, a man channeling all his energies through a long dark tunnel in which his breathless desire to win is the only light. The bear's face shows none of this direction, instead looks expressionless as always, perhaps even dumb, with the flat brown bear eyes staring down at the basketball as if it is some flying saucer just landed in his hands. He puts the ball to the floor, lets it bounce, then catches it again with both hands; some of the giants on the home team bench hoot.

"Time, man," Barnett says to the bear in a hissing voice of the playgrounds, the streets, the hard gray concrete that makes sneakers shriek and whistle and spark.

As the bear begins a hesitant dribble, Barnett stands back with his hands on his hips and his pelvis jutting forward, a look of extreme amusement on his face as his colleagues on the bench yell their approval of his cool. The bear chugs along toward the basket with a clumsy, uncoordinated dribble and dragging feet, concentrating on the bouncing ball as only animals can concentrate when life is at stake, with a fullness of their beings excluding all else, a hunting lioness first scenting a lone, lame gazelle in the brush, eyes keen on the horizon, ears straight up, or a prairie dog scenting a coyote, standing statue-still except for the wiggling nose and the same focused, far-seeing eyes. (This approach functions for animals with other animals, the predictability of behavioral modes, an equality of senses, of knowledge of terrain, of desire to survive. The bear, forced to rely on his poor animal nature against a towering, trained basketball player, will have to transcend mere keenness of eyes and precision of nose to fast break and rustle the ropes with the basketball.) The bear dribbles to the outside of the key, and then Barnett is upon him in two swooping steps, an octopus on defense, his massive hands undulating in the air, swinging and flailing in front of the bear's face. With his feet planted on the orange lines, the bear tries to put the ball up over his right shoulder, but Barnett's two hands and grimacing face are there; then he tries over his left shoulder, and meets the same immovable, frightening impediments. Then he lifts the ball straight up over his head, as if he were about to balance it on his nose, and opens his long-toothed mouth in Barnett's face, his sweet warm breath affixed to Barnett's features like a death mask. Barnett reaches up, grabs the ball from between the bear's novice paws, and runs like crazy, clearing the key and making his way toward the basket, before the bear can move. Slowly, comprehension dawns over the bear's face, nothing so obvious as the lifting of a thick fog over an airport or the light bulb popping out of the comic-book character's head as the "Eureka!" issues from his mouth, but a resolute blinking, a setting of the shoulders, a sudden animal knowledge of the game, a realization that the prey is within reach. Barnett approaches the basket and shoots an easy lay-up, a fast two points, and he tips the ball to the bear as it falls through the whispering net. The coach and other members of the team speak listlessly in the stands, shuffle their feet as they lose interest in what appears to them to be a one-man hot dog show.

Clumsy and precise, the bear dribbles out past the key and surveys the court, noting (without conscious measurement, as animals and trained athletes do) the dimensions, the orange lines, the yellow three-second area like a trap around the basket; Barnett stands under the hoop, fiddling with the strings of the net with fierce nonchalance. The bear stays very still at the free throw line and raises his hands and the ball up over his head. His dim bear vision can hardly make out the basket up ahead, the transparent backboard decorated with gray tape, the white net, but the way there is as illuminated as a nighttime runway: the padded orange bottom of the upright, the metallic yellow right below the hoop, the bright orange of the hoop itself all glow with a startling black light poster luminosity. The bear throws the ball in a high, space-shot arc toward the basket gleaming like a candle, and gasps sound from the stands along with cries of "Long!" and "Short!" and high-pitched metallic whistles before a moment of silence as the ball whooshes through the basket. Barnett leaps away from the net just in time to avoid getting hit over the head by the flying ball.

"The animal got lucky," Barnett yells to the stands to quell the stamping and applause, then takes it out. He dribbles past the key with languid grace, bouncing the ball as if it

were a yo-yo attached by some gossamer, near-invisible string
to his index finger, completely under his power: he dribbles
behind his back, switching hands at the blindest, dead-center
back spot; he dribbles between his legs, so that the ball seems
to be some small alive creature trying to avoid getting
crunched by the giant's white canvas feet; he dribbles low and
mean, and high and saucy. When he reaches the top of the
key, he stands behind the curving orange circle and dribbles
bodaciously, one foot out to the side, one hand on a hip, his
head cocked at the bear in challenge, as if he may try one of
his patented long shots that never fail to bring sighs from the
crowds and curses from the players on the opposing teams.
But instead of putting it up, he approaches the basket once
more, and the bear picks him up, defensing with his flashiest
dance moves. The backstroking bear arms look like churning,
anarchic windmills to Barnett, the invisible-rope climbing
looks like an attempt to pluck the ball from upraised hands;
the bear Twists low as if faked out, preparing to leave his feet
in a daredevil block, only to swivel again out to the side Barnett picks to shoot around. The bear's feet dance Mashed
Potatoes around Barnett's sneakers, Shuffles and Boogalooes
and Stomps until the path of Barnett's approach to the
basket becomes decorated with the ornate paisleys the bear's
claws scratch in the highly polished surface of the floor. Ten
feet from the basket, seven feet, and the spectators see that for
all the bear's finessing footwork and air-churning arms, Barnett will go for the cripple lay-up over the bear's head and
make it easily, probably every time until the twelve is
reached and they can all have a good laugh over the match.
As Barnett picks up speed and the ball slaps the floor with increasing force and velocity, the bear jumps, seems to hang in
the air for a moment with his toes pointed downward in the
best balletic tradition, his arms ringing his head like a halo.
In the air he bends, reaches, grabs, and turns his furry body
into a rolling ball heading straight for Barnett's feet, a tum-
bler now rather than a dancer, and he hits the ground sound-
lessly just as Barnett is about to let loose his favorite shot, a

sweet quiet little banked number imitated at all the playgrounds in town. The man's shoes squeak bone-chilling complaints, putting on the brakes when he sees the bear's move,
then take off in a frenzied, long-legged leap out of some
cartoonist's imagination, all limbs flying in different directions. The ball sails off over the basket like a bird looking
for a better place to roost, and the bear, whose roll ends with
him standing again, hardly winded, lumbers over to the far
corner of the court where he retrieves the ball and starts to
head once more for the key while Barnett lies in a heap under the hoop.

"No harm, no foul," the coach yells. "Get up, you turkey."

"Fall back, baby," one of the players yells, "the bear's got
the hot hand now."

"Hell, he can't keep makin' 'em from back there," Barnett
says as he sits comfortably on the floor, head resting on bony
knees. The bear throws up another suborbital satellite which
floats gently through the basket and Barnett rubs his eyes,
then his calves, then stands with the unhinged look of a man
whose sports car has just been turned into a stepped-on tin
can in a car crash. Unnerved and proud, he misses his next
three shots and still refuses to guard the bear, who runs his
total up to ten with ease as Barnett's face grows strained, his
eyes large and limpid and looking ready to cry.

Barnett comes downcourt like a car careening down a rain-
slick mountainside with washed-out brakes, leaning into his
run at a lightning bolt forty-five-degree angle, pummeling
the ball to the ground with each dribble so that the sound is
akin to machine-gun fire, slapping each rubber step with a
shrieking that leaves tire tracks behind. The bear manages to
guard this rampage by running backward as fast as he can,
pumping his knees all the way and waving his arms to help
propel him along the slick floor, but even so he slips and
slides and momentum more than perseverance drags him
along in front of teeth-gritting Barnett. Ten feet from the
basket, Barnett zigs as if to go inside, along the baseline, and
the bear zigs with him; but when Barnett zags back to ap-

proach the basket from a better angle, the bear finds himself weightless and hurtling through space, his heels daintily tickling the floor, his paws grabbing handfuls of sweaty air. Barnett, without his snorting, grunting opponent, instantly becomes a loping gazelle, a floating ballerina, on his approach to the basket, spins and stretches and gently and noiselessly caroms the ball off the backboard and through the basket on a perfect reverse lay-up.

"Long," someone yells, and the rest of the Wolves giggle. The bear, crumpled in the midst of the first row of seats, gets up, shaking himself like a wet dog trying to forget the recent smell of soap; he rotates his ears in an attempt to clear them of the hornets who've just moved in.

"Call it quits, suckah?" Barnett asks the limping bear who now whips his head back and forth with such fury that bear spit flies from his open mouth like a hurricane rain, like a monsoon at the height of its season, a thick, globby downpour which lands in gouts upon the polished wood surface, then skids and relaxes into long, thin, viscous stripes like the slimy, half-alive growths on the sides of aquariums. The coach tosses Barnett a graying towel, which he pushes around disdainfully with his foot as the bear continues wailing away with his head, making a low moan similar to his ice cream cry in roundness, though not in tone.

"Play or forfeit, animal," Barnett says as he kicks the towel past the sidelines toward the home team bench.

"Whoooooo. I'll play," the bear says softly. "I always finish my gigs." He catches the ball Barnett throws head-high and ambles out past the key, dribbling with his deliberate, concentrating clumsiness which no longer evokes the hoots of the other players: they know Barnett has to come out after him. The bear has the hot hand and, unguarded, will win the game.

Just outside the key, at the place that seems to magnetize the ball and send it flying supersonically toward the metal hoop, the bear stops and, still dribbling, eyes the sky as if on the lookout for a flock of ducks for dinner, or for the marshmallow movements of storm clouds. With years of practice at being cool behind him, Barnett strolls out to the key too, looking at his teammates, at the empty seats on the other side of the court, at his beautifully shaped fingernails. As he comes upon the bear, who still dribbles patiently outside the key, a look of mild surprise transfigures his face, the look of someone who has just run into his elementary school best friend on a street corner after years out of touch with that person's fortunes, a pleasant and passionless look that precedes a handshake and a pat on the back, a few meaningless words, and then a passing once more into the separate worlds inhabited and a resumption of memory, of relegating that other person to a nonliving past softer colored than the present, slightly blurred, like the background scenery of dreams.

A flash of hands ends the idyll, dark hands crossing and slapping and grabbing in a speeding blur and a soft whispering swishing like a flock of butterflies coasting through a still summer afternoon. The bear emerges from the skirmish with the basketball slamming onto the floor in front of him, both he and it heading toward the hoop like a pounding rain, leaving Barnett standing where the bear had been, holding his hands a foot and a half apart as if he were about to dribble a black hole in space, sink an invisible twenty-footer. The bear drives like he is the spearhead of an invading fast break of Mongol hordes, inventing basketball as he runs, putting the leather to the floor with a new mastery, a craft approaching art, his footwork undifferentiated from his beloved dance, heels twitching out and in, every so often a tiny two-step, a jiggling knee. The pure spirit of the game has him now, of running and jumping, of making rhythmic, foot-slapping noise, of the feel of the ball hitting hand as regularly as the beating of your heart, the pounding of your lungs, all separate from competition, from other men and beasts, the muse of the sport demanding beauty as much as any other self-respecting, accepted, and recognized Greek quasi-goddess, demanding clarity of vision, demanding living metaphor as an offering, settling for no less than perfection. The bear runs right up under the basket, defies gravity as he Twists his body away from the floor in a hairy corkscrew, feels the ball in his hands as light as a balloon, lighter, lighter, almost soaring up to the rafters with him in a crazy delirium. The bear invents the slam dunk to a chorus of oohs and ahs, and wins the game.

The bear walks toward the sidelines with an airiness in his head nearing the intoxication induced by powerful drugs, his vision blurring, his knees wobbly, a slow-motion ambling walk which seems to bring the sideline nearer in a wavy dialectical mode, three steps forward, two steps back; the dark tide of other players meets him halfway, engulfing him with slaps on the back and on the paws, with chin chucks and cheek tweaks and fast talk, and Big hugs him and kisses the side of his muzzle. He is twisted around and around in congratulations like an unblindfolded pin-the-tail-on-the-donkey gamesman, finally allowed to reach a standstill when the coach appears in front of him, outlined in swirling squiggly lines and with four vibrating eyes scattered across his face.

"Let's go upstairs to da offices," Mahoney says. "If you can write your name on a contract, you've got yourself a good steady job with more travel opportunities dan da navy and more broads around dan da air force, not to mention dis fine group of hooligans who wouldn't pass to you if you were alone under da basket and already hanging in da air. You'll bring in more fans than our ladies nights, bald-head nights, and paraplegic nights put together. Come on, baby. We'll get you shirts and shoes and all da peanuts you can eat."

Disoriented, confused, the bear allows himself to be led away from his teammates, the exaltation of the game already slipping away, being replaced by a prickling of the hair on the back of his neck, a tingling of his claws, which any Ford employee could tell him is no big deal, only the slightest incubating touch of alienation of the laborer.

In '69, we were the kings of basketball." Big speaks in a whisper, his hoarse voice weaving contrapuntally around the syrupy high sweet songs of Marvin Gaye blasting from the huge stereo, songs about the transcendentalism of physical love strangely belied by the flaccid giant sitting on the couch, and by the lumpy form of the bear on the floor, his back legs widespread in a parody of human sitting posture, his front ones balancing his oversized chest and broad back, like a hairy fulcrum or a geometric diagram in a junior high school textbook, by plumping down in the exact center of the back-leg isosceles triangle. The bear strains his head forward to hear Big's words, and tilts his head from one side to the other, raising and lowering his ears at the same time as if he were an alert dog, a gargantuan imitation of the world-famous RCA logo, "Bear Listening to His Master's Voice." He makes every effort to control the clicking of his back toenails as his toes dance to the music, his ankles twitch, his calves ache with stifled steps: an intelligent beast, he has to concentrate to discern the deeper meanings that sometimes surface from the overworked miasma of human speech, and in Big's tone he apprehends a seriousness which demands attention, which negates Dance. Big interprets the blank, open look on the bear's face as concern (he already knows that the bear loves him, since animals do not conceal their love as some people do), and continues to speak of the past, which always looms larger, both frightening and comforting, when the speed has worn off. "When we played at home, you could see the road team's knees knocking when they had to stand up for the starting lineup. Baby, we mesmerized them like snake charmers do to cobras, we had them dancing our game, we had the moves. No one could touch us. Mahoney was the toughest forward in the league, and with an outside shot. Hell, I scored forty-eight points in one game, just battering the heads of all those little guys standing under the basket with their mouths open and their hands up. I was still young, and thought it would go on forever. Then Coach retired, Mahoney retired, and we got all these rookies, all the time smoking weed and hotdogging it as if passing had become extinct in college ball. In 1970 we couldn't break five hundred, one rookie slashed another with his blade, the new coach badmouthed us on TV, and I was traded for a flashy guard, two draft picks, and cash. Cash! No more glory of the sport. Just survival, making the cuts, getting the points. So I started speeding, started sweating electric diamonds on the court, running down two pairs of shoes a week. Man, they called me Mister Hustle. I threw up anything inside of twenty-five feet, and got traded and traded, 'cause I was so valuable to any team. Then some smart boy in the commissioner's office thought up the expansion of the league, good for the sport, they said. Late in the '70 season. And I became even more valuable 'cause all those punk teams needed the big man, the center to stand under the basket and take the beating for all the other ants flashing around down there. So here I am. Rich. That's all you gotta be these days."

The jingling of coins in worn pockets comes into the bear's head as an audio image, confusing him because of its dimness and connection with a past, unremembered part of his life, of his career. The corresponding visual image that pops from his head like a candy-colored light bulb or undotted exclamation point is the ice cream cone, the lost delight, as lost to him as the '69 season is to Big, as much a part of a vanished past, a world inhabited by different animals, extinct species, fantastic dreams.

"Whoooooo," the bear roars dolefully, and Big rubs his eyes with gigantic fists like meat loaves, thinking the bear shares in his particular gossamer memory of a better time.

"Oh man," Big says in a whining, nasal voice full of compassion. "What you want? Whatever it is, I'll get it for you."

"Whoooooo," the bear cries; Big's lengthy arms extend toward the animal in an involuntary gesture of charity. "I would love some ice cream."

"Don't have no ice cream, man," Big says, leaning his face in his hands in disbelief and melancholy. "We'll get you ice cream after tonight's game. That's a better time for ice cream. You shouldn't eat so soon before playing, make you sick. Now let's get ready to go."

The bear still sits on the floor; released by his bellowing, his body sways more visibly to the blasting music, and he remains immune to Big's words. The thought of ice cream thrills him. Anyway, he's never needed any time for preparation before, can dance without a spangle or a tutu, without props or video magic, is one of the last of the real live shows, even more so since in the course of his hitchhiking travels he's lost his small trunk which held his clown collar and shackles, probably mislaid it on purpose to be rid of that slavery, in fact cannot even remember that he's ever owned such a piece of property and believes, in the present-tense manner of animals, that he's always been a free bear.

"Get your bag, sucker. Do I have to tell you everything?" Big says in exasperation at the bear's total lack of professional expertise at pregame activities. "And don't forget your shoes. Be some big fine if you scratch up the floor every game. Hell, think you could cut your toenails like a civilized creature. Never saw a basketball player with such teeth and nails. This game's gone to hell."

As Big switches off the stereo with a click and a menacing spark of angry static, the bear looks around the room, unable to remember where he put all of his new belongings (animals,

and bears in particular, being forgetful past the point of
socialism with their material possessions): what bear has ever
owned an athletic bag with a snarling silver wolf decaled
on its side; a brand-new pair of Adidas basketball shoes in an
extra-wide size manufactured specially for the giants of the
game, not even for the guards and forwards but for the centers
alone, the men with the size twenty triple-E feet which earthquake stadiums on fast breaks, which cause volcanic eruptions
on small Pacific isles when the center alights after a strenuous
rebound; a silver and white home uniform, shorts and T-shirt,
with the number double zero on the back like a huge pair of
eyeglasses, or like cartoon eyes waiting for the wandering iris
and pupils to be drawn in, in unmatched sizes, the shorts in a
man's size forty waist, big enough to accommodate the bear
stomach and staunch bear hips, the shirt in a mere large (in a
game in which the smallest men wear this size, the quick and
mobile guards, the harassing gnats, the outside shooters in
tune with all the meandering ellipses of the universe, the natural shape of planets' orbits, of stars' wanderings, of the
basketball on its cruising course to the orange hoop) because
of the narrower-than-human bear shoulders and tapering,
finely shaped bear chest; a dark blue and silver sweat suit in
the same unmatched sizes, as if one man were to wear the
smallish top, another, a seven-footer, to wear the great baggy
pants, especially beloved by the bear when Mahoney pulled
it out of a tissue-papered package because of the gleaming
material like something unimaginable to bears, like the night
sky in the forest, a genetic memory held in deep reserve by the
urban bear, existing in near remembrance as the thrill of
swinging through viny trees lives in some humans' heads, the
stretching of arms, the excitement of loose legs, the wind in
their eyes; a strange and necessary collection of wristbands
and headbands, Ace bandages for knee and thigh and ankle, wraparound swathes for the arm and for the stomach, all
of these like baby toys to the bear who longed to swing them
in the air and catch them in his teeth, to shake them back and
forth in his powerful jaws as he might swing a fresh-killed

rabbit in the wilds; and a group of socks of varying lengths, all dashing with their silver stripes at the top, which the bear perceives as a kind of disguise for his feet, one of the points of this game, he's sure, to make his clawed and flat bear feet as human as possible, as clothed and manly as can be. The bear searches the room with his dull eyes, knowing the shining silver of the club logo on his bag will attract his gaze much as a lightning bolt in the forest would, but he sees nothing out of place, nothing that does not belong in the spartan elegance of Big's living room, a room full of man things, of large pieces of furniture, a couch, a chair, the stereo, of dials and gauges and jumping needles and buttons to push and pull and twist and turn, of massive wood and highly polished chrome, of black and brown without nuance, without shading, the flatness of leather matching the ungrained wood for a look much like Big's skin.

"I don't know where my bag is," the bear says, and Big slaps his broad smooth forehead with one gigantic hand.

"And how many of the plays the coach taught you do you remember, hey man?" Big asks.

"Whoooooo," the bear cries, in genuine despair, no wanting, no remembering, a feeling similar to the void he drops off into when he falls asleep, a wide yawning chasm of nothing, the depth of his animal nature overcoming him with its vacuum, with its limitations, with its natural ability only for love, and for mindless suffering (not so much unlike humans, only they think constantly about love, and suffer all the more for it). Big throws his arms straight out and stands up, his body like a great flag of night in a new wind; then he embraces the bear.

"Oh, man," Big says, his mouth filling with the bear's neck hair as he speaks, "we'll find your things. Man, I get so mean sometimes when I'm off that stuff, and so mean when I'm on it. Lemme go take some. Then we'll find your suit and make it to the game. We'll cream those suckers, you wait. Nothing like pro ball to get you up. Just wait till you get out there, all the huffing and running and sweat, all those dotted lines on the court, everywhere, until you begin to see them in the air, the arc of each shot in slo-mo instant replay, man, it's beautiful." Big disappears into the bathroom as if he were the galloping spearhead of a fast break, leaving the bear sitting slouched with bear unconcern on the living room floor, bewildered by the changeableness of human nature (though he fails to perceive it as such: instead the image that sweeps through the dark movie theater of his mind is a darkening sky at sunset, filling speedily with the deep red and purple gloom of night, with great lunging cumulonimbus storm clouds, a sky portending many things frightening to animals, sending them scurrying and scuttling, hurrying to safety, to protect their young, to the solace of warm tree trunks and thick-scented caves). The anxieties that any rookie would have about his first professional basketball game, the gurgling stomach clenching and unclenching like fretting fists, the exalted heartbeat, the cool sweat unlike the sweat of exertion or the sweat of fear, a sweat leaving the body feeling clothed in a smothering layer of sticky Handiwrap, a sweat similar to that left in the wake of exotic tropical fevers, debilitating and thrilling, leaving the pulse racing, the skin contracting into grainy nodules like the thick sands of the Sahara, never occur to the bear; in fact, Big's hug leaves him elated in his confusion, and he rises, balances his bulky body on one toe, and begins to spin, the syncopated music still playing in his head. Bending his knee and rotating his hip, he lowers, lowers, until his posture resembles that of a Russian folk dancer more than a rock and roller, but quickly he exits the dizzying turn, leaps into a rope-climbing Monkey, then gives a quick look over his shoulder to see Big coming out of the bathroom; plopping back to the floor in a position approximating the one he was in when Big left, he looks up expectantly, his head cocked, his ears ready for audio clues. When Big jerks his shoulders, neck, and head toward the front door, the bear obediently stands up and follows the giant out, hunkering along on his thick padded feet so comfy on Big's shag carpets, then out the door and down the concrete path to Big's tiny sports car. On the front seat, the shining flight bag with the snarling wolf on its side waits for them.

In the locker room, everyone suits up quickly in the grim metallic quiet associated with professional killers for hire or CIA men studiously dressing up as hippies to infiltrate a demonstration, in contrast to the bear, still nude, fumbling with his shorts and shirt. In a perfect bear imitation of Charlie Chaplin, he puts both his legs through one skinny leg hole and trips when he attempts to take a step; then he sits down to pull his legs out and try again, and ends up with his legs straight up in the air with his shorts wound around them like a glittering Möbius strip; once he gets them off, he seriously considers the structural implications of the shorts and determines intelligently that one leg to one leghole must be the prescribed method, and promptly puts them on backwards, so that a tightly stitched, uncomfortable crotch hugs his bear behind and a large, baggy area adorns his front. By this time, all the other suited-up players stand around him, watching in fascination.

"Good thing this cat ain't got no jock strap to worry him," one of them says, and the others laugh.

"Can't wait to see what he'll do with the shirt," another says as the bear tugs at his bound butt, then at his sagging front waistband.

"Man," Barnett says, himself the picture of on-court nattiness, a silver and white striped headband keeping his long, frizzy, wispy, shining hair from his brow, the stark white of his brief uniform making his skin shine near-purple in its brownness; his socks are pulled to his knees, the stripes arranged like precise orbits, the paths of moons around his calves. "Turn those things around before I start itching. If you gonna be a basketball player, you can't be no fool." The bear holds out his arms in supplication and surprise, his blank eyes asking for help; Barnett reaches his magnificent basketball-god's hands out to the bottom of the bear's shorts and gives a strong tug, sending the pants crumpling to the floor like a puddle of liquid mercury around the bear's feet. "Now turn them around, turkey," Barnett says, and stands over the bear with his arms crossed on his chest as the bear daintily steps out of the shorts and follows his instructions, ending up with a perfectly fitted anomalous covered-up lower body, gross thick thatches of brown hair protruding both above and below the elegant human pretension of the shorts.

"Arms up," Barnett then commands, and when the bear complies the complex T-shirt with its distended armholes and neckline slips easily over the bear's head, entangled only for a moment on his wiggling ears; with the impersonal hands of a physician, Barnett tucks the shirt into the bear's shorts. Big and Barnett then slap hands intricately, congratulating one another on what they have come to consider their own invention, their Frankenstein's monster, their hirsute idiot child. The others, intrigued by Barnett's performance, begin to search the bear's flight bag, finding the myriad bands and bandages and socks, waving them in the air like tiny lariats. As the bear stands innocent and pleased at the camaraderie he has caused, a mass idea occurs (just as a scientific breakthrough discovered in the six months' night of a Norwegian laboratory will happen simultaneously in a sun-warmed laboratory in San Diego): to dress the bear as a little girl might dress her favorite doll, to decorate him as one would a Christmas tree. Hands fly around the bear, and white and silver ornaments, and poking fingers; in a futile animal hope, the bear stands stock-still, but this only makes a better Christmas tree of him, and when the team steps back en masse to admire its handiwork, the bear is an inspiringly silly sight.

The bear stands, adorned like a hairy mummy newly discovered by graverobbers, the pharaoh of bears, the shimmering fop of beardom. All up and down each arm, wristbands of various widths, in the team's white and silver stripes, twist around him like the asp-bracelets Cleopatra wore. Around his head, just below his ears and above his eyes so that his fuzzy face hair tickles all four of those organs, two thick head-bands weave through his fur, compressing his skull with their elastic force so that his head aches as if with heavy thought (severe money worry, or sexual anticipation, or hunger: all the ills that give men headaches, the ills that bear heads are empty of, hence the absence of migraine in bears though not in some of the more inbred, tiny types of dogs and Oriental cats which always look worried). His legs too are wound with bands and bandages, shining and trailing off behind him like a bridal train; around his waist, a cummerbund bandage marks the meeting place of his shorts and shirt. The bear stands as if frozen, all the constricting bands on his body acting like a winter's layer of hoar and frost; his muscles, unused to the bondage that professional athletes accept, strain tense and silent as if waiting for the approach of an old, well-known enemy, and his eyes gleam like the glassy black marble eyes of stuffed teddy bears (the best way to trap a pet: dress him in tight clothing, an immediate immobilizing force not unlike that of curare, only less fatal).

"Jeez Christ," Coach Mahoney says as he walks into the locker room, dragging a big red hand over his cheeks and mouth and chin, "watta buncha ninnies. Perhaps I should remind you guys dis is not a class in interior decorating or fashion design. Perhaps I should remind you dat da Dallas Outlaws are waiting in da other locker room ready to cream you guys' asses."

"We tough and ready to play, coach," the Earring says. Mahoney grabs the loose end of the bear's sash and pulls, sending the bear flying and dervish-whirling down the locker room aisle until this particular dance ends in a short, shimmy-ing Boogaloo, a flash of heels and knees before the bear bows and sits to a chorus of applause and cheers.

"All right. All right. Very nice," Mahoney says. "Maybe we should hire da Rockettes too, bet we could pick dem up for a song dese days."

"Me and my bear are ready," Big says, and Barnett slaps his hand once more. "Don't even need to warm up."

"Yeah, yeah," Mahoney says, "I can hear your blood buzzing in your veins. You run over da plays wid da bear?"

"This cat ain't no dummy," Big says; Big never bothers to memorize plays anymore, never learns the give-and-goes, the outlet passes, because there's never anyone waiting for the plays to happen. Only hotshot rookies driving inside and under, and assists when the guy with the ball gets punched in the nose and throws it to the first friendly face.

"Don't pick on the bear, man," Barnett says to the coach, who throws his hands up in the air in dismay.

"Hey, don't go sensitive on me. I love dis bear. Dis afternoon on *Sports Talk Back* I called in to announce our new secret weapon, and da show was flooded wid calls after dat asking ticket prices, seat locations, and whether dey could come here widout getting mugged. We might have ten thousand here tonight. Da owner even loves da bear. But we still would like to win a game every so often."

Through this, the bear sits like a buddha, contemplating shoes and socks. The long, thin spaghetti tubes of the socks and the rubber-bottomed, laced-up flat shoes seem in no way related to his fat and furry feet. In a dim bear way, he realizes the problem transcends his intelligence, his dexterity, something in the very essence of his being; he moans softly to himself as his claws become entangled in the shoelaces, as the socks crawl up his arms like loving snakes.

"Do I have to wear these?" the bear asks in a soft voice.

"What's wrong, baby?" Mahoney says. "Listen, bear. You go out dere widout shoes, you'll come back wid bleeding stumps for toes, and I'm not even sure bears have toes to start wid. Dis is a tough game. Dis is not just dancing."

As if the sun were about to shine through a battleship fleet of storm clouds, the bear nearly has a human revelation: dim shapes coalesce and disintegrate in his head as his whole life, the past he can never remember and the overpowering present, begins to take sides, to turn into two teams, the dark jerseys and the light jerseys as distinct as two rival basketball teams on the shining hardwood surface. The teams are outer strife and (apparent) inner peace, though in reality this apparent peace moves toward strife as ineluctably as the coming of the great bear void of sleep, and when closely examined is as ethereal. The bear nearly sees himself as a creature at odds with his environment, a state antithetical to animal nature but common to man: were his brain a twist more convoluted, he might discern the inapplicability of his forest genes to urban living, the ineptness of his hands for donning shoes and socks, the inescapable tension of being sui generis in a world where mere differentness is reason to assume immediate guilt. Of course, the unnaturalness of his surroundings has corrupted him (but where is a natural place for a bear these days? in Yosemite with the gaping tourists? in cartoons? in zoos? in interior decoration as bearskin rugs, fangs agleam?), has enabled him to hover near the luminous world of thought, half-aware of the misery of his animal state, unaware of its meaning. The children always poking him, the women examining his back for zippers and seams, the drunks pulling at his hair, all the boors coming closer to the truth of his existence than the believers, the obvious (in this case, that everything is sham, artifice, contrivance: something dressed as something else, for whatever reason, must be found out) overcoming the subtle (a dancing bear!): his proximity to an analysis of his condition causes the bear to become what they thought him to be, a man in a bear suit, even metaphorically a sad state of being, of imprisonment.

As Barnett slips two pairs of striped socks over the bear's heavily furred legs, then laces up the ill-fitting gym shoes, the coach paces up and down an aisle of the locker room, shuffling and stomping his feet in rhythm with some unheard tune, or perhaps to the slap and brush soft shoe of his thoughts.

"All right," Mahoney says, "I'm not going to say much to you guys tonight because, what da hell, I don't get half as much money as any of you turkeys, so take it as constructive and loving criticism, and don't get upset. Nate da Great, man, you gotta watch dose behind-da-back dribbles, man, dey're looking for 'em, man, deir hands are so close to your butt dat if you dribble in front you're liable to get da league's first goosing foul done to you, and I don't wanna haveta see you blush." The team settles down onto the benches in the locker room, smiles on their faces, their eyes glazed and dull as if they've been watching the daytime educational children's shows on public television for many hours. "Hey, Sweet Lou. You get da same lousy two points if you shoot from six and if you shoot from twenty, man. One of da finer points of da game, thought I'd point it out to you. So when dat lane is open and da other team's center's standing around picking his nose, don't stop at half-court and take aim, man. Instead think of my blood pressure and my ulcers and my receding hairline and my hopeless weight problem, and remember what a thrill it was in college when you'd drive and all dose fans would cheer and dose little girls wid short skirts and pom-poms would jump up and down so you could see deir asses." Lou takes aim at an imaginary hoop with an imaginary basketball, weighing it in his careful hands, his eyes hawk-keen, while the others, uneasy in the knowledge that their turns are coming, tickle his ribs and stamp their feet in forced hilarity. "My buddy, Earl da Pearl. Da little men, we call dem guards in dis game for no good reason I could ever figure out, dey dribble da ball downcourt looking all da time for da open man, you know, da guy standing around wid his chin balanced on da hoop and his eyes half closed from boredom. Guards are famous for getting lots of assists. Dat means tossing da ball to other guys who can score. Now, man, dere's Big collecting dis ridiculous paycheck to keep him in drugs and, man, he's just standing around dere under da basket thinking about comparative religion and Kierkegaard and stuff, and a shrimp like you dribbles right into da key, collides wid da other team's center who's been standing around thinking about dis hot mama he's left in his hotel room who's probably going through his pockets at dat very moment, and you get da charge, dey get da ball, and I get a stomachache. Just think about it, man." Nate reaches across the bench to tug on Earl's jiggling foot; the bear listens, entranced and fascinated, at this verbal, theoretical approach to the game he's never really played, realizing at the same time that the coach resembles him more than any other man in the room does, his bulky chest, deep-set eyes, heavy arms. He sees the coach as a bear in a man suit and immediately feels a kinship for him. "Easy Ed, man, I love your two-handed set shot. I love your hang and dunk. Man, your hook shots are hot. But dese are not free throws, man. At da line, we take it slow. We look close at da hoop, lift our arms in dat direction, let go of da ball, and if da wind's in our favor, we get a point, sometimes three to make two, sometimes one and one. Dere's no competition, man, dat's why it's called da charity stripe. And dere's no style points awarded, not like at da Olympics." The locker room begins to resemble a monkey cage at the zoo more than a collection of professional athletes because of the chuckling and gouging and mock punching; the bear catches the animal high spirits, begins to feel a lightness in his chest, a low hum in his head, but at the same time feels afraid, the prickling fur on the back of his neck, and becomes wary. "And da rest of you guys. I hear dey're gonna have air conditioning on tonight, it's gonna be chilly out dere. So move around a little on defense, you know, nothing spectacular, just to keep da blood moving. After all, you're valuable pieces of property and da owner wants me to look out for you, see you don't catch chills. And watch dose twinkletoes out dere. If we wanted Fred Astaire and Gene Kelly, we'd get 'em, hey, nothing's too good for dis team. When you got da ball, you pound it on da floor if you wanna walk wid it. No cute little bunny hops when you're just standing around wid it waiting for your illegal moving screen to pass by. Dat's about all I got to say. You'll all be getting engraved invitations to my wrist slitting in da mail." The team rises and files out of the locker room, an air of easy jocularity about them. The bear hangs back, waits until the coach starts his walk, head down, as if approaching his own sentencing for heinous crimes against humanity, or his own electrocution in Sing Sing, and falls in next to the coach.

"Kid," the coach says, slinging his barbell arm around the bear's shoulders, "it's all fundamentals in dis game. Dat's what it's all about." The bear shakes his head intelligently, as if he understands the joys of a fundamentally sound team for a basketball coach, and the coach and his bear pass out of the locker room and into the arena, white lights full blast, the early throng of fans clutching hot dogs and beer and calling out the names of their favorite players. For a moment the bear believes he's felt the sight of a hunter's rifle upon the back of his neck, and crouches and spins to discover the enemy only to find no one there. The coach stands back, arms crossed on his chest, shaking his head in admiration for his newest player's reflexes. The bear looks around, feels muscles contracting and relaxing in readiness for flight or death, then ambles off to the court, his shoes scratching an uneasy Samba on the hair of his feet, to join his teammates while the fans gasp and point and jeer and laugh, throw hot dogs and dimes and pages of their programs at the spectacle as the house organist plays "Take Me Out to the Ball Game."

The team has already begun its impressive series of pre-game practice relays, a full-throttle lay-in and rebound, after which the player hurtles a wrap-around-the-back pass to the next man in line, a dribble-and-dunk combination that has turned into a fancy footwork competition with a variety of hanging-in-the-air moves designed to simulate antigravity astronaut training, and outside shooting practice, throwing in the high, arching shooting stars with the physical affectations of the trade, a twitching foot, a loose and supple wrist, a toss of the head as studied and effective as Bogart's lisp. The bear gets in the lay-up line, at the very end behind Sweet Lou, who's already taken his second turn, during which he dribbled the ball between his legs, back and forth, all the way under and past the basket, making his teammates think he'd completely forgotten the purpose of the drill, had become hypnotized by the rhythmic slapping of ball on floor so much like a heartbeat in its resonance and regularity, before he arched his back, looked over his right shoulder, and put up a reverse lay-up which brought gasps from the reverent group of devoted early fans. This time when the ball thwacks into Lou's outstretched hands, he bends his knees until his calves are at forty-five-degree angles to the ground, aims his head down, and dribbles like a madman toward the basket as if following an invisible line drawn on the court. Five feet from the basket he launches himself, the ball held on the tips of his fingers at the most elongated, outside reach of his arms so that it seems to be pulling his body along after it. A dunk must be imminent, the air becomes electric with the power and concentration inherent in the art of dunking, but at the last moment Lou's body relaxes, seems sweetly suspended rather than held aloft by the tensing thrust of muscle and tendon, and he gently lets go of the ball over the basket, raises his arms and points his toes in arabesque, then lands in time to catch the ball and swish it backwards into the waiting furry paws of the bear.

The ball slaps into the bear's paws, and the crowd roars; used to the adulation of the masses, the bear shuffles his feet, his heels flying in and out as he waves the ball in front of his burly body like the coyest stripteaser, and the roaring, the yelling and four-four clapping, heightens. Coach Mahoney sits at his designated place on the sidelines, his face in his massive hands, his legs widespread to support his elbows and upper torso, perhaps remembering a murderous fast break the team he and Big played for in 1969 would run, with no announcer's tongue fast enough to comment on it until it was over and only the devastating results could be reported like a casualty listing after a major natural catastrophe.

When the bear puts the ball to the floor, the crowd becomes even louder in its appreciation of the Wolves' new secret weapon; people press up against the railings which divide cheaper seats from more expensive, closer-to-the-action seats, stand on vacant seats, fathers hold their children straddling their necks or hanging on their shoulders for a better view. The bear is an instant star. He dribbles cautiously toward the basket, his ill-fitting gym shoes squeaking with each step from his weight and deliberation in movement, appearing to be merely a bear dressed up as an athlete, a carefully trained gimmick, a joke, a publicity man's bright idea, and the crowd eats it up, stretches its arms out as if to touch a bit of the wild animal on the loose, yells loud and unintelligible combinations of syllables as if communicating with a primitive being on its own level. Three feet from the basket the bear leaps; with his arms overhead holding the ball, he scissors his legs in time to a Marvin Gaye song heard only by him, points his toes, lifts his right knee to his chest, and sloops the ball through the net, catching it on his own way down and passing it off to the next man in line before his pointed tootsies touch ground. Even the masses can discern the difference between a bear and an artiste and, after a hushed moment, the chant begins: "Bear, bear, bear, bear," and the bear takes a low, long bow and starts back for the end of the line when Mahoney removes his face from his hands, looks around the arena with great sorrow in his reddened eyes, and calls to the bear.

"Hey, bear," he yells, "get over here," and the bear, after taking a second bow when the cries for him fail to abate or diminish, trots up to where the coach sits, the inscrutable bear expression on his face like a mask. Experience has taught the bear never to speak in front of crowds of humans, so he looks at the coach's large, bearlike face awaiting whatever instructions are to be offered, which he will then carry out unquestioningly, in the docile dog manner of the domesticated bear.

"You're benched, man," the coach says mournfully. "Come sit here next to me and play dumb. I just can't do it. Dis ain't no circus, dis is pro ball. Animals do not play pro ball, no matter what some sportswriters say. Da owner is gonna kill me, but I can't let you into dis game. For da sake of da old days." The bear looks up the court, where Big spins a basketball on his upthrust index finger, then to the crowd which still chants "Bear, bear, bear," before he sits down next to Mahoney to await the beginning of the game.

The pregame ritual which began in the locker room talk, then the intricate practice regimen designed, by its unerring display of skill and fortitude, to scare hell out of opponents, continues as all but five of the players for each team sit on the long, uninspiring, much-fabled bench while the five starters, the chosen players, the ones with the most grace and artistry, with the sharpest elbows and the sneakiest punches, the ones who for no apparent reason can run that much faster than the others or put a basketball through the whispering net from twenty feet with that much more mysterious ease, strip off what remains of their sweat suits with the unselfconsciousness of children about to go skinny-dipping and assemble in a studied, random fashion around the yellow circle painted like a helicopter landing site in the middle of the court. The bear watches, fascinated.

A small man in a zebra-striped shirt steps in among the giants, chats briefly with Big and the other center, who crowd into the middle of the yellow circle; the bear relaxes, lets his muscles go slack, his jaws hang open until his tongue slops out one side and his long yellow tooth tips show (animals having no notion of a future, they can relax completely as if relaxed forever, and be fierce as no man can be because the moment of hunger for blood becomes eternal). Then the centers tauten their bodies as if they have been struck by whips, the small man throws the basketball up between them, and they leap, their feet magic and flying, inspired by a wish for antigravity, for release from the earth, and the bear jerks forward. Electricity buzzes all around the bear, the sound perceived not merely by his twitching ears but also by each hair on his body, by his damp nose, by his sharp, keen teeth: the feel of the forest, of animals on the hunt, of two predators meeting for a fight to the finish in which one must inevitably become the prey, of tight feline bodies, heads down, eyes shining cat-yellow in the night, and hungry. All this the bear feels with his entire body, and it frightens him.

As if hypnotized, the bear watches the game with intensity equaling the speedy, violent, single-minded direction of the players on court, but he can't understand it. Unlike the patterns of nature, which have a fluid continuity of form, a sameness for eons slowly turning to a similar, gracefully altered sameness, the scrambling of basketball—the high and low posts and everything in between; the pick and rolls; the mad three-on-one rushes downcourt; the switching off one-on-one defenses which sometimes produce perfect symmetry, little man against little man, medium-sized man against the same, giant against giant, and sometimes create situations out of silent comedy, with a guard badgering the stomach of a center who blithely puts the ball into the hoop with a twitch of his long fingers—looks anarchic to the bear: with eyes genetically created to see the slow trends of forest existence, the growth of baby trees after a rainy season, lazily looping, buzzing flies, the movement of clouds over the mountains, the change in size of the deer herds from spring to winter, from year to year, these intricately planned basketball plays terrify him with their flying legs and arms and bodies. He sits next to the coach with trepidation of the animal kind, not the sweats nor the migraines but a body readying itself without self-consciousness for battle and death. Time expands and contracts in a manner Einstein could never have mapped as the bear observes minute-long time-outs that seem to stretch for hours, plays that run with manic speed before his eyes until he can't tell who has the ball, who is beating up on whom, which team is which despite the different colors of the uniforms, the bodies blending into multicolored streaks with white tennis shoes on, colliding and bouncing off one another in a parody of nuclear reaction. Lights flicker in a specially engineered satellite up above, counting the bouncing balls and bodies, minutes, periods: the bear feels barraged with stimuli, a dazed laboratory rat after a particularly hazardous maze run on LSD. Before he knows what has happened, halftime arrives.

"All right," Coach Mahoney says, back in the locker room. "Fifty-four to forty-six is not dat bad. Dese guys must be tired from deir road trip or something. If we watch dose fouls, we might have a chance to catch up fast in da beginning of da third quarter. Big, when you block dose shots, no reason for you to put your fist in da other guy's teeth. Lou, I appreciate your effort on da drive, but when da other guy's just standing dere wid his feet taking root and he's snoring, don't bang your head into his chest. Dat'll be charging every time, man, and wid your hot dog style you ain't getting away with anything. And defense. What can I say? It's half da game, dat's what da writers say, stopping dem from making baskets, even dough it doesn't show up on da old lifetime stats in da NBA Guide. But you've heard all dis before."

Big, just returned from the toilet for his usual halftime refueling, asks: "What about the bear?" and eyes widen, mouths open to give birth to opinions, heads turn to the coach to see what his answer will be.

"Da bear plays," Mahoney says, "over my dead body. And dat's a pretty big impediment for you dead-footed turkeys to step over."

"But the crowd loves him, they're ca-razy for him," Barnett says, rising from the bench and holding both his gigantic surgeon's hands in the air like a master orator.

"I don't even mind him so much anymore," Sweet Lou, the Earring, says.

"Well I don't mind you, so we're all liberal here," Mahoney says, and rubs his beefy hands over his face so the cheeks shifts like a mountain range over an active fault line, tilting his nose first to one side, then to the other.

"He's the coach," Big says, a voice from the old days when basketball coaches were benevolent despots unquestioned in their realms who owned the bodies and deserved the respect of their players, men more powerful than the team owners, who feared their leaving, listened to their suggestions, thought of them as parts of their families; coaches in the sixties were lifers who coached for the same team until the game ate up their insides, giving them all the endemic basketball-coach diseases, diseases of the nervous bench sitters, the ulcers and heart disease and high blood pressure and tension headaches, and then became executives for their teams, general managers who engineered trades and draft choices to make their teams as skilled as possible, coherent units aching for the touch of the court on their shoe bottoms, of the ball whistling through fingertips, for the inaudible ticking of the twenty-four-second clock. With the passing of that era, with free-agent hotshots naming their price, their team, their coach, their terms, coaches became another transient commodity, fired and hired for their box-office-enhancing possibilities, a nomadic corps of sufferers, of martyrs to the game, having to become as changeable in their loyalties as the seasons, unable to sign leases on apartments, to buy homes, to let their children develop lasting friendships with the kids down the street, gypsies not by choice (whoever heard of a basketball coach quitting?), unlike the players who auction themselves off, go where the most money is. Coaches don't have to worry merely about putting together the best possible team anymore; instead, they have to think about potential flash, drafting the hot dogs whom the people will pay to see, the guys who can fly through the air from the top of the key to the basket, do triple corkscrews, then dunk without getting winded, rather than the sure little guards like gadflies on defense, with the shots that look all too easy on offense. Coaches who make the game look too easy get fired; coaches who get their pictures on the first page of the sports section because of their funky names for long-lost plays and their belief in transcendental meditation get raises. Mahoney sighs.

"Dat's right, I'm da coach at least until tomorrow, so I can still fine you guys tonight. Insubordination. If I decide to play da bear, in he goes. Until den, I don't wanna hear about it." The bear looks up at Mahoney with incomprehension, his eyes more blank than usual at this display of tenuous power, of mutiny, of loyalty, feeling less and less that the coach and Big actually are his brothers: he discerns a turmoil in them he can neither identify nor understand. When the rest of the team charges out to begin the second half, the bear hangs back, becomes the last member of the home team bench to take his seat, not the place of honor next to the coach this time but the last seat on the bench, in isolation. He watches the game with continuing confusion and new detachment, the feeling of impending death vanishing, his body relaxing into usual bear posture, the slumped shoulders, the arms hanging stupidly down between the back legs, his muzzle jutting forward, quiet as a buddha counting his own heartbeats.

As the bear watches, the Wolves fall further and further behind, turning the ball over with a panache which almost becomes style, a studied parody of the art of basketball, and the bear can hear the coach groaning and grumbling at the other end of the bench, shouting at the refs on even the most obvious calls against his team, shuffling and stomping his feet on the floor as the point gap widens and more and more fouls are called, most of them against the elbow-throwing Wolves. The third quarter disappears into the fourth, and the topography of the game begins to change as different-sized players are substituted for those in foul trouble or already fouled out. Like a child's game of musical chairs, the personnel manning the bench changes as well, until most of the starting five sit with the bear cheering on their even less talented teammates. Nate and Ed need servicing by the team trainer for small cuts and abrasions, Earl has his leg wrapped up in a mile-long bandage, then sandwiched by a giant ice pack, and only the perennial Big still stays on the floor blocking shots, rebounding, shooting, his eyes fiery from love of the sport and from drugs, the guys on the other team clearing a path for him when he goes up for the big hook shot. Still the

Wolves lose ground, and Mahoney's sufferings at the end of the bench come to resemble the painful death throes of a victim of rattlesnake bite, the sounds he makes become those of a swollen, parched throat, the gestures violent aberrations of a suffering nervous system. The bear watches as the game becomes less beautiful (if it ever was: the first half seems to him, at this point, to have been precise and artful compared to the physical excesses before his eyes) and more a rumble.

Suddenly a whistle, and the manic play turns into a casual milling around with Big at its center, his arms hanging limp by his sides, looking heavenward at the scoreboard; he makes a lackadaisical gesture of "it ain't my fault" as he walks to the sidelines, and Mahoney leaps up with his beefy hands in the T-formation, swaying and jumping and snorting and stomping to attract the attention of his flunkies. With only four men on the floor, the Wolves watch as the fouled man makes both of his free throws; then the Wolf closest to the basket grabs the ball as if it were an infant he has just abducted, smothering it in his hands to keep it from crying out for its mama, and calls for the time-out. Two minutes left in the fourth quarter, with the Wolves down by twenty-two, no replacement center on the bench, and all three big forwards already fouled out. Mahoney wipes the sweat from his forehead with the back of one of his obese hands, then sits in the middle of his crouching and standing players with a face so devoid of emotion that the brain behind it has to be working overtime and more, whirling through possibilities and coming up with nothing. The bear sits trancelike at his end of the bench, unaware of the club turmoil, until he gets bopped on the head by a flying Coca-Cola cup like a guided missile, then looks around to discover the crowd's mouths moving like one, chanting a single syllable over and over, and, when he concentrates, he can understand what they are saying: "Bear, bear, bear, bear."

As if the team were performing a carefully choreographed dance routine, one end of the circle of players opens gracefully and uniformly to include the bear, and many hands beckon him; he rises, enters the magic circle, and it closes behind him with the soft squeaking of gym shoes on wood. He feels trapped, his muzzle crinkles up into a snarl while his eyes maintain their inscrutable look, the ferocity in his nose not yet contagious to the rest of him.

"Bear, man," Mahoney says, his head downcast, "I got no choice. I gotta play you. You're taking over for Big, so here's what you do. When da ball hits da glass, you pull it down if you can. At either end of da court, you get right in da middle of things, right under da hoop, and stir up trouble, don't worry about fouls 'cause we ain't gonna win dis one no how, and you ain't gonna foul out no matter how hard you try in dese last couple of minutes. Dat thing you're doing now wid your nose. Do dat all you can at da guys on da other team, especially when you go up for rebounds. Never put da ball to da floor; when you get a rebound or a pass in da backcourt, get da ball to one of da little men fast. Den get downcourt as quick as you can. Understand?"

"I don't want to play," the bear says, very softly so none of the fans will hear or, if they do, they could never know who spoke, just a disembodied voice from a circle of men surrounding a bear.

"Sweetheart, you gotta play. We made up a contract dis afternoon. Listen, I've been your friend. Big's your friend, man, you know dat. Are you really gonna let us both down like dis?"

Like a woman devoted to a bad-news lover who forces her to do terrible things, the bear considers this. "Okay," the bear says, and the coach mops his brow once more, then drags his hand under his nose. "I'll play this time, for you two guys, even though I don't go in for this kind of rough stuff."

"All right, all right, enough of dis statement of aesthetics," Mahoney says, his hands, flying like overfed pigeons, alive with play possibilities. "As far as I'm concerned, you don't have to throw elbow one. Just stand under da basket and let dem push you around if you want. Dat's fine for a team like dis. A bear center. Me, who loves dis lousy game so much, sending in da first animal in history." Somewhere up near the scoreboard an elephant trumpets, a huge jarring honk which sends the bear, bustled and shoved along with his team-mates, scurrying onto the floor to await the last bone-breaking minutes of the game.

A Wolf inbounds the ball, and the bear obediently ambles over to the basket and stations himself under it, his muzzle still curled up around his nose so that the bottoms of his long yellow teeth show, but nobody notices the bear's snarl. Bodies circle around him with dizzying speed, and portions of them hit him, snag his shirt or shorts, brush his face; the bear can't tell the teams apart from the middle of things any better than he could on the sidelines, maybe even worse because a nausea, a seasickness creeps into his stomach and his head aches. Trying to still the violence inside him, the bear lifts his hands up to his ears; at the same moment, for no apparent reason, the ebb and flow of players moves away from him to one of the Wolves' little men about to shoot from the out-side. When the guard sees the bear free, under the basket, with his arms up, he throws a straight quick pass directly at the bear who, he assumes, will leap up for a sure-thing dunk, a quick two points. Like a comet hurtling through a crowded universe, the ball zips past outstretched hands, turn-ing heads as it flies, on a magnetized trajectory pure as geom-etry. A slap, as the ball smacks into the bear's nose and bounces off; he grabs it with a howl of pain, one of the Out-laws scoops up the loose ball, and the nine human players hustle off downcourt, the Wolves minus their big center on defense. The bear stands, still under his team's basket, hold-ing his nose with one paw, his head with the other, until he sees Mahoney stomping his feet, pointing and yelling: "Down-court, downcourt, you dumb animal! Get dose rebounds, move your hairy feet!" and the bear begins to run, forgetting his nausea and shock. The crowd, delighted once more with these antics, roars and throws papers, cups, programs, which rain down upon Mahoney and his first-string bench warmers; with the bear under the opposing team's basket on defense, the high pitch of excitement increases. But the bear finds defense even less appealing than offense.

The weave is on, the dizzying square dance of man-to-man defense, of passing and driving, of fakes and counterfakes and finally the shot, and then the grueling jumble of rebounding bodies, and this time the bear at first feels delight, like being inside a popcorn popper, the same isolation he experienced at the lonely end of the bench, only joyous, fun, unable to discern between the two teams but appreciative of the action, the switching of partners, the pairing and unpairing of giants. And the bear is now the privileged one, with the best seat in the house, right under the offenders' basket; he can even follow the pinball path of the leather from hand to floor to different hand, being brushed by outstretched digits, arms, whooshing past open mouths, the single object of desire. Until whumph, an elbow comes crashing into the softest part of the bear's middle, the part unprotected by muscle (bears cannot do sit-ups: a physiological fact), and the bear doubles up in pain as his whole world goes blue, the color of breathlessness. The opposing center grabs a rebound which would have fallen right on the bear's round head and passes it back out to one of his little men because of the crowd under the basket, namely the bellowing bear.

"Whoooooo," the bear cries, and the refs look at one another in embarrassment and perplexedness, aching either for the blessed arrival of the instant replay camera in live sports so that all vicious fouls can be detected and rectified or for the bear to shut up. As the refs silently confer, the little man drives up the middle, elbows the bear in his roly-poly hips, and lays the ball up and in for two points. Mahoney comes off the bench hollering, the bear continues his cry, and the refs start to point and yell too, first at Mahoney ("T" they yell in unison, this time not for "time-out" but for "technical foul"), then at the bear ("T" again).

"Another display like that from either of you and you're out," one of the refs says, sternly, to the coach and his center.

A couple of Wolves hustle the bear away from the key

so that the other team's best free-throw shooter can take the two technicals. Mahoney, rubbing his face as if he could change his countenance with his hands, wipe off a little fat here, a little excess jawbone there, stomps back to the bench where he sits with his face entirely submerged in his big red mitts.

"Bear!" Mahoney yells from the bench, suddenly drawn from his reverie. The bear trots over amicably, recovered from his bout with one of basketball's errant elbows and ready to take his place once more in the popcorn popper. "You're out of da game. You're not cut out for basketball, you sissy. I'll put in one of my midget guards to play center before I'll play you again. Now sit down on dat bench and keep quiet!"

"But, man, the bear just got his first taste of the action," Big says. The Outlaw makes his first free throw with ease, whooshing the ball through the net as if he were the only man in the universe while the crowd whistles and boos.

"Da bear is out. It's bad enough we got sissies who can't play defense, who miss three weeks with a sprained finger, who think dat a shot's only good if dey fly through da air before dey reach da basket, who need a million bucks a year to play. A center who's a bear and who cries when he catches a little bit of da elbow ain't no basketball player in my book. Let da owner sue me. Da bear is out."

"You're makin' a mistake," Big says, putting his arm around the bear, but already the coach is engrossed in the perfect free throwing style of the Outlaw shooting the second technical, the high arc of the ball at apogee, the straight and thrilling downward course toward the inevitable net, the passage through the hoop without the crass sound of leather on metal. The game starts up again with the Wolves defending on the inbound pass minus their big man, or big bear.

The bear looks up at Big lovingly, as one looks in a dream at a long-dead parent or spouse, eyes turned skyward even in sleep and a warm flush spreading on one's cheeks as if a caressing dream hand has passed across them. To Big, he seems about to cry giant dark brown tears.

"Hey, man," Big says, "you don't have to stick around here, you know. You can go shower, undress, fool around in the locker room and stuff. I'll be in there in a minute when this fiasco's over, and we'll go get us some dee-licious ice cream, just like I promised. Coach won't mind if you go early. Hell, this game's good as over."

Dipping his muzzle slightly in an approximation of a nod, the bear looks once more at Big's face as if attempting to memorize its contents for some future examination in the quietude of remembrance, then rises and heads off toward the locker room. The dwindling crowd chants "Bear, bear, bear" as he leaves, and throws what's left of its programs and its last-quarter hot dog wrappers down upon him as if it were raining confetti upon an astronaut newly returned from kangaroo-hopping exploits on the moon. Unaware of the formalities marking recent celebrity, the bear fails to raise a hand or even a finger in greeting, makes no eye contact, signs no autographs, reveals no new romances or money-making schemes (like bear basketballs and gym shoes, bear-autograph T-shirts, bear testimonials for beer, bear contracts to do play-by-play or even color for a national network during the play-offs providing his team doesn't gain a berth); he hunkers into the locker room without personal fanfare, sits down for a moment on a metal bench which freezes his bear butt even through his shorts and fur, then begins to remove his basketball suit. Images materialize in his movie-screen consciousness, all scenes of carnage, of the crunching jaws of mountain lions in the soft necks of deer, of coyotes gorging on carrion, of owls swooping on newborn squirrels and the screams of those helpless babies, like the high-pitched sound of the night itself. A species memory, each of these, for the bear has all his life lived in the company of humans, but the power still moves him, a feeling of disgust, of wrongness. His head feels leaden as an anvil, resonant as heavy metal, and when he shakes it his ears ring. He packs his new clothes into his Wolf bag, and with the bag tucked under his arm, he trots down the hallway and out the back door of the arena, dodges honking cars in the parking lot (more cries of "Bear, bear," hands popping out of hastily opened car windows to tug at his fur, programs and pencils poking at him enthusiastically), until the bear reaches the highway. There he puts his expert thumb in the air and cools his brain with fragrant night sky, as useful as morphine for him, as filled with the powers of forgetfulness which anyway run rampant in his fuzzy brain. By morning, Big, the coach, the elbow in the stomach will be phantoms; by next week, cobwebs.

The bear feels an emptiness, what lovers would know to be the ache of loss, but with an animal's lack of cause-and-effect discernment, of self-analysis, of self-knowledge of the psychoanalytic type, he knows only the void inside himself, as if some essential organ has been ripped from its mooring and the body, in attempting to nurture the wound, can only cover it over with layers of hurt in much the same way that oysters create their pearls, making instead no shining jewel but only a bright, hard, encased nothingness where the mythical heart (the one that breaks, that sheds tears of blood, that dies so many little deaths in the course of everyday life, that is immortalized in most sixties rock and roll songs) should be. The point is that as the bear stands on the highways trying to catch lifts to wherever these cars might want to take him (though the germ of California lies dormant in the deep and dark recesses of his brain), he feels a pain quite different from the dumb physical suffering of animals, the metaphysical ache of lost love opening a black hole in space in his guts which threatens to suck his whole being through its windy vacuum turning him inside out with hurt. The bear keeps moving, as if motion itself may heal him or at least make him forget about his discomfort, the excitement and uncertainty of life on the road, the weirdos who offer him rides, the highway patrolmen who do W. C. Fields double takes when they see him at the roadside with his hairy bear thumb up in the air, the cars that put on their brakes and do screeching flip-flops like fish out of water to get a better look at him, but instead of being a balm the cool breezes of the highway whistle around and through him as if he were hollow, as if he really had this big echoing wind tunnel where his insides should be.

The bear stands at the side of the highway with an expression of blank hopefulness on his face (a brightening of the eyes until they come to resemble hard-surfaced, shining marbles, a straight-up set of the ears) similar to the expression that might be discovered upon the face of someone recently released from a state insane asylum, his hairy thumb high in the air like a banner, his Virginia Wolves flight bag clutched under his arm, close to his chest, as if it contains his favorite memories (if, indeed, he has any). The bear stands straight with his thumb pointing in the direction he seeks to go, a simple approach not by choice but because it's the only method that has occurred to him, looking like a wooden bear totally out of place, supposed to be outside of some tobacco store to replace the outré wooden Indian that used to be there. Sometimes he doesn't blink for minutes at a time, his eyes filling with brown viscous liquid from the road fumes and grime, finally overflowing into oily tears which stain the fur around his eyes a deeper color than the rest of his body. The worst part is that only the real weirdos stop to offer the bear rides. In fact, the whole hitchhiking scene has changed into a weirdo scene, unlike the benevolent underground railway of hip tips on travel and drugs it was in the sixties, the right to hitchhike unmolested then an established, inalienable right much like the right to vote or to speak the expletives of one's choice, the roads crowded with long-haired dirty smiling hikers holding out thumbs adorned with guitar pickers' two-inch-long fingernails, or an index finger and a thumb from which sprouted magically a smoldering joint ready for the lips of a friendly Volkswagen driver. People hitchhiked with guitars and dogs, with backpacks and steamer trunks, with pregnant girl friends. They all got as many rides as they wanted. Then the decade changed, and a lunatic fringe began to creep into the hitchhiking scene: a sudden awareness of the vast possibilities of a captive audience of passive, humming marijuana smokers, and the grabbers and the flashers, the speeders and the rapers, the guys with the crew cuts and the black Plymouth sedans took to the roads, a resurgence in cross-country driving by the silentest minority, the perverts, and the art of hitchhiking became as precarious as the art of walking in the city alone at night with the sound of insistent footsteps behind you and home still blocks away.

Most of the perverts cruise for the pretty girls in tight jeans and tank tops, the girls always brushing wispy silk strands of hair out of their reddened eyes, and some cruise for the young boys dressed the same way and with the same unselfconscious mannerisms, much as such predators as wolves and lions cut the weak, guileless young from the antelope herd, mesmerize them with yellow gleaming eyes like cold metal, then move in for the ignominious kill. But only the real weirdos pick up the bear, the ones whose aberrations lie outside the realm of the sexual, whose synapses misfire dark sparks, circuits crackling, blood flowing way too hot or way too cold. The bear snoozes in front seats only to wake up to the shock of pain, finding that a lit match, flame side out, has been stuck into the soft, thick fur of his belly; or a guy who looks like Mr. America, an all-right family man cruising by at thirty miles per hour, turns into the original fiend, taking curves at seventy, the stretches at eighty, and all the time looking at the bear out of the corner of his right eye, as you might observe the stranger sitting next to you in the movies who keeps doing bizarre, unmentionable things; or the more banal version of these types, the four-wheeled variety of the Ancient Mariner, all with life stories and a half to tell the bear, who nods in rhythm to the tires turning beneath him, becomes hypnotized by the white and yellow dotted lines that disappear beneath the car as if it were devouring them, the stories of minor and major surgeries, minor and major love

affairs, faithless wives, children on drugs: a finite number of
stories, the bear finds, a finite number of twists and turns to
them, few trick endings (though, with an animal's patience,
he never becomes bored: the perfect friend). No one offers
him dope to smoke (the guys with crew cuts in black Plymouth sedans do not smoke dope, are not into anything that
makes them feel pleasant and dreamy: they're into whites or
reds, ups or downs, anything that makes them mean as hell,
that makes the hairs on the back of their necks rise up straight
as if with static electricity, that makes their blood tingle, their
nerves stand up and shout insults, their fingernails sensitized
to the slightest change in steering wheel pressure, their eyes
glazed hard as kiln-baked clay, as mirror), offers to take him
to the nearest ice cream parlor (he has nearly forgotten the
delights of ice cream, though he would begin to salivate if
anyone spoke those two resplendent words), asks him about
his childhood. The inner, mysterious ache, coupled with this
onslaught of exterior pain and constant threats, makes the bear
feel like a magnet for all the floating torment of the universe,
which he pictures as a vast, amorphous cloud much like the
pictures in astronomy textbooks of the Milky Way, dotted
with the sharp points of stars, the burning radiance of planets,
all dangerous and frightening and beyond his understanding.

But the bear notices a relaxation in his body, a slight warming of the empty space inside himself when the beat-up red
Datsun with a young, long-haired guy inside it stops for him,
the car's engine chugging like a bad imitation of a motorboat,
coughing out threats of failure or death, giving earthquake
rumbles which rock and shake the whole little car.

"Hey, man," the guy says. He has long, thick, light brown
hair, the color teenage girls in the early sixties called dirty
blond when trying to dramatize their own drabness, a holey
T-shirt with UCLA emblazoned across its chest in navy blue
letters, faded blue jeans with holes in them at the knees,
around the pockets, over the thighs, so that they seem to be
held together by spiders' webs which cling, sticky and glu-
tinous, to his lightly haired skin; he wears on his head a blue

and white ticked engineer's cap with almost worn away orange lettering reading SOUTHERN PACIFIC right above the bill, which shades his eyes and gives them a moronic look, a lack of light and life. His face, bland, kind, soft, is the type owned by the rock stars who sing for prepubescent girls.

"Hey, man," the bear says, and tosses his flight bag onto the back seat. The bear knows the rituals of hitchhiking conversation, and waits.

"Where you goin', man?" the guy asks with friendly unconcern.

"Where *you* goin', man?" the bear asks back.

"To Alamosa, man, home of the Great Sand Dunes National Monument and of flying saucers," the guy says in mock-travelogue voice while he pushes the buttons on his radio with expert, fleet fingers like a secretary's on a much-loved IBM Selectric, hammering through classical and country and news stations until they linger, adoringly, over one button, poised now like a pianist's fingers before beginning a favorite Rachmaninoff crescendo sure to bring all the rubes in the house to their feet for the Chopin encore: rock and roll, and the bear's toes dance a little as they have not done in days and weeks (or maybe years, time weaving and stretching and bending and contracting on the highways for bears and humans alike, though the bear is especially lacking in this department, the judging of spans of time, more so than the dogs who get to know when the time for mama or papa to come home from work is growing near, or for the sleek house cats for whom the machinations of the outer world, of time, gravity, and the coming and going of humans, fail to matter because the whole cat universe is comprised within the slit of iris set in the yellow of the eye).

"I'm heading to Alamosa too," the bear says without pause, though he has no idea where or what Alamosa might be, knows only what the guy has just told him, which makes little sense: sand dunes? flying saucers? Sometimes humans put together combinations of words which mean absolutely nothing to the bear, ring no bells, light up no lights. The bear tilts his head to one side, pricks up his ears, in an attempt to comprehend fully and completely whatever answer the guy might make.

"Far out," the guy says and, as the Rolling Stones begin to sing "Brown Sugar," the guy reaches up into his hat and pulls out a neatly rolled joint, lights it with the car cigarette lighter, takes a couple of deep drags, and offers it to the bear without taking his eyes off the road.

"I can't," the bear says, overwhelmed by the combination of the Stones and the dope, and embarrassed to admit to this stranger that the only way he could partake of the much-coveted joint would be if this guy were to breathe the candy-sweet, dark-brown-sugar smoke into the bear's nose and mouth, warming his esophagus, his nasal passages, tickling his lungs with the many-legged smoke which would creep down into his chest like a friendly centipede. His heels twitching a funky four-four rhythm on the beat-up carpeting of the Datsun, the bear feels bold enough to lift his elbows in and out in time to the song, shake his head from side to side, and the music, like the marijuana smoke, begins to weave around in the vast open spaces of his aching soul, soothing as a magic healing balm.

" 'S cool, man," the guy says, flipping an ash out his open window. " 'Hey, Brown Sugar, how come you dance so good,' " he sings along, tapping his foot while it's on the gas pedal so that the whole car dances forward in a herky-jerky motion in time to the music, tires letting out high-pitched sighs at every second beat, engine groaning in a backup vocal.

The Rockies bloom like hallucinogenic flowers from the Colorado landscape, rising straight and poppy-colored and hazardous, and the bear gets light-headed from the marijuana smoke hanging in the thin air like a gauze curtain. Up and up, higher and higher, Colorado blossoms into the sky like a mushroom cloud, the essential shape of the place an incline, rivaled in geographical and metaphorical up-ness only by Nepal, which rises to untold heights due to the Himalayas and to the famed Nepalese hashish, both of which make religion and spiritual experiences that much easier in the cool, attenuated air. The orange colors range from bright tangerine, found nearest the highway, from which spring exhausted plants resembling ragged men crawling across the desert in search of an oasis, to deepest brick in the highest, farthest away, most mystical expanses of mountain, definitely the places where Indian medicine men would hunt for peyote, would have visions of eagles and serpents and any combination of the two. The bear sees shapes in the mountains which cause his fur to prickle, his skin to itch as if infected by vermin of the most insidious type: there, a puma about to spring right out of the rock, its lithe body outlined in the orange granite to the subtlest curves, its paws enormous, clawed, vicious; there, a huge, clumsy beast the bear can't recognize (a prehistoric sloth of the type that must have traversed this area in its jungle days, before the seismic quaking of the earth gave birth to the jutting mountains, an animal sitting back on its haunches like a thoughtful man or bear, its large stupid head tilting to one side, the thick lines etched in the mountains from wear, from lightning and pouring rain its heavy, matted coat), and the bear becomes excited by this, feels drugged by his surroundings, an exalting, heightening drug that quickens the breath, makes the eyes feel maddened and unworthy in their limitations. The guy driving sees none of this and experiences nothing but the usual cheap marijuana buzz which helps him to drive, to follow the center lines with a humming fascination, his shoulders rounded toward the steering wheel, head jutting close to the windshield, over the dashboard as if magnetized to the engine, to machinery, to hot metal. The car labors in slow motion, until the bear can feel the wheels turning, each revolution like fingers grappling with rope, and he begins to feel panicky, as if he is on an out-of-control roller coaster, the ultimate in cheap thrills gone wrong, but then he looks at the driver who has not changed his expression since the ride started, who sits in the same posture, perhaps willing the car through the Rockies, and without conscious decision the bear resolves to remain quiet, to sit still, so as not to hinder the mystical experiences at hand (being a sixties bear, he must believe in mystical experiences, in their daily aspect, in their unavoidable transcendentalism).

Finally a plateau, a small dirt turnout engineered so lost tourists can stop and take pictures of the terrifying view afforded to the braver ones who get out of their cars, clamber out into the sage to feed the ticks and mosquitoes until, ten feet from the road, a steep, fast trip to the void for any tipsy high-heeled mama or frivolous, hiding child, a drop-off into orange granite the color of drying blood on a head wound. Since this is not Disneyland, no Kodak Picture Spot, there are also no daily cleaned rest rooms, and not another car in sight on the infinite, snaking road clutching at the mountain like a hungry boa constrictor at a baby lamb; the guy gets out of the car and walks to the farthest elliptical end of the turnout to pee. The bear hunkers over to the side of the turn-out too, a few feet away from the driver, and lifts a back leg on a small scraggly plant resembling a wild head of hair. The clouds hang below them like the fluffiest penicillin growing on a month-old loaf of bread, the blue sky stretches forever until it is pierced occasionally by a craggy tip of a Rocky, the stolid granite heading right for the sky holds them up on its veined surface eternities old, the silence in the thin air begins to whistle around their heads and ears: a disgustingly male moment ensues as the two pee into nature, exposing their sensitive, hidden genitals to the elements and to each other, two small, liquid-bearing mortals amid all this vastness, silence, rock. The instant male camaraderie of the urinal springs up between them (women never seeing one another in public rest rooms, never getting down to the funkiest of facts about one another, never surreptitiously judging one another's organs, these being non-pull-outable), and the guy smiles at the bear for the first time, showing crooked, slightly buck front teeth and eyes that wrinkle up into smaller versions of the smile.

"Hey, I guess you're really a bear, huh?" the guy asks as the bear stands back up, resumes his nearest-to-human posture, his dancing posture.

"Yes," he says, as usual rather frightened by the denseness, the total lack of forest smarts he discovers in most humans.

"Far out," the guy says. "I'm Hank. What's your name?"

Again the bear becomes aware of his ultimate separateness from humanity: "I don't have a name," he says as the guy zips up his pants, looks at the bear as if seeing him for the first time.

"Far fuckin' out," Hank says. "Your parents didn't name you? That's radical."

"I don't remember my parents," the bear says, embarrassed, "and the names I've been given by humans never seemed to be the right one."

"You played pro ball?" Hank asks suspiciously, eyeing the Wolves flight bag with slit eyes, as if getting the feeling he's being hustled, will be asked to contribute money to a foundation for nameless bears, or be held up by a gun magically pulled from a pocket in the realistic bear suit (for what? his beat-up Datsun? his engineer's cap? his small marijuana stash which the bear can't even smoke?) and left stranded in the Rockies miles from any civilization: both read like plots from forties movies, cross Hank's consciousness as small-screen, television versions of the original epics, complete with commercials, and are quickly dismissed because Hank, like the bear, grew up in the sixties and knows all men to be brothers, with men and bears fitting into that category somehow when they've just peed together.

"Yes. But mostly, I dance."

"Oh, yeah? You dance, like, ballet, or what?"

"Hey, man," the bear says. "I've played gigs all over the

country, and I only dance one thing, just rock and roll: if it ain't the Stones, or Martha and the Vandellas, or the Supremes, or old Chuck Berry, I don't dance it."

Hank moves his feet excitedly in the dirt of the turnout, creating a small orange cloud which rises to his knees, coating his blue jeans and the patches of skin that show through the holes, and claps his hands once. "This must be karma, man. I'm in a band, on my way to meet up with them right now. I play bass, you know, electric, but come look at this," he says, exhilarated, grabbing the bear by a hunk of arm fur as if it were a shirt and dragging him over to the rear end of the little car. He opens the trunk to reveal something the bear can't relate to at all, a huge, black, nearly human-shaped something wedged into the small trunk at an obscure diagonal, something which a more educated bear might guess to be a coffin, a folded-up gondola, or (electric light bulb popping out of the top of this educated bear's head) a musical instrument case. Hank looks at the bear's face, expecting excitement, and sees instead the usual bland bear look, expressionless and, especially now, dumb, eyes rather sodden and flat, mouth hanging slightly open so the tips of the long yellow teeth show out, the pink beginning of the tongue; disappointed but without his original fervor dimmed, Hank jimmies the bruised black case until it snaps out of the trunk, leans it up against the side of the car, throws two latches so that the cover swings open with an audible whine in the thin air conducive to small sounds, opens like the top of a vampire's coffin, like the long-unused gate to the yard of the neighborhood haunted house. Inside the case, gleaming and looking alive as only good wood can look, wood waxed and shined and rubbed and thumped until, over the years, by osmosis, it begins to look strangely like a man, a jazz man, who would talk New Orleans jive if it could speak, would wear stingy brim hats and skintight pants, would hammer syncopated beats on tables while waiting for food to be served, would whistle at women with big asses enclosed in narrow skirts, is a stand-up bass, the first the bear has seen.

"It's my Big B, man. I'm learning to play real bass, do those old-time blues riffs for the band. It's about fifty years old."

The bear looks and looks at the bass, and finally realizes why he's getting this odd, déjà vu sensation (if bears get such a feeling, can recognize the misfiring of synapses as a supernatural experience important in unknown ways to their past and future lives): the bass looks like him, its growing roundness around the middle, its pinhead upper, its deep brown tones, its fat solid bottom, and the bear pictures himself living happily in a cave shaped like a bass case, form-fitting as a corset, a revolution in bear habitats. Across his movie-screen consciousness comes a vision of himself in the forest carrying his house on his back, a bear mobile home, the anomaly of the vision and yet its absolute rightness, the black case as battered as old skin among the trees, the small mammals, the bright-colored flying and perching birds. He reaches out one large hairy paw toward the body of the bass and tentatively smacks it (with the same motion his uncivilized brothers might use to swat a spawning salmon out of the downstream current and onto dry land for supper), and it makes a rich, echoing, hollow sound which reverberates into the pad of his paw, up through his arm, and sets the vast emptiness inside himself to echoing sympathetically: without coming to any real conclusion, without the spark of synthesis that marks man as a thinking beast and bear as a dim one, in a piece of brainwork most similar to a bear looking up on a foggy forest night and seeing, in a sudden and dramatic parting of the mist, a shining silver moon like a scissors cut in the universe, the bear knows the stand-up bass to be the music world's representative of pain, the archetypal instrument of da blues, its deep thunking tones the sound of the emptiness of the soul, of the heart when love has left it. He drags his claws across the strings to let loose a twanging chord like a moan.

"Hey, man," Hank says, obviously pleased that the bear thinks his instrument is far out, "I'll teach you to play it if you want."

"I couldn't," the bear says, holding up his arms as if they were inanimate things not connected to himself, showing the clumsy, long-clawed paws.

" 'S cool," Hank murmurs.

"But maybe you need a dancer," the bear says, amazed at his own effrontery.

"Hey, yeah, maybe we do," Hank says, letting the new idea wash over him like a breaking wave, the sensuous approach of ideas when under the marijuana spell. "I mean, I'd have to talk to the others about it first. But you're coming to town anyway. You can crash with us for as long as you like, and we'll see what happens. Like, just let it flow, you know, man?"

"Yes," the bear says, understanding only that the bass has begun to disappear into its black outer skin, then into the trunk, that it is time to return to the chugging little car and hit the road, though he has no feeling about this one way or another, accepts it as a matter of course, seeing the dark brown instrument which he had started to think of as a relative stuffed away, setting out once more on the road to anywhere. He settles back into the worn front seat as Hank guns the engine, spins the wheels in the dirt of the turnout creating a dusty whirlwind around them much like the one that sent Dorothy and her animal companion to Oz, finally reaching concrete, the tires whistling relief, and heading up once more.

Then a trickle of gas stations, maybe one every five or seven miles, almost invisible to the seasoned traveler used to the high sheen, the superchrome and sun-catching white of the giant off-the-freeway stations with the four-foot-tall black plastic letters advertising their inflated prices half a cent lower than the guy's across the street, these nearly unseen because of their decrepit condition and anachronistic signs, a tarnished flying horse about to plummet off a roof, a half-mast seashell, the pumps the old round-top type, with rusted nozzles, taped-up hoses, chipped concrete around their bases, broken windows in the offices, rest rooms right out of nightmares, the ladies' room key sticky, suspect. The bear senses the coming of some low-level civilization, and is glad to be with a human much as a woman welcomes male companionship when she finds herself walking down a dark street, in a dubious section of town, on a moonless night: with a human, he can cruise any city undetected, looking like a mere pet, a tame oddity, willing to be a second-class citizen if his rights include the right to remain silent, to walk unmolested, to snarl at the surreptitious kicks of children as any wild bear might. Though now a free bear, he willingly puts on the pretend yoke for the sake of his own safety; there are no organizations to protect the civil rights of bears since they have none, so he's forced to become a nigger bear, the Stepin Fetchit or Eddie "Rochester" Anderson of bears in an unenlightened world full of starers and pinchers, and hair pullers and face makers, a tough world for animals on their own in the cities. And low-level civilization is actually even more dangerous, because pretensions to liberality exist in direct proportion to population, the bear baiters throwing fewer sneaky elbows, exhibiting more healthy, genuine distrust and animosity.

"Are we getting near a town?" the bear asks, remembering from some dim past a collar and a leash, reaching up to his neck with both paws as a passenger on a bucking airplane hitches at his seat belt as if it will keep him from a fiery oblivion.

"Hey, you're pretty smart," Hank says. "If you can call this a town."

When two of the rickety gas stations appear facing one another on corners, the bear sits up straight in his seat, and then the town happens, growing up out of nowhere like a sunflower sprouting out of a crack in a concrete sidewalk. A restaurant, a church, a bar, a school, all gray and beige and created as if on a small scale, for people of less than normal size or less than normal aspirations; two more restaurants, another church, a women's clothing store, a barber shop, a Bank of America with false, graying Doric columns holding up its doorway, its windows barred to keep Wild West robberies from occurring; another gas station, a bar, a cowboy clothes shop, and the town disappears as quickly as it materialized, the dusty orange ground of the Rockies, looking to the bear like a fallow field which next season might sprout diners and country churches and gas stations (the bear being, of course, an urban bear, unused to the ways of the country, of small towns, and finding them slightly humorous and unreal), reappearing for as far as his dim bear eyes can see.

"Ain't it the pits?" Hank says, snapping the radio off in distaste as the stations scramble, whine, crackle, and a country western lament starts where rock and roll left off, as if the car has passed through some time warp, some invisible barrier right out of a science fiction film which changes the nature of life as we know it. "Good thing we're staying out by the dunes, away from all this lowlife."

Farther up, the whole landscape looks red around the edges to the bear because of the thinness of the air, his own exhaustion, the incredible orange cast to everything making the bear suspect he's been transported to someplace in outer space, Mars the Red Planet, the deformed sages and browned, sagging cacti looking extraterrestrial too, or as if they've never been alive. Then a forest sprouts out of the orange dust cloud as aberrantly as the town did, without warning, and the bear glances over his shoulder to make sure of the astonishing change, to check and see that the whole orange trip hasn't been a hallucination (since urban areas do not mirror nature in changeableness, cities being made up of all the same stuff in various stages of death and decay, the poorer sections of town missing only the new paint job, the shiny-glassed windows that the richer sections have, all changes gradual and matters of patina rather than radical departures: in his Zen way, the bear realizes this without realization, and decides without decision that he prefers the city for its constancy, though it may be a constancy of dread, of watching out. At least there he knows what to watch out for). The new shade cools down his eyes and brain, green a color of relaxation, of introspection; sheep wander among the trees, moving in a mass as if their fluffy wool coats were connected by gossamer threads, nibbling at the forest floor, straying out into the road in a group when one of the front sheep sees a particularly delicious-looking weed morsel thriving at the highway-side. Further off, cows stand still in pens, unblinking and stupid, and horses stamp feet, rear heads in magnificent dumbness. The bear wonders at the nature of these domesticated beasts, at the dullness of their eyes, their obvious thoughtless devotion toward the humans who feed, house, train them (this wonder taking up a millisecond of his consciousness in a fleeting vision of a team of straining, yoked oxen).

"Look how clear it is today," Hank says, surveying the heavens as the car seems to make a turn without his expending any effort, as if it knows the way. "Gonna be a far-out night tonight. We're nearly there."

A ranger in a miniature log cabin kiosk in the middle of the road sticks his head out a window, then waves the Datsun past with a supercilious look on his face, a look betraying his belief that the national parks should not be for everyone in the nation and that, if asked to volunteer, he would be glad to be the one to decide who gets in and who stays out.

"This, man," Hank says as he steers the car along small twisting roads past parking lots filled with recreational vehicles like great whales, picnicking families in among the trees, station wagons, and in the distance, nearly blending in with tree trunks, an amazed deer or two, "is as high as you can get and still be legal. Ever seen the Great Sand Dunes before?" Hanks asks, his voice excited, full of possibilities.

"No," the bear says, still not knowing what the hell sand dunes are, the first word conjuring up faraway, dim memories of California beaches, long flat stretches of yellow punctuated with trash cans and lifeguard stations, the second meaning nothing at all, no association, just one of the many funny sounds humans seem capable of making when they find their mouths hanging lax and free and empty.

"Well, this'll blow your mind, man, will freak you out, will do all those things that haven't happened, for real, in nearly ten years now, you know, when everything all of a sudden sorta changed down there." Hank's voice becomes louder as the car's coughing increases, sputtering up the last steep grade as if it were the ultimate loop of a roller coaster, causing the bear to bring his paws up to cover his eyes, no thrill-seeker in the human sense, no climber of mountains because they happen to be there, no death wish or pain wish, no surreptitious interest in kinky sex: a bear interested, at this moment, in inner peace, and not in a gravity-defying roller coaster ride to a blown mind or a freak-out.

As the car stops, quivers, and makes a noise like a hungry stomach, Hank says, "There it is," and the bear looks, removing his paws from his eyes timidly, slowly, afraid that he has been kidnapped to someplace truly dangerous: his toes, flat against the worn car carpeting, have no dance left in them, instead ready themselves for flight into the trees if necessary. What he sees is beautiful and eerie, and instant pictures from who knows where come into his head, pictures blurred and mysterious and magical, seen on a small screen years ago, seen again today: a lunar landscape, soft and of the purest white, perspective disappeared into vastness, size unjudgeable, the flow of perfect, shifting ellipses more lush than any sea waves, more dangerous in their deception (1969 the year of the Moon Walk, that giant step for man and for bear, the end of sonnets written to the moon, demythification: the perfect way to end a decade, with men kangaroo-hopping around, opening their cosmic beer cans in antigravity, leaving satellite kitchen midden, toy flags, Oscar statuettes, squeezed-out tubes of toothpaste food for posterity). Of course, the bear watched the Moon Walk in 1969, America stopped down dead and held its breath for Baby Face Neil Armstrong in his Frankenstein boots and 20,000 Leagues Under the Sea hat, a venture full of cultural resonance, full of genetic memories; the bear runs out into the white white sand, halfway up the nearest slope, feeling his heart pounding in his hairy chest, his lungs expanding and contracting, his feet sinking into the velvet sand, meeting no resistance, squishing as if into foam, shaving cream, bubbles, and though he has run only about fifty feet he feels exhausted, ready to assume the archetypal pose of man laboring across the desert, flat on his chest with tongue hanging out of mouth and encrusted with sand like diamonds. As he flops down his whole body bounces as if in slow motion from the cushion of sand like the softest goose-down pillow, his arms and legs rebound into the air, his chest relaxes, and into his head comes "Hey, Brown Sugar, how come you dance so good," complete with chord changes and lead guitar, and he has to dance.

He rises Twisting, and when his heels launch out into a slo-mo funky Mashed Potato sand flies six feet all around him and he looks just a little like a hairy Botticelli Venus born out of sea froth. Head up, eyes closed, he shimmies his shoulders until they brush the sides of his jaw, he lifts his legs high so that he looks like he's on a shape-shifting trampoline made of liquid or bits of glass, he goes down low into a Hully Gully, then Monkeys on up, grabbing air filled with the sand like rhinestones; he Stomps a few light steps, jumps and twirls on his toes so he looks like a giant furry corkscrew about to bore into the white sand, then falls to his knees in a move sure to make any crowd come to its feet and start clapping in time to the steady bass line, and while still on his knees begins to Swim through the flying sand, first freestyle, then leaning back at an incredible angle, his spine straining, backstroking with a blissful look on his face as if the water were a cool blue seventy-five degrees, the sun were out, and Acapulco were all around him, tropical flowers in hot pinks and reds, girls in bikinis, a piña colada waiting for him après dip. He stops, opens his eyes, and sees five human figures standing next to the red Datsun, quiet, watching him, so he trots back down toward them on all fours, enjoying the sand on his feet, its springy texture, its Danceability.

The first thing the bear notices as he galumphs up to the parking lot is that two of the humans look exactly alike: two small, slight women with identical features, long wispy brown hair, small eyes weighed down by heavy, dark eyelashes, a dark brown mole at the left corner of each mouth, two rounded, childish chins. Again the feeling of hallucination, since the bear is well aware that men look exasperatingly different, that sometimes it's even hard to tell that they belong to the same species. The other two, beside Hank, seem far less anomalous than the matched set of women: a short, muscular man with Brillo pad hair and round wire glasses, and a black man, as tall as Hank, with the same birthmark as the Our Gang dog, a huge dark spot of skin surrounding his right eye like an eyepatch, like a magnet making it impossible to look him in the other eye. The bear stands up in front of them and takes a bow.

"Far out," Hank says, softly and breathily, like a spoken whistle.

"Far out," the two women say at once in sweet high voices that should belong to sixteen-year-olds on first dates; one reaches out a tiny hand and strokes the bear's chest.

"This must be a sign," Hank says, and the others shake their heads; the bear shakes his too, as if to shoo butterflies out of his ears, because the old time warp feeling has returned, the feeling that he's back a decade in the good old days, that at any minute joints will be passed around, talk about the Grateful Dead and the Jefferson Airplane and Janis Joplin will begin, that perhaps the whole group might even get into serious hallucinogens. "I picked him up, right there on the highway, like a vision, man, right after I'd gotten my bass. This bear was *meant* to join us."

"Let's see the bass," the black guy says.

"Hey, yeah," Hank says, then turns to the bewildered bear and says, "this is Bobo, our lead guitarist who's also teaching me to play the stand-up. That guy there's Wayne, on percussion. He has lots of hostility to release because he's short." Wayne smiles at the bear, and the two women giggle. "And those are our singers, Cassy and Polly. And dig this," he says to his group, indicating the bear with an emcee's broad armsweep. "The bear's got no name. Isn't that hot?"

"Far out," one of the women murmurs. The bear thinks she must be Cassy because she stands closest to Hank, a learned bit of human logic or etiquette which doesn't always work, like most human logic.

"Yeah," the other says, in a voice that combines Marilyn Monroe grown up and Elizabeth Taylor in her child-star days, a cartoon voice so pure and high it could only be the voice of some prancing Disney bird in a tutu, an anthropomorphic vision of femininity done all in pastels and graceful as only animation can be, the boneless, muscleless, painless grace of man's imagination. It rings in the bear's ears long after the words have been spoken, as if he had a vibrating tuning fork sending plaintive messages to Venus stuck up in there, inside his brain, and he shakes his head to quiet the hum of it, and sand flies from his face and ears, sand lodged in his thick fur, encircling him in a glowing, sun-catching aura like that a fine gem might have. "But what do we call him?"

"Dude, get out that bass," Bobo says, his one magnetic eye serious, directed. "Lemme see this baby, make sure we didn't waste our money on some hunka junk."

"Hey, it's beautiful, man, and it sounds like a little bit of heaven," Hank says, and drags the bass out of his tiny car trunk once more, thrilling the bear with the sight of the gleaming instrument as tall as a man, as round as a bear (has the bear unknowingly been questing after some synthesis, this bear-man combo? If so, the answer would have to lie in music). Hank stands up behind the bass, disappearing except for his white hands wrapping around it so that it looks like an even more bizarre incarnation of that multiarmed Hindu goddess, and runs off the classic eight-note boogie from high to low and back again, and the bear's knees move in and out as Hank repeats the riff, then shifts it up a half-tone, sending shivers down the bear's twitching spine, then back down to the original eight-note span, only in double time, his fingers beating back and forth on the strings as quickly as the strings vibrate so that finger and string seem to be one, hard for the bear to tell which actually makes the music. The women send their heads, dreamily, to and fro, head nearly meeting shoulder on each pendulum pass, Wayne taps his hands on his thighs,

the whole group becoming part of the music-making process
except for Bobo, who watches and listens with back straight,
eyes on the small portion of the instrument that makes contact
with fingers, head tilted slightly, looking like a spot-eyed mon-
grel waiting for dinnertime. Just as the bear feels Dance coming over him like an orgasm, head to toe and back again, the
riff ends, having reached its own predestined, obvious conclusion, the limitation of the only ten notes Hank knows.
The bear's body goes slack, his jaw hanging open, his tongue
lolling out in disarray, his eyes dull: looking for the moment
like any zoo bear, any potential national park comedian, any
furry mugger of menstruating adolescent girls on camping
trips. The women scratch behind his ears as if he were some
tame mastiff sitting before a fire, the whole scene one of dis-
traction, of exalted feelings gone awry, of missed trains and
buses and subway connections, of phone calls never returned,
letters never written.

"Well, man?" Hank asks, sure of his powers, his bass sha-
manism, even within the confines of his small knowledge.

"That's some far-out piece of wood," Bobo says, scratching
the dark brown spot surrounding his right eye, the skin there
thicker and at the same time more sensitive in the psychic
sense to good and bad vibrations, certainly to the big fat
rolling sound waves sent out into the troposphere by the new
bass. "What you think, bear?" Bobo asks, throwing his eye
upon the bear, who snaps to attention like a boot camp
trainee, his mind called back from the depths of the void,
from vast dreamlessness, from an out-of-body experience
brought on by the sudden ending of music.

"For such a simple riff, it was hot stuff," the bear says,
aware that he is being tested, something humans do over and
over, to each other and to their animals.

"It was okay," Bobo says, though he looks at the bear
with a new discernment, his human eye clear and friendly,
his dog eye narrowed as if seeing eagles on the horizon.
"Hank's got a lot to learn, but he's gonna be one groovy bass
player."

"Hey, man," Hank says in thanks, hiding away the sacred stand-up before any ill humor should fall upon its glowing surface like young girls' skin.

"Let's go smoke some," both of the women say at the same time, then begin laughing and speaking in a foreign language the bear has never heard before, a language full of consonants, of hard stops, of words that sound like the names of dragons in old English legends, like Vikings' names, like monsters made up of various animals' body parts put together in haphazard fashion for terror appeal in ancient Greek and Roman myths. Tilting his head so as to get a better pickup, the bear listens closely (his animal need to make sense of the universe, his ability to concentrate completely on any one of his senses should his life or his lucid perception depend upon it), but still hears nothing resembling any words he's heard before (since animal knowledge is completely a posteriori, separate from instinct and intuition when it comes to dealing with man, even the putting together of two previously known words might stymie a tame bear: no language abilities, no differentiation of one language from another, no spelling, knowing only what he has already been taught and no more, a Berlitz school of past experience, and at the same time a constant tabula rasa, self-erasing, in need of reminders for even the most basic facts).

"Don't worry about it, man," Hank says, noticing the bear's auditory discomfort. "They do it all the time. Hey, no one else understands it either."

"They thought we were retarded when we were little," Cassy says to the bear, looking at him with extraordinarily pale eyes like shining stars between the heavy, dark lashes, "because we talked different from everybody else. We just knew how to talk to one another from the start, our own language. There are whole books written about us, linguistics, psychology, anthropology. They made us learn English and thought we'd forget our language, sent us to special classes right up until we were sixteen and ran away to become rock and roll singers in San Francisco."

"Idioglossia," Polly says in her exact version of Cassy's voice. "A private language developed by twins or close siblings who have had little or no contact with other children or the outside environment. Only two or three other cases have been documented. We're, like, dinosaurs, y'know? We're missing links."

"They think they're hot," Bobo says, waving both his black-outside, white-inside hands at them as if shooing flies away from his dog eye. "They're not even such good singers."

"We sing just like Janis Joplin," Cassy says as the bear notes that her mole sits just a little closer to the corner of her mouth, that Polly's eyebrows arch a little more over her eyes, which gleam like opal. "Not only that. Any other girl singer would get tired, singing nearly every night like we do when we're on tour. But," she says to the bear, "y'see, we switch off nights, like we're just one singer but really there's two of us."

"Yeah, she sings one night, I sing the next, and everyone thinks we're the same girl. Like we're underground, y'know? They'd still like to find us, to study us some more and stuff," Polly says.

"Hey, let's go smoke and then wait for the lights," Hank says, and begins to walk to the other end of the parking lot where a giant repainted blue, banged-up school bus stands looking like a hulking hairy mammoth out of some daredevil of a nightmare. A tension lingers, the ride in, the bass, the proving of good taste, the pseudo-insults, but the bear knows that even third-rate marijuana will dispel that as quick as an air conditioner pushes the hot air out of a one-room apartment; and, anyhow, the bear feels too overloaded with new information to think for very long about what's going to happen in the area of group social interaction. He is seeing two women identical as paper clips who can communicate with one another outside of the banality of everyday language: a species unto themselves, as bears in the forest communicate by look and moan with other bears, as lionesses on the hunt make low purring noises understood only by other lionesses, as house dogs know the mailman-bark of the dog next door, and then prepare to greet the mailman themselves. Part of a group once more, and a group with at least two members deserving future study (the bear finds Bobo with his spot eye interesting among regular humans as well), the bear forgets all about the wind tunnel where his heart ought to be, the black hole in space in his gut, and hunkers along after the five people toward the big blue bus.

"I bet the lights'll come tonight," Wayne says to solemn looks and nods as they reach the bus. "This is a portentous day."

"The You-Eff-Ohhs," Hank says in his emcee's voice, as if introducing the newest rock group from England, and the eyes of the five people turn to the skies though dusk is barely beginning, the sky tinted rosy as if by watercolors, a mere wash of hue rather than the full-on, hallucinatory reds and purples of a real Colorado sunset, the air so clean it becomes prismatic, the night vapors so strange that anything can happen between this mortal coil and the firmament, and does. There are crazies other than urban weirdos, and they find themselves drawn to the sites of (super) natural phenomena: to the Oregon and Washington territories, to take suspect pictures of the cameo-appearing Bigfoot, and to Colorado, to watch the unidentified flying objects.

After having weed puffed up his nose by both twins, the bear's loaded. Their faces come as close as dreams, hovering about his big head like hallucinations. The bear examines the twins through the brown velvet smoke, their thick, animal-fur lashes flicking at his nose and eyes, the one (is it Cassy or Polly?) with the chocolate mole closer to her mouth (which the bear can see with one of his eyes as she covers his nose with her mouth) breathes her redolent breath into him. And then the other, whose brows rise and fall with her breathing as if in constant surprise, puts her mouth over his snout while the guys of the group pass around big fat joints designed to light up even the most mundane skies with kaleidoscopic effects, to turn heads upside down so that you feel like your feet are rooted in the stars. The bear, supine, watches as each group member grabs a flat combination of plastic and metal from a pile of such contrivances near the bus's front door and hikes out to the very beginning of the sand, the dividing line between concrete parking lot and the unknown. Deck chairs: for watching Fourth of Ju-ly fireworks from the front porch, for sunbathing on the beach while the kids play in the surf under the watchful gaze of sun-blond lifeguards stationed a hundred feet apart, just enough room for their bikinied groupies to stretch wall-to-wall; a middle-class staple of support, sagging seats for sagging rear ends, brought out to watch for UFOs in the very center of America, which is guarded by radar on all sides, riddled with military tunnels, protected from anything mysterious and airborne and watchable from deck chairs at the farthest edge of the Great Sand Dunes National Monument. The bear follows the others out without first grabbing one of the odd contraptions which clunk together in high-pitched tones that make his claws itch at their marrow, so he lays himself down at the small, childlike feet of Cassy and Polly who sit at the center of the group, one bound to her left by Hank and Wayne, one attended to by Bobo (and, anyway, a bear bottom would not fit in a deck chair, too broad across the hips, the gigantic sockets where the back legs fit into the pelvis looking dinosauric when seen as a skeleton; bear weight, too, is enough to crush even the hardiest specimen of folding chair made for the relatively straight posture and light weight of the human race instead of the slouching, bottom-heavy tonnage of bears: a polar bear in a deck chair being a vision worthy of some 1920s surrealist or of a refrigerator company's ad man).

Night comes quickly in the highest parts of the Rockies, something to do with the thinness of the air, an atmosphere loving the dark as much as the dusty musty atmosphere of an old movie theater does, a kinship to darkening, to the dimming of lights. Indeed, the bear becomes aware that the vast panorama of night sky like a black movie screen is much like his own consciousness, that looking up into the sky and waiting for something to happen there resembles his thought process: the lack of control, the joy of revelation, the anticipation until revelation comes (what bear before ever engaged in such epistemological observation?). He looks up and the night sky becomes his black mirror, for there, above him, are more bears: Ursa Major and Minor, which appear, to men, to be ladles rather than bears (men always thinking of their stomachs, of the implements that help fill their insides), but instead, to the bear, shine bear-ness out of the great void, a gentle, female bear-ness surrounded by lions, hunters, bulls, and twins. He sees their shapes, larger and smaller, feels their rays on the skin parts of himself, his nose, the pink insides of his ears, the pads of his feet, which he turns up toward the sky in a gesture of supplication and identification; feels them so much, their power, their essence so akin to his in isolation and vulnerability, that he closes his eyes and can still see them, now etched in his consciousness like pinpricks of light coming through the swirling foggy depths of his brain. Drugged and heady from marijuana and stars, from the soft cushion of sand beneath him, he keeps his eyes closed for uncountable minutes (time for straight bears being filmy as gauze, ethereal as moth wings, unknowable as the books of Dostoevski; for head bears, enjoying the peculiar timelessness encouraged by marijuana smoke, time disappears until bear life is eternal or nothing, not that it matters either way so long as the floating continues) until a chorus of gasps, of oohs and ahs wakes him from his sleepless reverie lying upside down, paws pointing to the heavens, legs straight up, like a cartoon dead bear, a man-in-a-bear-suit dead bear, and he opens his eyes without changing position, a good move known by all animals in dangerous situations, a brief still survey of an unknown danger being wiser than a blind run into the inevitable traps of men and other beasts.

Something hovers overhead, although it appears to be made of stuff more gossamer than mist, looking like a water stain upon the smooth satin surface of night sky: a cigar-shaped stain, though its ends suddenly contract into points so that it looks like a pursed mouth, then spring back out into

flat stubs like babies' fingers. From the other end of the parking lot, from another group of watchers in deck chairs and on
the patios of mobile homes, a man yells out "Halllooo," which
sets off a series of yells in various known and unknown lan-
guages, plus machine noises making the old dit-dit-dots of
code which cut the thin night air with as much surprise as a
Bowie knife, the high-pitched siren call as anomalous as the
thing hanging overhead. From somewhere else in the dunes,
light flashes out a brief signal, obviously people very prepared for this type of happening, someone determined to
make contact with his klieg light stolen from a Hollywood
movie premiere allowed to shine for an instant and then
obliterated by an old wool blanket. The shouts sound more
and more like the calls of wolves to the bear, and the picture
of that lonely animal raising its head to the full moon sky
crosses his stoned consciousness before it's replaced by a picture of men doing the same, lifting small white faces made up
mostly of open mouth to the night, to a fat flying cigar the
bear feels he might almost touch if only he could get his feet,
which seem frozen in position pointing to the sky, to move.

Still the thing just hangs there, blasé as hell, traveling incognito and not wanting to be recognized, until the shouts,
the attempts at coded messages, even some clown with day-glo
orange painted semaphore flags out in the middle of the nearest dune waving his arms like a poppy in a hurricane, all give
up, fold up their chairs and chaises, shake fists at the sky (a
universal message if ever there was one), return to their mobile home cocoons, jaded and weary and certain the thing is
dumber than they are. The bear and his group, however,
do not move, the bear out of a personal communication, hypnotized by the sky, the others out of a faith that only those
who grew up in the sixties can have: a willingness to believe
in anything someone else truly believes in, and if twenty people, a hundred, a thousand believe in it, all the better. They
look up and up, the brown velvet marijuana smoke still circling in their lungs acting like an invisible cushy pillow for
their necks, cradling their heads; the bear remains on his

back, head resting in the soft white sand, feeling light and suspended as an astronaut in an antigravity simulating chamber. The night turns still and friendly, no rabid attempts at any type of primitive contact (what possible meaning could SOS ditted and dotted out from a dim green earth have for a floating, gigantic cigar from someplace farther and more unimaginable than the vast recesses of the void of the bear brain?), the night more complete, past navy blue to true black.

The quietest metallic humming, as from a very discreet electric typewriter, fills the air, tingles on the insides of the bear's ears, on the downy cheeks of the twins, on Bobo's dog eye, and the hanging thing turns the coldest color, a lethal yellow the color of live electricity, the color of Weimaraners' eyes. This warms slightly to an arctic blue as they see or imagine the thing quivering, vibrating like a mass of just-conjured ectoplasm over a séance table, then orange, so hot and bright they all close their eyes against their wills and still feel the heat through their eyelids, as if the sun has come a million times closer than ever before, as if their eyes were eggs frying in a skillet.

"There!" the bear says, the first to open his eyes when he feels the cool night air on his nose once more, something alert and animal in him cuing him as the humans sit still and eyeless as ancient Greek statues of unseeing gods. They blink, their eyes open just in time to see the thing not darting away, as they expected, no whoosh of wind from some cosmic backfire, no deafening roar of engines, no blinding white flashes; the thing just shrinks in size until it is an orange speck in the night sky, a poppy petal floating on the wind, shrinks and shrinks until it disappears. The bear's ears ring as the heavens are shattered by silent speed, slashed by the pointed tips of the flying cigar.

"Wow," Hank says. "Like, man, I can't believe my own eyes."

"Far fuckin' out," Wayne says, rubbing his woolly hair with both hands.

As the women speak to one another in an unearthly language made up of too many consonants, their eyes alight, the bear certain a keener insight, a clarity lies in their mysterious words, Bobo says: "A sign. This is some kinda omen. We're ready. The Ungrateful Wretches begin touring tomorrow. And the bear comes with."

"Hey, all *right,*" Hank says, and the men slap hands, which in the dark merge and come apart with a strange neon afterglow, a trail like that a comet leaves. The twins squeal a guttural word full of *g*'s and fall upon the bear, tickling his armpits, his stomach, his thighs, rolling over and over with him in the sand, the bear worrying that he will crush them, flatten a tiny arm, a leg, a nose, but they feel as resilient and cushiony as the sand, and his breath begins to come quickly, as if he has run a long way, his tongue lolling out so that it collects sand in its moist pores.

"C'mon," Hank says as the women and the bear disappear into the darkness of the first sand dune. "We gotta get some sleep. Up at dawn, y'know, get right on the road. Get into Denver and find a gig."

Sighs in the night, panting, and they all move off one by one in the direction of the bus, looking like disconnected cars of the same train, like wraiths, ghosts related in life by the nebulous connection of blood, in death by the mute comfort of one another's presence. The bear, elated, excited, stirred in strange ways, drops off to sleep instantly in the corner of the bus they designate as his, a thin twin-size mattress thrown on the floor, flashing off into the void as quickly as the hovering cigar, an electric, irritated sleep in which he will moan and growl and open his eyes though only the whites, the sleepwalking nonseeing part, will show, the rest of his eyes turned inward to dreamlessness, to deepest black.

Intermission

The van looks like a monument to cross-country travel, caked with layers of dust like strata so that you can trace the course of its trip much as geologists trace the history of the earth by the subtle variations in the layers of stone, its colors obscured by dirt, revealed only through the graffitic artistry of precocious children: orange shines through the letters of arithmetic love matches, of character descriptions of anonymous Bills and Bobs and Lindas, of basic profane and impossible orders, making the car look like a confused bulletin board on wheels rather than a real, practical vehicle that's brought two tired people to El Dorado, the promised land, California. If it were bronzed just the way it is, the finger-traced writing in the dust, the bald, slick tires, the full, overflowing ashtrays, and placed on a concrete pedestal somewhere right in the middle of the country, Kansas, say, or Colorado, harried husbands in station wagons full of kids and dogs and camping equipment, traveling salesmen with racks across their back seats for hanging the latest fashions, the newest in men's suits, and college students driving out to UCLA would salute it in passing as a memorial to the unknown motorist. Instead it sits on a side street in Hollywood, in the real grungy down-and-out Hollywood rather than the Hollywood of your dreams, parked in a red-curbed no-parking zone though no cop will mess with it, will stop to write out a ticket

for fear of getting mugged (in Hollywood cops cruise in
locked-door patrol cars making menacing faces, looking mean
and surly, and trying not to see street crimes in which they
might have to involve themselves: Hollywood cops are very
proud of their manicures, of their clean, unused guns, of the
shine on their bumpers and chrome, of their impeccable
driving).

Across the street, in the barren, black leather interior of
the Little Detroit Inn, Ray sits gloomily looking like the
Great Stone Face, another kind of monument, imported from
Easter Island and imbued with much more mysterious, enigmatic meaning. Five empty beer mugs sit in front of him (too
early in the day to start in on the gin), coated with the fuzzy
froth left over from the real beer, and a sixth, unstarted,
gold gleaming mug waits under his chin, though he looks like
he's forgotten all about it, a man thinking about past glory, a
used-up athlete remembering the last World Series he played
in or the last touchdown pass he intercepted, an executive
down on his luck after being caught embezzling small
amounts of company funds to pay his gambling debts, a Las
Vegas lounge singer whose voice went bad before he could
make that hit record (all kinds of ways for a man to end up
looking like Ray, though Ray emerges as a sort of champ for
being the only ex-bear owner among these has-beens, an atypical fate deserving of six beers in the afternoon, of a setting
concrete face, of existential despair). Joy steps out of the
ladies' room, a wooden doorway marked with stick-on letters from which the a and the e have fallen off and probably
been trampled underfoot, sees Ray in his beer oblivion, peers
around the smoky, prematurely darkened room, her eyes at
about human knee level (looking for a lost child? a missing
purse?), until, in a corner, by the bar, she spots the chimp.
The chimp sits with its legs widespread, its sailor suit getting
grimy and stained from the dust, dirt, and alcohol residue
left on the floor from clumsy drinkers wearing motorcycle
boots; the small navy-blue-ribboned sailor hat it's supposed to
be collecting spare change in lies a foot away from its finger-

like toes, forgotten, as it studies one forearm, then picks at the
exact spot where it feels the nibbling flea, then pops the offending vermin into its mouth for an instant combination
death sentence and dessert. That finished, it scratches its head,
hoping to find more meals crawling upon its body; a look of
stupid animal fascination stays on its face, the lowered, taut
eyelids, the straight-line mouth of concentration, and its ears
wiggle. Joy stomps up to Ray, her arms hanging tense at her
sides, then shakes his shoulder with one of her hard little
hands to rouse him, get him to raise his eyes up to hers.

"I told you to keep your eye on the chimp," she says in a
low voice, as if not wanting to let the children hear mommy
picking on daddy.

"I can't believe it," Ray says. "I can't believe I've gone
from a bear who could take care of himself to a monkey that's
worse than a baby. Look at it sitting there in the corner playing with its toes. Jesus Christ, I used to be a pretty good
drummer too," he says, and pounds on the tabletop around
his used beer mugs, making an interesting two-toned double
time using the tips of his fingers and the inside of his ring
bands to hit the table, the first sound a soft thud, the second a
sharp tattoo, a real professional job of table pounding. He
finishes the riff by unsnapping and then snapping his pockets.
"Hey there, little fella," he calls out across the room to the
chimp, which doesn't even look up, its big ears like wiggling
conch shells obviously useless in the midst of such ardent concentration; Joy runs her hands over her gray face, skin like
the ancient papyrus scrolls found in the pyramids and just as
inscrutable. Two big motorcycle-jacketed guys at the bar turn
around ready to fight if those words were directed at them,
maybe even if they weren't, but Ray looks so harmless and
drunk-comical that the butch types decide he's not worth
their energy and, besides, they're having a good time watching the monkey. Joy, seeing the glances both Ray and the
chimp are getting, the black leather vibrations coming from
the direction of the bar, gets up and grabs the chimp, who's
been nibbling its ankles, by a wrist as an irate mother

might drag a frightened child up to sit on a department store Santa's lap at Christmastime; the chimp drags its feet, then lifts them off the floor to hang happily from Joy's hand by its wrist, making little clucking noises and finally twirling its body around in midair like a hairy gymnast so that it can hook its back legs under Joy's arm and ride like an opossum to the table.

"That guy who sold us the monkey gave us a bum deal," Ray says to Joy and to the chimp when they get back. "Since we got it we been putting out more money for its upkeep than it brings in, hell, it brings in peanuts. The bear was a gold mine compared to this gorilla." His stiff wooden mouth forms itself around the words with particular zeal, like an evangelist with a wired jaw, as if he thinks that the chimp, like the bear, will understand his taunts, bridle at them, perform all the more brilliantly because of them (people rooted in the past, fixated in a particular year or month or season, have trouble with the shift from then to now, see them as one flowing entity like a Möbius strip, fail to recognize the change in characters in their lives, the falling of leaves from the trees, the gray hairs growing on their own heads), and he stares into the chimp's dumb, beady, merry little eyes as if expecting a retort. The chimp sucks a toe, scratches its head, pulls on the tie of its sailor suit as if it's never seen the tie before; this tightens the collar, choking the chimp, causing it to cackle in amusement at the discovery of a cause-and-effect universe.

"It's just a baby, you know that. The guy said its parents were in that famous chimp act, almost like it has a pedigree. Anyway, you should just forget the bear. He's gone. And you didn't like him so much when we had him," Joy says. "You picked on him all the time."

"Hey, little fella," Ray says in a mock-daddy voice as he chucks the chimp under the chin; it grabs his fingers, pulls them, mouths them, then lets them go as uninteresting and returns to chewing its own toes. "Me and the bear got along fine, we understood one another. This monkey doesn't understand anything. How're we gonna make it with this monkey as our breadwinner? It can't even remember its hat. That bear knew how to wring a customer dry, really knew the suckers. And could he dance."

"Just give it time," Joy says as she holds the chimp to her as if it were an infant, cradled in her arms and serene for a moment before it grabs a handful of Joy's wispy hair and begins to taste it, pull it through its widespread teeth, tickle its own nose with it. "The chimp's just got to learn the ropes, grow up a little. Then it'll be spare changing with the best of them." Ray's face shows no agreement, no amusement as he sips his beer, then removes one of the cigarettes from behind his ear, twirls it as a gunslinger might twirl his Colt or as a hot dog drummer might twirl his stick before starting some star riff: the cigarette moves from finger to finger as if traveling up and down a ladder as Ray sits expressionless, and the chimp can't resist, throws its little body across the table, its long arms reaching and grabbing, and beer mugs scatter, beer flies like rays of sun, and Ray slaps the chimp's face or the chimp's face meets his hand in its cross-table dive, then pulls his hand away to save the cigarette from certain death, the inevitable chewing the oral chimp seems to subject its whole world to, the constant taste test. He snaps and unsnaps his pockets, pats his pants, then in a back pants pocket discovers a crunched-up, sat-upon book of matches looking like a found relic from some caveman's kitchen midden and lights one up as Joy retrieves the chimp to her bosom.

"Here, little fella," Ray says, his voice friendly though his mouth betrays nothing, hard as rock, smileless, "wanna have a bite of this?" as he proffers the lighted match. "Yummy," he says as he makes the small flame dance in front of the chimp's fascinated eyes, a monkey's Svengali, but Joy holds the chimp, its arms pressed to its sides, and it wriggles in frustration at having to let such a tasty morsel escape, something that could only tickle the tongue with delight, would feel as marvelous as having a buzzing fly trapped behind the jail of teeth, strafing and divebombing and crashing off gums and palate as the chimp would sit in happy, meditative satisfaction, its primary organ of pleasure getting all it could take.

"Oh, Ray," Joy says with exhaustion, tolerance, depression as Ray lights his cigarette just before the match burns down to his yellowed fingertips, with a flourish that causes the small flame to bend parallel to the table and not straighten up again until it's right under the cigarette, a trick that further impresses the chimp. Ray pokes the cigarette into a corner of his mouth which molds around it like half-hardened clay, and leaves it there where it seems to wax and wane, puff and rest by itself while Ray drinks beer and talks around it, a relationship similar to that the rhinoceros has with its tiny pilot bird.

"Boy, were we dumb," he says, his hard gray eyes lit up in his dead face, "getting this monkey. A monkey can't cut an imposing figure in crowds, just doesn't have the size and the personal magnetism. Monkeys are jokes, you laugh at them as you pass by but you don't stop to look. There's no artistry involved in being a monkey, all the monkeys in the zoo do it equally well. And they're too much like people, only work when they feel like it. I say we try to trade up, maybe get a kangaroo or some great big ugly snake, something that'll stop traffic, make people wanna drop quarters and even dollars like the bear did when he was really groovin'. What ya say?"

"I was just getting attached to it," Joy begins, eyes downcast at the bundle of joy in her arms, looking like any number of classic pietàs, and she intends to say more, to comment, perhaps, on Ray's lack of humanity, on the harshness of his spirit as reflected in his stony face, on his inhuman treatment of animals, but she stops because one of the hulking motorcycle-jacketed chimp admirers from the bar saunters over and stands next to Ray looking solicitous, shy, and ridiculous because he holds the chimp's discarded hat in one of his huge hands.

"The monkey left this," the motorcycle type says, looking like an abashed suitor come to ask papa for his daughter's hand in marriage, and he gives the little navy blue cap to Ray, who tosses it at Joy and the chimp; the chimp looks pleased and amazed to have this forgotten plaything back (the fact that it's supposed to collect money in the hat hasn't really gotten through to it yet: hat as receptacle too abstract a concept for a prepubescent chimp, while hat as toy seems perfectly reasonable and correct and delicious) and it puts it in its mouth, savoring first the edges of it, then the tassel. The suitor watches in fascination, stuffing his big hands into his pockets and shuffling his feet so that his boots make spine-tingling, floor-grating sounds that cause the insides of Joy's eyelids to itch and burn.

"Why doncha sit down," Ray says, a genteel drunk host, looking up at this black-clad monolith of a young man, his hair road-grimy and falling into his eyes, his face reddened by wind and pimples, his head small and overwhelmed by the features upon it, a large-toothed mouth, a long nose, heavy brows, the body large, muscled past the point of abundance, the type Ray picks out as a mark right away with an IQ assumed to match his shoe size, a willingness to believe any song and dance Ray might come up with, a real potential flimflam. "Hava drink."

"Thanks. The reason I came over . . ." he says as he drags the wooden chair out and away from the table (the kind of guy at odds with the universe, who creates grating noises of discomfort wherever he goes, who sits in your living room trying to be friendly as vases fall from spots on shelves from which they haven't been moved in twenty years, as the piano tuning goes sour in the middle of a melody, as seams pop on the sofa revealing old, yellowing stuffing, as your dog bites him; a young man suited only to the road, where nothing can go wrong with the wind rushing by him), sits down with his legs spread wide, his big chest hunched over, as he prepares to finish his speech.

"What's yer name?" Ray asks, accentuating his drunk's accent now, playing with the mark already, computing the amount of money in his pockets, the brain in his head, figuring in his slide-rule mind the direct or indirect proportion between the two and the possibilities for altering the placement of the former.

"Uh, Jimmy," the guy says, sticking out that huge right hand for Ray to shake, and Ray, like a doddering antique, pries his right hand away from the handle of the beer mug and shakes. "What I wanted to say . . ."

"Mine's Ray, and this is Joy." Ray pats Joy on the shoulder with mock devotion, but she doesn't raise her eyes from the chimp, "and I suppose you've met our pride and joy, our little darlin', our monkey."

"Pleased," Jimmy says, smiling to show all of his rabbit teeth, long and pointy, and simultaneously Joy and Ray realize that this person is maybe eighteen years old, a kid trying to look hard and streetwise, and Joy feels some tenderness for him, while Ray's eyes light up like the jackpot sign on a slot machine, his mouth twitches into his wooden Mona Lisa smile which communicates no mirth nor delight, just discomfort and perhaps a fear that the motion might make his face crack and fall off in crumbling plaster pieces, a smile that moves no portion of the face other than the mouth, causing no lines to crease the cheeks or widen the nostrils, no happy crinkles at the corners of the eyes, this responsible for the ageless quality of Ray's face, the eroded stone quality that ancient statues have when only missing arms or noses reveal their true antiquity. "What I wanted to ask you was, I heard you talkin' 'bout getting rid of the monkey."

"Yes, it's true, we might have to part with her," Ray says, his voice full of syrup and melodrama. "See, Joy and I decided a while back to remain pure, to stay out of the capitalist mainstream that was exploiting our brothers and sisters, to not pay income tax, all that stuff. So we got this dancing bear who we had a symbiotic relationship with, really cool. We fed him and clothed him and gave him a place to sleep, and he danced in bars and on corners and brought in the bread. That worked out great till we lost him."

"Hard to lose a bear, man," Jimmy says earnestly, trying to stay in the conversation since he expects to be dealing soon.

"We didn't really lose him," Joy says, the voice of reality, and Ray disapproves of her speaking up, gives her a vitriolic look as he wipes beer fuzz from his upper lip. "He ran away when he got sick of symbiosis."

"Yeah, I dig," Jimmy says, since he doesn't have the vaguest idea what these guys are talking about. "So then what happened?"

This part being extremely delicate, the tear-jerk part which could make the deal, Ray considers carefully, the Clarence Darrow of the Little Detroit Inn (though no one but Joy would recognize the inscrutable look on his face as one of concentration, the slightest clues showing themselves and then seeming to evanesce as if they had been imagined by the watcher: the eyes moving as if in REM sleep, a small circling of the pupil as if tracing the course of a ferris wheel, a tightening of the already thin mouth, a tautening of the forehead as if thought were a muscular exercise to tone up that area, all in a trice), and Jimmy, bored with the story and the storyteller, watches Joy and the chimp instead while the chimp sleeps in her arms, its fingers and toes enmeshed in Joy's hair, its head thrown back so that the cavernous expanse of mouth is laid open revealing the square, flat chimp teeth designed for chewing contemplatively on vines in the jungle, mashing grasses, happily gnawing carrion bones.

"Well, we were just so bummed I can't tell you," Ray begins his tale of woe, "we were like lost souls, we just sat around drinking and smoking and talking about what a great bear he'd been, and it seemed like we might have to take real jobs, get back into the mainstream, ugly stuff. Then we met this guy, a real lifesaver, who'd inherited this baby chimp from his uncle who'd been a monkey trainer who'd died, see, this guy didn't know the first damn thing about animals and was looking to unload it to anybody, you know, most people'd mistreat a monkey, keep it locked up in a little cage, make fun of it. So it was lucky we found it, since we could give it a life of freedom on the road, of being treated like an equal, if you know what I mean. But it's just not bringing in enough, still learning the ropes, and I don't know what we're going to do with the sweet little thing."

Jimmy's had enough, not used to talk but to the vibrating sound of engines under him, the scuffling lament of tires on asphalt, his ears filled up with the buzzing of a thousand flies, his body jamming, in constant motion like a tuning fork; all this sitting still and listening makes him aware of his battered nerve endings, his specialized muscles, and he feels his whole body emitting a high-pitched whine like that of complicated machinery when belts turn and gears lock in oily precision (this the sound of a road man, no soft skin on him anywhere, brains like scrambled eggs from the constant frappé motion), and the sound fills up his head till he feels it ricocheting against the insides of his skull. He claps one hand down on the small table and speaks. "I wanna buy your monkey. How much you want?" At this his friend from the bar comes over, pulls up a chair, another big hulking kid but with snub features and eyes the blue of faded denim.

"They gonna sell you the monkey?" the new guy asks, and Jimmy smiles again.

"This here's my friend Roger," he says, chummy, his own voice drowning out the revving in his ears.

"Howdy," Roger says, smiling and showing evidence of orthodontia, of parents attuned to the vicissitudes of physical beauty and willing to spend money and time in making their son conform to those standards (though in the end he winds up palling around with a guy like Jimmy whose parents never looked at him twice, who never had a meal fixed for him by a loving mother, who grew up wild without dentist appointments to fill his afternoons) and end up having to write him off as a big question mark in their existences, something sprung from their own bodies which they will never understand.

"Not for sale," Joy says quickly, shifting the chimp in her

arms so that it moans, sighs, then snuggles in again, nose covered with Joy's hair.

"But we heard you talking 'bout getting rid of it, and we'd be glad to take it off your hands," Roger says, his eyes now the color of icebergs beneath which cold cold waters flow.

"Yeah, we got money," Jimmy says, sweeping the air with one hand to indicate limitlessness, a calculable quantity to someone on the road used to the stretch of highway before and behind, the snaking of unending blacktop.

"Now just a minute, honey," Ray says, no love in his voice, instead the voice of a hanging judge, one who knows the sharp cutting edges of life rather than the gray areas of decision, "let's hear what these guys have to say."

"No, you're not doing it to me this time, Raymond," Joy says, her hands tightening around the chimp until they look like bone covered by a thin layer of the finest silk. Ray sits perfectly still, his eyes like snakes' eyes, flat, expressionless, full of ineffable hatred, then lifts his nearly empty beer mug to his lips and downs its remnants, an act of finalization, termination, an end to jiving and dealing; Joy quivers slightly as if from cold rather than from fear of reprisals, and can't meet his eyes.

"Well, boys, you heard what the lady says," Ray says, now mock-friendly in a used car dealer's manner.

"All right," Jimmy says, looking not at Joy or Ray but into the ice water eyes of Roger.

"Pleased to meetcha," Roger says, lifting a hand to his forehead in salute and not removing his gaze from the peaceful, sleeping face of the chimp. They shuffle out of the bar like a Tweedledum and Tweedledee brothers' act in leather, their boots knocking on the concrete floor in precision fashion, their long lean black-clothed legs flashing left, then right, with Jimmy, slightly taller and far less menacing, in the lead, Roger, a cockiness in his walk, a strut, following.

"You stupid bitch," Ray hisses. "We could've made a killing. You blew it, and all for that dumb monkey."

"Sometimes I think you don't have any feelings," Joy says,

her voice trembling, tender, filled with motherliness, but nothing assuages Ray's anger, softens the hard geometry of his face.

"So what're we gonna do now? Your monkey didn't make us any bread, we've got no money for gas, for food, for anything. The only thing it does well is sleep. At that, it's great, but that does us zero good."

"Let's get out of here," Joy says.

"Yeah, and go check into the Hilton," Ray says, but Joy, humble, has already risen and waits with her back to him for the sound of his chair sliding across the floor, the familiar sound of him checking each of his pockets and ears for cigarettes, matches, change, roach clip, a quiet patting building to a crescendo of snapping and unsnapping of shirt pockets; when she hears all this, she begins her walk to the door, dozing chimp baby in her arms.

Dusk only makes Hollywood look grimier, the air full of visible particles of night which cling to buildings, to people, giving the scene a soft-focus look as if photographed through cheesecloth. The daytime foot traffic, tourists and unemployeds, has not yet given way to the even more seamy nighttime walkers of the streets of Hollywood, a collection of hustlers of anything that can be hustled, of things illegal and semilegal, of the pleasurable, the frightening, the deadly (Hollywood turned from the glamour capital of the universe into a down-at-the-heels parody of itself, the name-stars inlaid into the sidewalks unnoticed by the shufflers, the runners, the strung-out cruisers of the boulevard): dusk seems a safe time, cars crowding their lanes like lines of crawling ants, the temperature higher than during daylight because of all the steaming, grinding engines and fretting drivers, sweat and carbon monoxide being released into the atmosphere and making it glow electric yellow if viewed from a weather satellite, traffic helicopter, flying saucer. Honking, yelling, the change of lights from red to green and back though no cars move, the air shimmering with heat and bad feelings, and Joy and Ray and their monkey step out onto the sidewalk paved with stars and rub their eyes, slightly drunk, disoriented, and full of rancor.

They will their concentration in the direction of the most straightforward route to the van, as if a magnetic force will then draw them toward it; the chimp, half awake, head bobbing like a newborn human baby's rubbernecked head, fingers Joy's mouth and nose with dreamy hands, the lighter-than-air hands of sleep. But before they can urge their somnolent bodies into action, dark figures fly through the air, thuds sound. Joy finds herself held from behind, strong male arms around her, forcing her own arms back so that she nearly drops the chimp. She sees Roger leap out like a shadow in front of the surprised Ray, sees them stand quite still, two marble statues of men depicting an ambiguous scene: about to converse, to shake hands, to walk past one another on the street (having a sixties sensibility, a mind that encompasses no physical violence except that done by cops to cool people, except that done in words by men to women and vice versa, she remains calm, no blood pounding in her veins, no twitching muscles, and just watches). Roger takes a big step up to Ray like a batter takes toward the ball when he's about to hit a home run and slugs Ray on the chin with one large fist, sending Ray sprawling on his rear end onto one of the sidewalk stars (and Joy recoils at the sound of hand on chin, a sharp crack like the one that might be made by a housewife beating a dusty rug), the star inscribed "Maurice Chevalier." Ray sits on the star, hands down on the sidewalk behind him as if he is still trying to break his fall, legs straight out and spread before him, eyes to the sky in case any interesting phenomena should take place there, perhaps another flying fist coming his way. Roger grabs the chimp out of Joy's arms, Jimmy lets her go, and they run off down the street as no cars stop to help the victims or catch the assailants, an everyday occurrence, the simplicity of violence, the predictability of life: Ray's bottom lip is split by a neat red line, a line like the pink margin-marker on notebook paper, as obvious and mundane; Joy's arms ache at the places where she still feels the hold of phantom fingers upon them and now her knees feel full of molten rubber, her stomach tingly. They both stare down the street after the two black-clad figures running, running, the suddenness and shock of the attack turning their perception of the world into a long skinny tunnel at the end of which two men in black become smaller and smaller. When the men disappear like the last dot of light on a turned-off television screen, Ray gets up, Joy moves to his side on cement feet, and they begin again to walk to the van.

Part Two

Ice cream! Like a miracle, like finding the right freeway off-ramp on an infinitely winding highway, like finding true love (something that has not happened since the fifties, when rock and roll was invented to memorialize the occasion), an ice cream shoppe grows like an errant weed out of the Rockies soil, a small run-down wooden storefront placed smack-dab between towns, making it the perfect hangout for rival high school factions and adolescent lovers before and after trysting: the Rockies honeycombed with inlets and turnlets, with coves that shine bright orange in the moonlight, with niches shaped exactly like pickup trucks. A hundred feet away, on a hazardous curving incline, the bear's nose twitches of its own accord upon his snout, and his toes begin to jiggle as they usually do when he hears one of the old songs, a song with a sinuous beat, heavy percussion background. Still he has no clue, even when his ears ache as if a whistling tea-kettle has been placed in each, and Bobo, who drives the bus, sitting in the front seat next to the bear, and Cassy and Polly in back, and Hank and Wayne in the Datsun filled with the band's musical instruments and amps and cords and wires, driving along behind the bus, following the same lazy spirals Bobo makes on the road because they are smoking the same low-grade marijuana, realize nothing, find no change in the quality of the air, in the great slooping currents of sound and smell that animals perceive as a fact of their sensual existence. The bear doubts his senses, sits quivering in the seat as if afflicted with fever, restrains his arms from waving wildly by an actual act of bear will. Then he sees it, his arms jump out the bus window as if to embrace a phantom floating on the air.

"Whoooooo," the bear cries, the most unearthly sound the loaded Bobo has ever heard. He swings the bus around into the unpaved parking area in front of the ice cream shoppe, thinking the bear has just seen a long-lost relative, and the beat-up Datsun follows them in. Before getting out of the bus, without saying a word, Bobo turns his magnetic dog eye malevolently upon the bear.

"This better be good, dude," he says as Hank and Wayne stroll over to the bus, as Polly and Cassy come out of the back rubbing their eyes like children in some fairy story just awakened from a nap to find either the wicked wolf at their door or a living room magically filled with candies and toys thanks to some thoughtful spirit of a godmother.

"Like, what's up?" Hank asks, a joint dripping lazy as maple syrup from the corner of his mouth. The low and secret speech of the women forms a choral background over which the bear can give his answer.

"Whoooooo," he bellows again, overcome with emotion for something he can barely remember, though he realizes his tongue has become hot and dry, and his throat works reflexively. It is something to cure this that he craves, something cool and sloppy, something mysteriously sweet. "Ice cream," he cries, the meaningless words for his affliction, or the double name of some past, beloved master. His body taut with the effort of thought, he strains out the bus window toward the ramshackle store, knowing only that, whatever it might be, there it is, waiting for him, or for his human companions to fetch it for him.

"Can you believe it?" Bobo croons in his singsong voice. "This here hairy dude wants an ice cream cone. Where do you s'pose he learned that trick?"

"I could go for one myself," Cassy or Polly says; at this moment the bear cannot tell the difference between them, in fact sees them as one small human whom he has, in his excitement, hallucinated into two. "Vanilla, or maybe strawberry. I bet they don't have too good flavors out here."

"Hey, it's all under control," Hank says in his emcee's voice as he sticks his hand into a pants pocket and comes out with a collection of change, quarters and dimes and nickels catching the sun and glinting like diamonds: the bear waits, breathless, expecting magic, expecting Hank to change the dead metal into living, melting ice cream (in some secret, dusty back alley of the bear brain; consciously, he's still in the pure reflex stage, the stage of animal wanting and slobbering).

"The bear wants ice cream, he gets ice cream," Wayne says. "Don't get so hostile, Bobo, man. Remember the omen."

"All right, I'm no bad guy. What you want, bear? Chocolate?" Bobo asks. "I'm askin' the bear, just so you don't get no wrong ideas, because I don't think it's so cool to let the bear go into this little Colorado ice cream place and order for himself. I'm not even going in there, and I'm slightly human."

All eyes upon the bear, waiting for his reply; to the humans, the bear seems to be thinking, his own eyes gleaming and intelligent, his ears straight up, his posture erect and approximating that of a man. Actually the bear's brain is blank, straining, like a weightlifter under a five-hundred-pound barbell, to summon up an image. Chocolate? Vanilla? Strawberry? (What are these words to a bear with the ice cream fever?)

"I don't know," the bear says, shaking his head slowly from side to side until his long nose nearly touches each shoulder. "Get me all three."

"Hey, yeah," Hank says. "A triple-decker for my man the bear. One vanilla and one strawberry for Cassy and Polly, a chocolate for Bobo. Me and Wayne'll take care of this transaction."

When the bear sees Hank and Wayne coming out of the ice cream shoppe with their hands full of ice cream cones, he experiences a wave of memory so sharp and intense that had he been a man he might have begun a seven-volume memoir-novel about remembrance with this feeling or, at least, would have noted the literary significance of the experience and thought about buying for himself an esoteric tea cake to celebrate. Something primal and deep and basic, as if a blow on the head has jarred loose from the cobwebs a memory of the first bear or bear-primogenitor, occurs, but the absence of any artistic sensibility in bears (save for this bear, and his only aesthetic is the Dance) makes Jungian memory impossible: instead, when he sees the ice cream cones in tricolor like some tiny nation's flag, saliva begins to drip down his muzzle and his head feels afire, gleaming white-hot with the single image, the ice cream cone with three balls of perfect symmetry atop it which must be his.

"Whooooooo," the bear cries out, and then, like a baby pronouncing his first word to the proud delight of mama and papa: "Mine!" He rocks from one bear buttock to the other, swivels his hips, does a fidgety sitting-down impression of a bizarre new dance in the eternity that it takes the free-floating ice cream cone to approach him (the bear fails to see the human attached to the hand which holds the cone, isolates the thing in space as it comes to him, a universe filled with one ice cream cone, a dim bear retina receiving only one upside-down picture). A moment of unparalleled Hitchcockian suspense as the cones begin to melt slightly in the hot Colorado afternoon sun, as the bear's triple-decker sloshes around like a set of ball bearings, just a little motion, the bear perceiving it only because of his complete fascination, obsession with the arrival of the cones. Closer, almost within reach of his hairy arms: if he looked at the others, he would not be able to understand their composure, their Buddhistic calm in the face of impending ice cream, their arms hanging relaxed and sure at their sides, their mouths held at usual posture, neither tight and strained nor open and anticipating. But of course he is totally unable even to remember that there are others around him, in fact, in an even more perfect Buddhistic experience, he has completely transcended his own body, left the flesh behind and escaped to ice cream Nirvana, the wonderful mysteries of the ice cream cone a unique bear-koan at essence, definitely The Way. Closer, closer, and it is his, he feels it dripping tricolor glop onto his hands, and without thought or premeditation stuffs the whole thing into his mouth, sending near-solid hunks of ice cream flying for a five-foot radius, turning the hair around his mouth white and light brown and pink, getting ice cream up his nose. Blinded by his own desire, ravening as a wolf, he chokes it down in a few seconds and then opens his eyes to discover that the others have barely started theirs, that they lick neatly around corners and edges, take little chipmunk bites out of the top circle of the cone, work architectural feats with their tongues, which they use to push the ice cream down into the cone, to arrange furrows and troughs, to flick the cool sweet stuff onto the roofs of their mouths before it touches their hot throats. He cannot remember what it tasted like, and he wants more.

"Whoooooo," the bear bellows again, and he puts his paws to his ears in a near-human gesture of misery.

"Y'see," Bobo says, "y'see what happens when you start dealing with animals? Turn this band into a fuckin' dog act. They're worse than people."

"What do you want, bear?" Polly says in her little-girl voice, sweeter because her throat has been coated with magical ice cream.

"Another," the bear says, reduced, in his voracious lust, to single words, unable to formulate sentences because of his animal single-mindedness, his brain contracted like a black hole in space into one thought preceding all others, preceding speech.

"Hey, man, you had a triple-decker, that's three times as much as any of the rest of us had," Hank says. "We don't even know if you're any good for the band."

Cassy whacks Hank across the back of his head with one small open hand, and says: "Men. Always looking for returns on their investments. Lousy capitalists. Karl Marx would buy the bear another ice cream cone."

"We read Karl Marx for a class we took at San Francisco State," Polly says to the bear. "We registered under a made-up name. We went to class on alternate days, and we each read half of the *Communist Manifesto*. But I think she's right. According to Marx, the bear should get what he needs."

"Since when is this a Communist band? Shit, those people's band days are over, honey. Now rock and roll is into money and playing Las Vegas, and don't let anyone tell you otherwise," Bobo says, his dog eye turning darker than usual, blushing in anger, menacing.

"The Grateful Dead is still a people's band," Wayne says softly, his hand over his mouth to wipe away an ice cream mustache.

"The Dead," Bobo says with reverence. "All right, dude, you know when you got me. Buy the beast another ice cream cone if you have to, the name of the muse cannot be invoked in vain. I ain't gonna fight with the Dead."

"All *right*," Hank says. "I change my vote. Another I.C.C. for the Big B. But this time only a single."

"Strawberry," the bear says, remembering suddenly that the middle of the cone had the most tang, enchanted his tongue most in its quick passage, had little bits of hard sweetness while the other two-thirds were smooth and bland, though glorious. A bit of bargaining worthy of the United Nations, whereby a disenfranchised hairy minority began with nothing and worked his way up to something because of Karl Marx and the Grateful Dead: all the bear knows is that Hank already walks toward the door of the store with change jingling in his hands, and that change, some silver and copper, can be transformed into ice cream once he passes through those portals. No wish ever to see the inside of an ice cream shoppe himself, to work his own deal, score his own stuff, peel his own napkin out of the metal box standing on the counter: all the bear wants is the end product, the edibles, unable to be anything but the overgrown child all his life, to rejoice in the flying carpet arrival of the hovering ice cream.

The independently cruising strawberry ice cream cone arrives, delivered as by an act of God into his greedy bear hands and, as the others work on their original cones, the bear addresses himself to his second. But he's learned: this time he teases the cone with his tongue, flicking out the pink serpent so that only the tip touches the top of the ice cream, stealing just a bit of the soft, cool, smooth, delicious stuff, so little that his mouth thinks ice cream is just a dream half-remembered, his throat hardly notices a difference when he swallows the melted morsel. A quick study in some areas, the bear laps his tongue around the circle of ice cream with true deliberation, whacking off chunks of it like a sculptor with some masterwork in mind; he whittles it down until all that's left is inside the cone, and then true bear finesse goes to work (cartoon bears with two-foot-long tongues used for searching out sticky honey in a buzzing beehive not being too far from the truth). His tongue, like a pile driver, dips in and out of the cone until all the ice cream disappears, leaving only the cone, perfect and intact, to be crunched between his long yellow teeth; he finishes seconds before the humans, whose small tongues and mouths work just as lovingly on the last of their ice cream cones. Feeling enculturated, homogenized (words for invisible acceptance into society always having to do with the processing of dairy products, milk metaphors), the bear slouches into regular bear posture, at ease and complacent with his new companions who eat ice cream cones just as he does.

"Can we get this show on the road now?" Bobo asks, the corners of his mouth coated with the dark brown residue of his ice cream cone, the same color as the skin around his spot eye.

"You don't wanna smoke a little first?" Cassy asks flirtatiously.

"Drug addicts," Bobo says.

"Like, man, we gotta get to Denver some time in the near future," Hank says, gesturing toward the horizon as if Denver, like Oz, lies over the rainbow.

"C'mon. You dudes, get back into the car. You chicks, go

smoke some weed and get mellow. You, bear, you owe me some consideration for my great compromise on your behalf. You stick around up front here with me and navigate, here're the road maps that'll take us to Denver," tossing a bunch of folded-up papers at the bear which, like reverse origami, come apart as they fly through the air and land on his lap in various stages of blossoming. The bus and Datsun start up simultaneously, causing a dust uprising like an invading horde of tiny golden insects; the bear looks back at the ice cream shoppe as they pull away, but all he can see is the vague outline of a small building, a building that might be a house, a school, a church since they all look alike in those parts, encased in a diaphanous cloth woven of dust, no remnant of ice cream-ness, but that's okay for the bear: his brain understands suddenness.

"You understand," Bobo says when the caravan is under way, when the bear becomes his only audience and confidant, "that using the Grateful Dead on me was an unfair move, man, totally unfair. I love that band. I met Jerry Garcia once. I mean, I saw him at a party, kind of a short dude. Who cares what he looks like. He's Jerry Garcia, y'know?" The bear fumbles with the road maps fluttering around him like Dracula's opera cape about to turn into a silky pair of bat wings: who ever told this dog-eyed creep that bears could read road maps? Constellations of tiny holes begin to appear in the corners of folds; where folds meet one another, whole towns and road junctions disappear.

"That's why we called our band the Ungrateful Wretches. Get it? We want to jam and boogie just like in the old days, make people get up and dance in the aisles, take their clothes off. Man, everything's changed, especially after they closed up the Fillmore. The Dead's all that's left of the old days." The bear, hardly listening to Bobo's nostalgic monologue, smothers in his flock of road maps, his wiry fur sticking through the tiny holes this folding and unfolding and refolding has caused, impaling the road maps upon him so that, with each small move of his body, the disturbing sound of paper being rent and torn crackles softly, until the bear stiffens, does the animal-statue trick that most untamed beasts in danger know without thinking: if you stand very still, maybe all that is bothering you will forget all about you and go away (good strategy in the wild, not so hot when the adversary is a holey road map subject to the caprices of the breeze blowing through the bus).

"How can you dance so good and still be such an inept animal?" Bobo asks, his dog eye glinting from the close-up view of the bear and road maps in distress; he pulls sunglasses down from the sun visor, so that he looks like a normal black man in shades, and the bear relaxes slightly, the wrath of a normal black man being bearable, the wrath of Bobo having in it the cutting edge of the forest, of the carnivore. "There I go, off on my Dead rap, talking to an animal, for Christ's sake. What can a bear care about the Grateful Dead?"

Strangely, the name sends a shiver of remembrance down the bear's spine, which causes the road maps to rip once more. In 1969, the archetypal San Francisco experience had to be going to a Grateful Dead concert at Winterland: the bear might have gone to some of these concerts, though just past cubhood and still highly impressionable, he couldn't remember if he tried. Cassy and Polly, Hank, Bobo, and Wayne had been to these concerts and they became enchanted by the combination of anarchy and control, of chance and will, of music and drugs that the concerts presented, and their own ephemeral butterfly youths.

"What songs do they play that are good to dance to?" the bear asks, trying to summon some image which will enlighten him, let him share in Bobo's secret.

"Hell, I don't know. I never listened thinking about dancing. Anyhow, they're a tripping band, not a dance band," Bobo says in disgust as he steers around a cow that has wandered away from its brethren through a hole in a barbed-wire fence and now walks the metaphorical high wire between the grasslands and the highway, an act as dangerous as any circus performer's. The bear looks into the cow's eyes as they drive by it, eyes as flat as a small sea turned brown by an oil slick, without intelligence, the bred-down, bred-dumb eyes of the domesticated beast, no relative of the bear: he recognizes nothing there of himself, as distant as this dog-eyed human hiding behind shades. "I guess we're finding our way to Denver by mental telepathy, or maybe by animal intuition. What d'ya say, bear: do we turn left or right here?"

The bear shakes his body as if his fur were wet from a morning plunge into an icy winter river full of sparkling, metallic fish for playmates, and the road maps that cling to him shred around him, freeing him from their spider-web grasp.

"I don't know," the bear says, his voice reasonable. "I've never been to Denver."

"You're lucky I'm a member of an oppressed minority just like you who can understand your I.Q. problems 'stead of a white man who'd call you ugly names and get real pissed off," Bobo says, removing his shades for the effect of his poisonous, one-eyed, dog-eyed glare. "I ain't never been to Denver either. So whatchya think, man? Animals're supposed to have feelings about such things, animals and women."

"I can't," the bear says, his body getting all riled and upset, the urge for flight itching in his toes just like the Dance does when he hears Marvin Gaye singing "I Heard It Through the Grapevine," his heart pounding a running rhythm in his chest, his brain scrambled into a mere receiver of signals: watch out for that tree, take that path, you'll be safe by that rock. An image of a terrified deer, followed by invisible and hungry pursuers, gallops through the underbrush of his brain, its eyes wide with fear, its dappled skin a blur of pale brown and white, its large ears straight back and quivering; the deer skitters, stops, looks both ways, then hauls off through a gap in branches, to the right. "That way," the bear says, sticking his hand out, his eyes closed tight, after the deer.

"All *right*, my man," Bobo says, pleased. "Don't ever let 'em say we're not as smart as they are. Pull your knife then, baby. That'll show 'em smarts."

"Lay off," the bear says, his voice low and gruff. "I've had all kinds of gigs, and none of them ever included giving directions. I'm a dancer, and that's all. I'm going in the back. You can find your own way to Denver. I'm going to relax." He clambers between the seats into the musty darkness of the living quarters of the bus, his eyes, adjusting to the change in light, even dimmer than usual; he trips over something small and round and falls on his chin, making a "whumph" sound as the air leaves his belly and chest through his teeth.

"Hi, man," Cassy says as she crawls from her place at his feet onto his huge, hairy plain of a back, holding onto each ear with a tiny hand.

"Look who's here," Polly says as she caresses the bear's muzzle, playing with the tongue that sticks out the side, through a crack between molars.

They lift him up, one under each armpit like a pair of bear bookends, and plop him down onto the nearest of the asymmetrically scattered mattresses that make the inside of the bus look like an aerial photo of multicropped farm country. Still they press up against him, cooing their private language into his ears until he becomes near-hypnotized with the guttural sound of it, with the tiny fingers creeping into the pink beginnings of his fuzzy brain, into his mouth, tracing the long yellow teeth, tickling the underside of his tongue.

"Doesn't he look pissed off," Polly says in English, though the bear perceives no difference, words having become a collection of sounds, of syllables, for him, an up-and-down melody that Hank might play upon his glowing stand-up bass.

"I bet that mean old Bobo's been picking on him," Cassy whispers through the bear's ear to her sister's waiting ear on the other side of the bear's empty head: bear as primitive communication device. "Wanna smoke?" to which the bear nods a yes to his matching set of earmuffs, and they set to cleaning and rolling with delight.

"You know," Polly begins, her fingers as busy with the defoliation of marijuana plants as they had been with the bear's own foliage, "when we were little, we were always dressed alike, exactly alike. Seeing her was just the same as looking in the mirror. We never thought there was any difference between us."

"Yeah, that's why we started talking alike. That's what one of those sociologists says. Just like thinking thoughts to yourself for no one else to hear," Cassy says. "Except that ours were spoken to one another. When we first ran away, we tried separating, living our own lives, but it didn't work. I'd always know what was happening to her, and she'd always know what was happening to me. Even if we tried we couldn't block it out, and it got to be dangerous, like a kind of double vision when you didn't want it, when all you wanted was to see single. So we thought we'd stick it out together, make life simple."

"Much better that way," Polly mumbles through the newly born joint that hangs from her lips like a line-drawing caricature of a cigarette. "We can pretend there's just one of us again. Then we don't get confused."

"You don't know what it's like," Cassy says as she watches Polly tuck stray wisps of hair behind her ears, strike a match, and light up the joint, her eyes crossing as she watches its tip burn bright orange, then dull to black, so she strikes another match to try again. "Looking alike in a world where just about everyone else looks different. We might as well be connected at the hip or share kidneys or something. We're already connected up here," she says, knocking on the side of her head with a diminutive fist.

"Yeah, everyone assumes we're pretty dim, like we each got just half a brain or something," Polly says as she draws her first deep drag on the joint, inhaling with the beginning of her sentence, exhaling with the end of it, making of speech a Zen breathing exercise. "And talking funny didn't help. Here," and she hands the joint to Cassy, then presses her mouth over the bear's upturned, coy nose.

"Mar-i-lyn Mon-roe," Cassy breathes, and the bear, already starting to feel stoned, hangs on each syllable, an odd collection foreign to his bear ears, perhaps, he thinks, some part of their secret language about to be revealed to him, some special women's code, Eleusynian, which he can learn. "We always dug her. Everyone thought she was dumb, just because she had these big breasts, and this little voice, and blond hair. But, y'know, she wasn't dumb. She was just adaptable, like women have to be. Men are born with freedom of choice, can be whatever they want because they don't have to be afraid of anything. Women have everything to be afraid of: being alone, being in crowds, not finding a good man, finding a bad one, having no women friends, the women friends they have betraying them, getting raped during the day, getting raped at night. So they adapt, y'know? If acting dumb's gonna make life easier and safer, they act dumb, and become real good at it. I read that in half of a sociology book for a class we took at San Francisco State. Marilyn Monroe adapted, y'know? She was a champ."

"Yeah, but what about the difference between real life and the flicks?" Polly says sharply, forcing the bear back from the floating state which the hypnotic rhythms of Cassy's speech sent him into: his head waggles on his neck, which suddenly feels reed-thin and vulnerable, and his concentration, contracted into a pinprick through the magic of marijuana, focuses on her mouth, which seems to be two scurrying lizards on the flat desert of her face. "In the movies, she got lots of guys and lots of money. In real life, she gave herself the big OD. We tried to get out of that male-defined society, and look at us. Outnumbered three to two (not counting you, bear), screaming our guts out on alternating nights fronting for these cool guys who think they're the whole show. I tell you, man, I feel artistically stifled. I don't feel adapted at all."

"Yeah," Cassy says, downhearted.

"I don't understand," the bear says. As he speaks, Cassy and Polly, who have been supporting his massive bear shoulders while breathing, in turn, the thick sweet smoke into his nose, retreat a foot or so to let their ears catch his words, and he plummets backward, a lead weight, onto the mattress and continues talking from this supine, undignified position.

"Why don't you leave? If you're good singers, you could get gigs somewhere else, without this band. You should be happy."

"When we first started this band, I was sleeping with Bobo, then Polly was sleeping with Hank, I switched to Wayne, then Polly was sleeping with Bobo, then Polly switched to Wayne, and I was with Hank for a while. It was heaven," Cassy says as if she were speaking of a long-ago dream, her voice light and ethereal as starlight.

"Now it's all business, and we're sick of it," Polly says; she takes an aggressive toke on the joint and blows so hard into the bear's nose that he coughs the smoke out of his mouth along with great gouts of bear spit turned brown and oily by the dope. The women pound on his back, on his chest, grab his thick, hairy bear arms and raise them toward the ceiling of the bus, hold his mouth open with lion-tamer hands so that they can look down his throat as if hoping to find, in magician fashion, doves, rabbits, unbroken eggs. The bus bumps over something (a deer body in the road? a flattened, dead-rubber piece of an exploded tire? a beer can magnified by the weight and bounciness of the bus into a bumper, a fender? or a hole in the road, perhaps a place struck by lightning in one of the Rockies' inimitable winter electric storms in which the end of the world seems nigh?), the bear gives one final explosive cough in midair, and with a bounce the two women and the bear are entangled once more, seriousness forgotten. They finish off the joint and prepare a new one for the ritual smoking, and the bear, with an animal's low tolerance for anything intoxicating, sees the bus spinning around him like that carnival ride that the bottom falls out of, leaving voyagers stuck to the sides like flies in honey, feels his limbs weightless and at the same time sodden, feels his nose to be an accurate compass pointing exactly to the North Star (which might be the upward-pointing nose of the constellation Ursa Major).

"Maybe we should have an affair with the bear," Cassy says, her mouth full of bear fur from where she has landed with her head against his chest (if the bear were any smarter, of, say, human male intelligence, though frequently even nine-tenths of that race fail to take the broadest hints as invitation, he might realize that Cassy could have spoken this in their private language if it were meant to stay private).

"Hey, yeah. We're twenty-seven, way too old for plain old straight sex," Polly says, extricating herself from under a bear arm. Do the women discern a gleam in the bear's eyes, that special shine that indicates someone has flipped a switch and turned on the sexual current, the 100-watt bulb of desire? The women might think they discern it, but it's not there, lust never showing in an animal's eyes: a slavering tongue, perhaps, or a high-pitched moan indicative of anything from pain to hunger, but the eyes don't change, unpatinaed as stuffed-animal eyes. The bear looks at them with interest be-cause of this new combination of syllables: no one has ever suggested sexual congress of any sort to or with the bear; per-haps a few drunks in bars might have made crass statements, but in his ecstatic dancing reverie they were no more than a part of the music, of the din that accompanied the dancing experience. And, having grown up in the cities, with only humans for companions, masters, friends, betrayers, he's never known that pure, unique state, animal desire (which, unlike human desire, is primarily triggered by olfactory stim-uli: no female bears in heat being taken for walks on the sidewalks of your regular big city, the hot thick smell of them floating on the air like an obvious love-cologne in a cartoon, a cruising orange cloud enveloping and turning male heads, no female bears in heat in the zoos for him to visit because, as soon as that delicate condition occurs, the offending animals are removed either to solitary confinement or to a special breeding pen so as not to horrify mamas and papas taking their kids for a wholesome day at the zoo with such obvious facts of life), so the bear's purity remains unimpaired, bears, unlike furtive gorillas, being nonmasturbatory mammals, un-interested in their own sexuality until odoriferous love like a thunderbolt strikes them down in the primeval forest. Then they do it and forget about it, the bear, on the sexual scale, clearly not built for love, his large roly-poly hips, his narrow shoulders, his goofy hanging arms, his stubby tail, an animal designed to carry the brunt of fairy-tale jokes, to clown, to bounce and jiggle like a basketball with head and limbs, but surely not to be a lover (despite the curious reputation: "Who's been sleeping in my bed?").

"What about it, bear?" Cassy asks, leaning against him with the weight of her whole small body. "You like us, don't you?"

"I like you," the bear says; the bus bounces in slow motion beneath him, circles counterclockwise above him, and his throat tastes hot, sweet, and sooty. No one has ever asked the bear whether or not he liked him or her before, a common assumption that animals like everybody, or nobody, leaving no room for a question either way.

"Well all *right*," Cassy says, rubbing against the bear.

"We can make you happy, bear," Polly says; both women remove some of their clothing, but human flesh is just flesh to the bear, whether there's more or less of it, different from his own (and, he cannot help thinking, slightly inferior) because of its lack of protective, hirsute covering, bringing no images of soaring eagles, shooting stars, blissful smells of a forest after a spring rain to his movie-screen consciousness.

"We can take you higher," one of them says, singsong; the bear has already closed his eyes because the tiny fingers start digging into his thick fur, soothing and restful, a scene of love straight out of the jungles where mama monkeys do much the same when they search for delicious nits in the pelts of their babies, doing a twofold service because they not only rid their offspring of vermin, they also provide themselves with a nutritious midday snack. They search through the fur of his lower body as he lies back, supine, half-stuffed teddy bear, a ludicrous sunbather at some exotic resort, a candidate for taxidermy, completely unaware of the object of their search, the previous arch discussion of ursine unsuitedness to love leaving out the most fundamental part, the relative smallness of unexcited bear genitalia, its downright minuteness in comparison to the leviathan proportions of hips, of thighs, of round head. Aroused, it's only slightly larger, albeit much more functional, suited for pure propagation rather than pleasure, built for speed rather than for comfort. In this case, invisible to two stoned women whose fingers, untrained in bear anatomy, might pass right over what they would otherwise know to be the object of their desire, thinking it to be part of one of the bear's great rolling muscles, protruding bones, or squishy little caches of fat. Under the wonderful anesthetic of the constant tickles, the bear soon snores away, nose up, mouth open, tongue lolling out and kicking up every so often like a dreaming cat's tail, and the women, just as hypnotized by the futility of their quest, doze off next to him, curled up against his sides while the grinding of the bus's struggling motor, the soft whirring of tires on highway, the bouncing and jerking and the magnetic inertia of stops and starts throw their calmed, buzzing brains into a still, dark, pleasant place quite similar to the vast void of bear sleep.

"Well, ain't this cute," Bobo says, his dog eye looking like a large hole in his face because of the increasing gloom of sunset, the lack of any type of artificial light inside the bus. "While you guys been snoozin', we got us a club date." The bear awakens in a flash, sensing adversity, but the two women, languid and unimpressed by Bobo's hostility, stretch, rub their eyes with fists like little mitts, gather small pieces of clothing which look interchangeable to the bear, able to fit on any body part, and apply these to the nearest naked piece of their own flesh.

"That mean we work tonight?" Cassy whines, a child grumpy after a truncated nap.

"That's right, honey You *are* a singer. Unless you want to hit the highway and thumb it back to S.F., where you might get a job waiting on tables," Bobo says. "How about it? You gonna get up and help, or do I have to stomp on you?"

"Okay, man."

"Jeez, what a Nazi."

"And how 'bout you, bear? You forgiven me for my indiscretions of this afternoon? Or you just gonna lie there like a sultan, smoke some opium, write some poetry, and wait for us workers to come home with the bread?"

"I'll help," the bear says, rising to his full height in an instinctual gesture of intimidation, then slumping back down into his normal posture. "What can I do?"

"Well, big strong dude like you sure could carry in amps and equipment while me and Hank and Wayne do the close work, the wiring and plugging and stuff," Bobo says, ingratiating, his magnetic eye looking nearly human. "C'mon, then," he commands, and the four of them walk outside into the purple and pink and brown mountain sunset, the remarkable sunset you see when you are that much closer to the heavenly bodies involved in the celestial changing of the guard, where the very air gets you high, makes your head tingle at its top as if some bubbles were trying to escape like the gushing froth of a just uncorked champagne bottle, makes your lungs choke out giggles.

In among forties-style office buildings (no chrome, no brown reflecting glass), restaurants, and shops stands the anomaly, the obvious recent addition making passersby yearn for the good taste of the old days. A small, charcoal-colored building with the modern architect's disdain for the crassness of corners: everything curves, the places where the walls meet, the entryway (of course down two steps, making the whole affair seem subterranean and very hip), the atrocious roof which rises half-domed like some Kremlin reject, and, certainly, no windows. Above the sunken, concave doorway like a mouth, the sign seems to bloom like a series of mushrooms from the loamy surface of the building: HOLLYWOOD, each letter gigantic, each made up of not neon, not paint, but thousands of tiny, clear-glass light bulbs with golden filament inside so that the letters seem to pulsate when viewed from more than twenty feet away, hurt your eyes when viewed from underneath, make the interior of the club seem gloomy by comparison, a sought effect, the slow adjustment of eyes taken into consideration by nouveau-decadent designers trying for a cross between Hollywood in the twenties and Berlin in the thirties; in smaller letters, half the size, right after the HOLLYWOOD and hardly noticeable in comparison, *Cafe* written in script and light-bulb-dotted just like its big brother, almost an afterthought. A rock and roll palace in Denver named the Hollywood Cafe would be a natural except for one thing: the absolute dearth of rock and roll talent passing through those parts. Young people come and sit at the small, modern California-style tables, buy piña coladas, and more often than not listen to recorded music because the Hollywood can't get anyone to come and play. So the unheralded arrival of the Ungrateful Wretches, certainly no big name, no record company backing, no album to plug, creates an instant stir, causes joints of Colombian marijuana to light up in the club manager's office, causes contracts to spring from file drawers, hands to shake, and an instant three-night gig to materialize better than any phony medium can summon into being the requisite ectoplasm hand over her wired crystal ball. As the bear and Hank and Wayne and Bobo cart equipment from the Datsun and the bus into the club, a small crowd of modishly tattered young people gathers, the box office opens mysteriously and a line begins to form, the air grows thick and sweet with the smell of marijuana as hands touch furtively in the ritual passing of the glowing ciggy. With darkness, the crowd grows larger, obviously stoned or the gleaming, living, hideously glowing Hollywood sign would deter them with promises of permanent eye damage similar to that gotten from watching the slow path of a solar eclipse.

Hank and Wayne wolf down hamburgers in front of the dressing room mirrors lit just like the ostentatious Hollywood sign: potential gigs always make them hungry, especially when they've been driving and smoking all day. Bobo, unaffected by this syndrome because of his dog eye, because of his more sensitive, more hostile, more excitable nature (closer to that of a trapped beast, of a leopard in a zoo), paces back and forth from the open door of the dressing room to the mirrored area taken over by Hank, Wayne, and their hamburgers, hamburger wrappings, discarded bits of bun, condiment containers, salt and pepper packets, crumpled straw snakes. His cowboy boots, worn only at show times, clatter on the tile floor in four-four rhythm so that the bear, even in bondage, shakes his hips. The bear's arms stretch to their utmost wingspan, each wrist tied with a long red ribbon, the ends of which the twins alternately hold in their teeth and in their hands as they try to lace the bear up to two tambourines. After many attempts, the bear has shown himself to be pitifully unable to hold tambourines, even one tambourine, and dance at the same time. By a gross contortion of his hands, he can hook his claws into a tambourine, but when he dances, they fly off like discuses, and the club wishes to avoid lawsuits and other related disturbances. Bobo suggested a single tambourine as the answer, but when the bear mustered his all in concentration to hold the small instrument between his flattened, pressing paws, his eyes crossing from strain as if the line of his vision, unimpaired and focused, keeps the thing in the air, he could not dance a step, dance flowing from a free-floating, unencumbered brain, certainly not from a bear brain intent upon levitation: he looked like a bear hero out of Ovid's *Metamorphoses,* about to turn into a tree, already half-rooted and growing a pelt of bark. So he ends up getting tied to the tambourines, the red ribbon going once around his wrist, then threaded through the holes of the tambourine, then down through a couple of digits and around the wrist again, uncomfortable and itchy, but Bobo says that a purely visual member of the band, a non-music maker, cannot be allowed, that everyone must contribute to the total auditory aesthetic; this sounds reasonable to everyone, and the bear accepts the handcuffing with docility and strain.

"Hey, Wayne won't mind sharing percussion with you, will ya?" Hank asks, making peace though no altercation exists. Wayne smiles and stuffs the last bit of his third hamburger into his widened mouth.

"The club manager really likes the idea of the bear," Bobo says. "He's sure we're the first rock and roll band with a nonhuman member, a real breakthrough. He says that if it goes okay tonight, and if one of you chicks screws him, that he'll do what he can about getting us a recording contract."

"Hey, really?" Hank says.

"I hope you told him to get lost," Cassy says, putting her fist up so that the bear's lace job becomes suspended in midair for the moment.

"You lousy pimp," Polly says. Before they begin speaking in their own language, spitting out consonants like sunflower-seed shells, Bobo holds his hands up in the air placatingly.

"Just kidding," he says, though he keeps his dog eye turned to the floor. "That kinda stuff doesn't happen anymore. Unfortunately."

"He doesn't mean it," Wayne says though this gets lost in a garbled mass of half-chewed hamburger.

"Doesn't matter," Hank says, "doesn't matter. Tonight's gonna be groovy, guaranteed. Who's gonna sing?"

"Not me," they say spontaneously together, then giggle and speak in code, words full of z's sounding like male epithets; their complete lack of awareness of the real world during moments of their secret conversation makes the bear feel invisible, the classic sensation of "pinch me, I must be dreaming," though in the bear's case he jiggles his toes in an unconscious affirmation of his existence: "I dance, therefore I am (*Salto ergo sum*)."

"What is this, a mutiny?" Bobo asks, throwing his hands up in the air, his hands which seem to the bear to wear white masks, which seem as incongruous as his dog eye. "Someone's gotta sing, the contract spells out two female singers to perform on alternating nights. The bear's not gonna sing, and I can't do all those pseudo-Joplin numbers, I'd break my throat. Shit, you know how long it's been since we had a decent gig?"

"No, how long?" Polly asks sweetly, as if seeking the answer to a troubling riddle. The bear perceives the rise in tension in the room as a human would be aware that the temperature has suddenly gone up twenty degrees: the fur on the back of his neck prickles, his muscles tense, his heartbeat accelerates in preparation for flight or fight, his head clears out fast as if someone has just turned on a wind machine, cobwebs shiver on their moorings, images flee, until a big blank space exists between his ears like a blank page inserted into a typewriter waiting for the first words to be written upon it, a tabula rasa, self-erasing, anticipating danger to imprint itself with rapidity, and with the grace of the kill. Bobo's arms flutter for an instant, wings or weapons, either way out of control, Wayne's chest becomes concave, his face pallid and hard as dry cement, Hank remains expressionless and interested as a sports commentator ready to describe one prizefighter beating another's head to the consistency of mashed bananas. The bear's blood hammers through his heart at top speed, sent from there to assignment at one of the vital organs to wait for death, though the preparation proves to be unnecessary, kind of a hot dog gesture his body can't resist, like a diver's double-gainer with a half twist when a simple swan would do.

"Oh, for heaven's sake, I'll sing." Cassy sighs. "You guys take everything so seriously." The bear's body deflates, blood seeking out normal paths so that his legs and arms feel full of armies of ants rushing to the remains of a picnic; Bobo, too, resembles an inflated balloon let loose, allowed to whoosh and sputter and shrink and wrinkle into a feigned old age, his predator's body, after the rage and readiness to pounce, flaccid and directionless, his cowboy boots silent upon the tile floor.

"Hey, all *right*," Hank says as if he has just engineered a world disarmament treaty. "I knew everything was gonna be far out. Maybe I'll even play the stand-up in a couple of numbers tonight."

"Man," Bobo says, wrath still evident upon his face, his

dog eye blooming darker than ever, "anybody plays that piece of wood, it's me. You just ain't no stand-up player yet, dude. Anyhow, I don't think Colorado's ready for a rock band with a stand-up bass. They just want to boogie."

The bear moves his arms with deliberation, listening to the tinkling of the tambourines (the image of a small gray hare caught in the steel shark jaws of a forest trap flies across his movie-screen consciousness) that attach to his wrists by pretty red ribbons. "When do we go on?" he asks, always professional. As if sleepwalking, moving through a dream without sound, motion slightly slowed, Polly begins to fix Cassy's hair, to paint her eyes and cheeks, then speaks in a soft, singsong, mysterious voice which might be a Hindu prayer. Hank and Wayne nibble leftover fries.

"This bear's the only one of you who's right on," Bobo says, his voice high-pitched and dangerous. He throws his arms around the bear's arms and chest in a wild embrace from which the bear cannot free himself, his paws useless because of the tambourine shackles. "You all think that all you gotta do is smoke dope and talk cool and you magically become rock and roll musicians. From now on this bear's my main man, and all the rest of you are amateurs."

"I've always taken my work seriously," the bear says, shimmying his captive shoulders within Bobo's grasp.

Wayne's eyes grow clouded with liquid, and he says, "I never claimed to be Ginger Baker, or even Ringo Starr," but Hank's noisy animation drowns him out: Hank stomps up to Bobo, who must loose the bear in case he needs his fists to defend himself.

"I practice that stand-up every day, man, and I drive our equipment around in that hot little car while you get the bus, and I put up with these babbling chicks, and I even found the bear who's now your main man, man," Hank yells to Bobo's magnetic eye which seems to be the seat of his consciousness, at least as far as conversation is concerned.

"We're not supposed to fight until we all become millionaire superstars with differing artistic visions," Wayne says.

The bear works and reworks this collection of syllables through the maze of his brain, much as a computer juggles an insoluble problem, sure that the answer lies in some unexplored region, before it overheats and throws up the tilt sign; Bobo and Hank look at Wayne as if they might have to beat him up, but then their shoulders relax from punch-out posture and Hank smiles into Bobo's dog eye, which fades from a deep chocolate brown-black to its normal medium brown.

"Right," Bobo says. "We split up after we make our first million apiece, and then all cut solo albums using the Grateful Dead as sidemen."

"Well, I'm ready," Cassy says, emerging from the dream like a butterfly from a cocoon, her hair curling on many levels like a diagram of strata, eyes kohled so that they look huge, cheeks reddened, her mole painted black and with tiny lines radiating out from it as if it were a black star in a pale firmament. "When do we go on?"

"Any minute, sweetheart," Bobo says, his voice all syrup, all 1940s Hollywood agent: incongruous for a black man with a dog eye. "Everything's set up on stage. All we need is for you to wail your little head off. Bear, can you handle those tambourines all right?"

"Yes, but I'd feel better if I knew your songs," the bear says, his hands feeling like they belong to some other bear, a classic horror-film ploy in which a concert pianist turns into a psychopathic killer because of an unfounded (who knows . . . ?) belief that grafted onto his own musical wrists are criminal paws full of hatred for mankind.

"No time," Bobo says. "Just wing it for tonight, and tomorrow we'll rehearse. It's not like we're doin' Mozart's concertos or anything. It's real old-fashioned rock and roll, I thought you had that in your blood."

"Hey, no prob for the bear, man, you saw how this guy can dance, he's hot stuff," Hank says.

"I'll do my best," the bear says, waiting for his legs to readjust to the demands of reality.

The sound of applause richochets around the small wooden room until it comes to resemble a full-fledged echo, ringing and buzzing with resonance in the bear's ears. Then a knock on the door, a real percussion solo which straightens all their spines and sends Hank's hands into a simulated bass riff on an invisible instrument, a kind of warm-up exercise. The bear needs no warm-up (artists at the pinnacle of their profession don't need to practice, to warm up, to rehearse: whatever they do is art, transcending time and place and circumstance. The bear, unaware of this, knows that Dance pulses through his veins, sees no separation between himself and the Dance, feels the Dance to be an inherent portion of himself, his soul, whatever the most basic unit of bear-ness might be); he follows Bobo out onto the stage of the Hollywood Cafe, and senses the presence of many beings sitting out behind the blinding lights as the musicians and the singer take their places by the already set-up microphones. Confused, startled by the assortment of equipment, the lights, the invisible audience, the bear stands at the edge of the stage until Bobo whistles in a high, clear, nearly inaudible dog whistle which the other members of the band don't seem to hear; when the bear looks at him, he inclines his head to the right of Cassy, where the bear then stations himself in readiness to boogie, to dance.

"How're y'all doin' out there?" Hank yells, one arm upraised, at the audience.

"All *right!*"

"Fucked *up!*"

"Rock and roll!" come voices from various parts of a room the size of which the bear cannot gauge, topless and bottomless and of infinite depth: like the light of the sun unfiltered by prismatic layers of atmosphere, the lights sting his eyes with blackness, make the world a world of shadows, of stark blacks and whites like the reversed world of photographic negatives. Cassy, the nearest one to him and the only one he can clearly make out, wears a startling halo, a thin shimmering nimbus surrounding her being like an aura, so pale yellow that it nears white, moving with her like another, ethereal layer of skin which must disappear in daylight, see-able only in the heightened atmosphere of performance and of music. The others move slowly, darkly, like black holes in the space of the stage; when a couple of trial chords and notes sound out to test the hookups and the amps the bear leaps into the air, his tambourines clattering, because the music surrounds him, hammers in upon his sensitive ears, feels like the pressure of water, twenty feet beneath the surface, to his body. The two shadows that are Hank and Bobo nod to one another, arms move in western shoot-out parody.

"Ya ready?" Hank yells again, and a rhythmic clapping comes from the infinite room, not from all of it, parts reticent, involved in something else, not yet giving themselves to the mere promise of music, but enough. "Far out!" he yells, and the opening riffs cut the bear's ears.

The first chords, repetitive, familiar, full of cultural reso-nance, send the bear's knees moving in and out sensually before he can even perceive the barrage of noise coming at him: from behind, out of the huge stack of amps, from in front, from the small screened boxes that send the sound of the music as heard by the audience back at the musicians, from everywhere, bouncing off ceilings, floors, faces, tables. The music frees him of the idea of tambourines, his hands flying off into the air like eagles; his ears straighten, his neck grows limp, fluid, his hips cut the air as a mermaid's pro-pel her through her thick liquid environment. When his heels Mash Potato, his arms windmill so that the tambourines ring out, he's lost in the music, an unconscious dancing machine; the lyrics begin and he's in heaven. The audience whistles, stamps, then as if in sudden, spontaneous inspiration claps along, the perfect, catchy beginning to a rock show: a woman singing "Johnny B. Goode," an unwritten rule broken im-mediately, nothing rock and roll audiences like better than iconoclasm. Cassy's voice, high, strident, on a rocky edge of something not human, something akin to the howlings and bayings of coyotes, something barely controlled: how it sends shivers up and down the bear's spine, how it twists his back into dancing postures never before invented, how it rolls his eyes back into his head as if trance is imminent, as if the whole world were this voice, as if all senses combined into one to tickle his ears past pleasure into a new, unknown realm where he can only dance off the druglike effects of this laser beam of sound, dance unceasingly until it might end.

The bear Boogalooes his whole body down Funky Broadway, his arms blocking arrows of sound that tingle and sting his skin way down past the fur, but this seems much too tame, too loose, too laid back a dance to go with this voice, and his bear butt snaps in and out, suggestive and quick, while his arms Monkey, the tambourines punctuating Cassy's singing with their four-four clatter. His knees grow weak, so he Jerks down into a slouching posture, his hands shivering at the tops of his arms, high as they can go, like captive butterflies; he rises with a leap, his legs scissoring, then falls into a split that defies gravity as it drags him back up to standing with its own momentum which sends him Twisting, outrageous calves and thighs and hips moving in contrasting directions.

> *He never learned to read or write so well*
> *But he could play guitar like ringing a bell,*

Cassy sings, which catapults the bear up into the sound-waving air again until he falls with his shoulders and upper back arching, then touching the ground while his hips and legs remain elevated and his arms backstroke wildly, punishing the tambourines, gyrating his hips like a supine Elvis.

> *People passing by would stop and say*
> *Oh my how that little country boy can play,*

and the bear stands again, this time with languor, all grace, and starts a Freddy, arms tracing circles in the air, legs shaking loose, thigh not attached to hip, calf free from the bondage of knee, foot tied to ankle by a rubber band. Each new dance feeling like it could last forever, like it could consume him with its perfection, its fullness, but the song moves on from verse to chorus and back to verse, and the bear's body tells him in muscle twitches and unknown spasms that he too must move on, that a dance of all one step is not the Dance.

With his head rolled back as far as it can go, his elbows swinging and strutting, he slides into a high-kneed Stomp, one foot kicking out in front of the other in parody of forward movement, a bear mime practicing his walking against the wind. Cassy's voice lifts higher with each chorus, the effect that of a rocket straining to escape the shackles of earth's offensive, limiting gravity, to escape to the void cruise of space, to infinite possibilities, and she points her child's chin at the ceiling to hit the notes, her neck showing strained and thin.

> *Go, go Johnny go, go, go Johnny go, go*
> *Go Johnny B. Goode,*

the first word a scream, a howl, a curse, a moan lifting the bear off the stage like sudden wings, turning his mime into a crushing back bend, then carrying him up on his toes, on ballet pointe for an instant, before the flow of the dance resumes as if nothing but a dream has interrupted it. For the last verse he falls to his knees, shimmying his hips and shoulders while his arms Swim every stroke of the civilized world, the butter-fly, the crawl, the backstroke, the breaststroke, the tambourines going crazy with the delirium of underwater, his knees numb to the hardwood, his feet twitching in air and rotating on his ankles, the movement free-flowing and un-related to reality like the flicking of a sleeping cat's tail.

> *Maybe someday your name will be in lights*
> *Sayin' "Johnny B. Goode tonight,"*

Cassy sings, her hips swinging, her back arched and sensitive to the crackling of her own voice. She looks over at the bear, at his holy-rolling, grabs the mike from its stand and struts

over to him, doing her own brand of the Dance, California
style, all limbs loose and sensual, each move of the hips a
rehearsal for sexual encounter. The bear senses her nearness
before he sees her, the electricity of his performance creating
a radar aura around him as potent as the electric fences that
protect the mansions of wealthy paranoiacs. With a motion as
lithe as the snap of a whip, he leaps up and dances next
to her, their steps unique but in tandem until, as if by acci-
dent, by the slightest miscalculation, their hips brush, right to
left, and the image of lightning striking both bodies simultaneously crosses the bear's black-as-outer-space consciousness,
his eyes nearly blinded by the metaphor, and he whirls around,
a full three-sixty, and does it again, this time left to right,
and Cassy swings into him with the ease of a pendulum, then
swings away, dancing a few light, febrile steps of her own,
unnamed steps without conscious inspiration, separate from
art unlike the bear's but with a magnetic, sexual appeal no
bear could duplicate (sexual suggestion for bears being a
whiff of something on the breeze; but the bear feels light-
headed as he sees her hips slowly circle above her legs, as
lissome as the rings of Saturn about their unchanging, luminous center, feels a tingling akin to that caused by her singing
and yet different, a tingling starting in his legs rather than his
spine, a chill calling for the right tender touch, the cure for
the fever). They bump hips again, side to side, then away with
an intricate walking Funky Chicken with the knees, Mashed
Potato with the heels, then back, butt to butt, then Swimming away, side to side while Bobo strums, plucks, pounds on
the electrified strings of his gleaming instrument as high-
pitched and ear-cutting as Cassy's screaming voice but with
the metallic edge, the machine hum that might cause dogs to
run wailing into the night after a phantom fire engine. The
emblematic riffs that began the instrumental bridge sound
again, and Cassy plants her feet as if her voice comes from her
whole body, or as if she were no more than an antenna, a
lightning rod, a receiver and transmitter for this voice which
is her essence, her audible soul sprung out through her mouth:

Go, go Johnny, go, go, go Johnny go
Go, oh Johnny B. Goode,

and the bear whirls on a single toe, his arms outstretched and vibrating the tambourines, a gorgeous pirouette liberated from the music, from the corporeal limitations of the body, before he falls straight as a two-by-four to the ground, his arms catching him in the ultimate pushup, then catapulting him up again where his legs scissor, then fall into a perfect split when his body lands without a sound just as the last chord, the last tremulous echoing of Cassy's voice, bounces off the back wall, the ceiling, the teeth of smiling and yelling faces and flutters to the stage at his feet like an exhausted carrier pigeon.

"All *right!*" Hank yells through a barrage of screams, thrown napkins, whistles, through aircraft and antiaircraft, the aftermath of the music as noisy and reminiscent of movie apocalypse as the music itself. "Rock and roll," Hank yells.

Cassy stands at the mike waiting, untransformed, a regular small woman without her secret identity as double agent; the bear remains split, legs like clock hands pointing to an early evening hour, his body limp, tambourines silent. What *danseur noble* would be required to solo immediately after a pas de deux? But when the first chords of the next song sound, the bear knows without knowing that his legs will propel him up, up again, that he will soar with the joy of Dance and forget the limitations of muscles and bones, that his eyes will close and his tongue will loll and the music will run through his veins in place of blood, faster than blood, jet propelled and outside the bounds of all natural laws, of the inevitability of gravity and of death.

"Shhh," Cassy hisses into the bear's ear, which startles him awake and ready to emit his loudest, funkiest fear moan, the kind he'd roar if a *Tyrannosaurus rex* chanced upon him in a primeval dream forest (that is, if the bear ever dreamed). Exhaustion sends him to the back of the bus after each night's shows while Bobo, Hank, and Wayne stick around the club to drink, smoke, talk to the women who catch their eyes, who return night after night to gaze at their favorite member of the band; after dancing two shows plus encores, their held-over act bringing in faithful and new fans, the bear's manic thrill, blood swiftly flowing like water in a rain-gorged river, like blood pushed by the speedy whispered inducements of drugs, head and feet connected not by a corpulent bear body but by gossamer, by cotton candy, and on his back butterfly wings enabling him short bursts of flight, gives way to limp stupidity and unawareness, to glazed zoo-bear eyes, to sleep so deeply entrenched in the bear void it's like antigravity floating in space, attached to the mother ship of consciousness by a slim silk thread. Cassy and Polly, after the shows, hang around the back of the club looking sullen, talking nasty to any man who might approach them, or return to the bus immediately to smoke and speak in their soft, sibilant, secret language which sends the bear to nondreamland, to sleep, quicker than a double dose of Valium.

"Are you coming with us or staying with them?" Polly whispers as the bear jolts upright, sitting like a stiff-backed marionette whose strings have just been pulled by an irate puppeteer.

"Whoooooo," the bear whimpers softly, a half-asleep plea for ghosts and goblins to depart, for scheming humans to have compassion for the all-out sleep of animals.

"You gotta decide," Polly says near-aloud. "We're tired of being bossed around by men, by that mean Bobo. We're splitting."

"Yeah," Cassy says. "We're hitching back to San Francisco, where we can make it as a solo act."

"Wanna come?" Polly asks in her stage whisper. The bear, in his postdance stupor, finds it hard to remember who they are, what they are doing in his night's sleep, what these questions they're asking mean. They might as well be speaking in their secret language, discussing the wonders of their special, peculiar double vision. He looks from face to face, his bland bear expression expressing nothing, and the women become exasperated.

"You're the only one we'd want to come. You're cool," Cassy says, her hands on her hips.

"And besides, he bosses you around worse than he bosses us. You're oppressed," Polly says, and the bear feels awakeness reeling around in his head like a drunken base runner, touching all the right spots but somehow not making contact.

"Okay," the bear says, his neck jerking around on his shoulders as if receiving the pulls and tugs of a phantom leash. Forgetting in an instant (did they ever exist?) the joys of dancing nightly for a live audience, head thrown back, eyes rolled up, tongue lolling, feet alive as a matched pair of frenzied jackrabbits: the constant gig, hope of all artistes in music-related fields, unending self-expression, black dreamless sleep when in life you have lived out all fantasies; domesticated bears, like house dogs, knowing the demands of loyalty better than the call of freedom, followers rather than leaders. Having no knowledge of prison escape movies, of the prerequisites of cinematic suspense, of "hurry" in general as a concept of time quickened by human need, he asks: "When do we go?" despite the small parcel each woman has by her side, one a beat-up backpack, the other a canvas drum, both bulging and odd-shaped from the collection of belongings stuffed inside.

"Now, man," Cassy says, prodding him in the chest with a tiny hand.

"Bobo 'n' Hank 'n' Wayne are out with some chicks they picked up after the last show. Groupies. If we work fast, we can be out of this hick town before they're even considering coming home," Polly says. "Well, if you're coming, stop dawdling and get your stuff together. We didn't have to ask you to come along, y'know. You're really one of them, a man, at heart."

The bear rises and, as his eyes adjust to the forestlike gloom inside the bus, he spies his Virginia Wolves flight bag, never unpacked, stashed in the same corner in which he threw

it when he first moved into the back of the bus, his night at
the dunes (though of course he doesn't remember putting it
there, doesn't know how it got there at all: he picks it up,
fits it under his arm, and his ownership of it resumes, no
questions about its life during the gap, no renegotiation of
contracts). "All right, I'm ready," he says, quite the bear-
about-town with his bag shining silver like a second moon,
soaking in and also reflecting the glittering drifts of street
light and starlight that find their way into the bus.

"Great," Cassy says, slinging her backpack over one shoulder. "California, here we come. Bye bye, hick city. Bye bye,
bus. Bye bye, Bobo."

"Right on. Huh, bear?" Polly asks, already imagining the
hot hard feel of the highway under feet, the adrenaline rush
as a car slows to offer a ride, the return to California to sing.
But the bear makes no response because he's noticing the way
the black building, the back of the club, seems to be a tangible piece of the night sky with only the doorway, the rear
entrance for the musicians and the help, cut out of it, perhaps a doorway to the infinite if it weren't the way to the
dressing rooms and kitchen and, as if he were within the
gravitational pull of a particularly appealing star, he can feel
himself drawn to the black building, would circle it like a
moon, but all he can do is stand in its back parking lot staring
in dumb animal fashion, eyes fastened to it like brown beady
buttons to cloth.

"Come on, man," Polly says, jabbing him in the ribs with
her small, sharp elbow. She looks all around herself, surreptitious and sly, a spy in the movies, a criminal on the
lam, and makes a low whistle by exhaling through her front
teeth, and drags her hand through the glistening night air
in a gesture designed by Davy Crockett to inspire straggling
and faint-hearted members of his troop. Sure enough, Cassy
and the bear traipse noiselessly after her like wraiths holding
their balls and chains in transparent hands, a nice straight
line of escapees from, perhaps, a combination mental hospital
and zoo.

After three brief and harrowing rides from dudes in cow-boy hats and pointy-toed boots, one with an eagle tattooed on his forearm, talons clutching a wavy, hairy olive branch, they find themselves plopped down upon a highway much as Dorothy finds herself deposited upon the yellow brick road: via mysterious incident as if out of a dream, with the help of midgets and fairies and animals, knowing only a general direction to pursue if they are ever to get home. The signs on the highway have long been defaced by gunshots, by highway sharpshooters trying their luck from speeding cars' windows with a belt from the brown-bagged whiskey bottle and a preparatory yahoo to ease the ensuing ear pain. But the highway number wouldn't have meant anything to Cassy or Polly or to the bear (who has developed an intense ani-mosity toward road maps and anything suggesting them, pre-ferring to rely on whatever instincts he might have left in the recesses of his bear brain, this city bear who would probably get more lost in your well-trod national park forest than a novice hiker who thinks moss grows on a special side of a tree trunk, who thinks he could navigate a ship or find his way home by perusing the skies until he finds the Great Bear, Ursa Major); all they can make out is the remnant of one magic word, WEST, which can only mean California to anyone with half a brain and experience on that golden coast, and the twins can almost smell the thick red brine of the Pacific Ocean as they stand with thumbs out in the middle of Colorado with only a city bear to protect them from male wildlife.

After midnight, and this Colorado night would be perfect for extraterrestrials to land their glowing, theatrical ships because of its velvet blackness extending in all directions like the magic sky at planetariums, a real celestial map to the stars' homes right there above the odd trio, but all they see is the black empty highway punctuated every so often by the simulated brassy starlight of car headlamps whooshing by them as if they were invisible: identical women and a six-foot brown bear at the side of the highway, the most visible hitchhikers east of Hollywood Boulevard. Pickup trucks haul by at near the speed of sound, the cab lights on so that the occupants can see to open their pop-top beer cans or to load their guns; station wagons filled with past-curfew high schoolers cruise more slowly, the heavy onus of injuring dad's car upon them at every turn, and orange glowing Unidentified Flying Objects hover from hand to hand in the silky warm darkness of inside. The two women and the bear stand at the highway side with thumbs up and out, but cars zoom by them, and the twins discuss, in their secret language, the situation while the bear remains stolid, silent, a veritable Gary Cooper among bears while the women chatter: caught in a highway limbo, no visible past with red brake lights disappearing down the road, no visible future approaching them in the form of metal and glass and Naugahyde.

"Maybe we ought to try some different strategy," Polly says, her little voice serious, and the bear listens in earnest, eager to understand each syllable of plot perfectly.

"Here's what we'll do," Cassy says. "You go hide behind those bushes there, so you can't be seen. We'll stay out here. Lots of guys are willing to give rides to chicks, but chicks with a bear? Then, when somebody stops for us, we'll tell them to wait a minute and we'll come get you."

"All right," the bear says. He hunkers away from the hot concrete of highway, the pavement still emitting the heat collected during the day when the orange sun shines down upon it, so that at night it appears to shimmer up in ghost form, rays flying up like phantom weed stalks as they do from the always burning sands of the desert. Though from the road the bushes look stickly and barbed, mean stubborn plants, the bear finds that they're soft and that they smell of sweet clean air, smell as green as forests and Christmas trees; he stretches out on top of them, and they mold to his body much as a water bed would, uses his silver flight bag under his head as a pillow. His animal's ability to relax in the most ridiculous of postures asserts itself and he dozes, a light sleep, sepia-toned rather than black, into which the intermittent drone of the highway intrudes like a dull hatpin into a half-blown-up balloon, never puncturing the surface, altering only the shape. Through the veil of sleep he hears the pickup pulling up along the side of the road, hears Cassy and Polly speaking in English to the driver, cowboy hatted and booted, to one another in code, small feet trotting softly next to him and away, then the sound of a truck motor hauling for all it's worth, Doppler effect in full swing, until it disappears audibly into the horizon. He awakens minutes or hours later (the night has become darker, with less depth, a flat black like the lacquered surface of a Chinese box) to find a piece of paper safety-pinned to the hair on his chest; a few lines of slanting handwriting like a brief haiku stuck together in the center of the page, and the bear pulls the safety pin free from his chest hair (unable to unclasp its delicate, to bear hands, mechanism, he must suffer the pain and indignity of this act of force) and examines the piece of paper, turning it over and over, looking at its blank back side, holding it longways and shortways and upside down, but still it makes no sense to him (though, from this clue attached to his own body like embalming directions attached to a corpse in a morgue, and from the immediate situation, the bear, being no dummy, being instead closer to the Sherlock Holmes of bears, can deduce his abandonment, though he cannot understand it). Not knowing what else to do, he opens the silvery flight bag and stuffs the paper in for unimaginable future perusal, returns to his bed of brush which remains in the shape of his burly body, a bear-shaped mattress, and goes to sleep, this time sinking into the deepest void, swallowed up into the black hole of his unconsciousness because he is back once more to the essential animal state of aloneness.

The dark blue Jensen Interceptor, a car like a bullet made to cut the night air, like a missile designed to flow silently through space, cruises at a speed well above the accepted highway standard, above moving violation level, but the bear, curled up like a bear fetus on the back seat, his nostrils filled with the near-tangible scent of leather, remains blissfully unaware. Sleeping a more dream-free and untroubled sleep than usual? Hardly, it's the same old antigravity drop into the void, though the possibility that a good job may be waiting for him at the other end of this ride, that he's heading back to California, would banish nightmares from the bleeding, bruised subconscious of any other out-of-work, on-the-bum, drifting dancer picked up in the middle of the United States (nowhere) by a Hollywood director in a very hot car on his way, at top speed, to save a movie begun by flunkies. The director talks nonstop about his life in the cinemah, thinking he has in the back seat the most interested of listeners, quiet and well-mannered, a bear after his own heart; revealing minutiae that would be found fascinating by only that hard-core group of Hollywood-novel readers, the ones who peruse all the gossip columns so they have the *clef* to every *roman*, who are up on the current jargon, who feel validated because their interest in film is both literary and visual. The topics of this monologue are not to be revealed

here, the point of view of the snoozing bear expressing all:
that this is no Hollywood novel, no production details to be
explained, no problems with key and nonkey grips and assistant directors; no affairs to be described in the most horrid
of avant-garde-Hollywood-sex manners, no use of the popular
slang for various body parts and techniques; no name-drop-
ping to lend verisimilitude to the plain blank page sullied by
black ants, no rock and roll stars just moved to Beverly Hills,
no femmes fatales, no famous profiles, no pretty-boys in pent-
houses; instead the bear sleeps in the back seat of the dark
blue Jensen Interceptor, missing what could be the opportunity of his life were he a blackmailer, a legman for a
columnist, or anything other than a bear artist. Does an exhausted dancing bear have a chance in the New Hollywood,
no matter how great his talents? At least he has the good
sense to sleep through the director's chat instead of butting
in with items from his childhood, well-used jokes, bits of his
recent past, stories of the screenplays he plans to write when
the rigors of real life allow him to settle down before that
most restful instrument, the typewriter. The bear dreams of
no screenplay, the vast movie screen of his consciousness tem-
porarily blank.

Perhaps the story told in this chapter doesn't really happen
in this manner, perhaps it's truly much more unexalted, in
much shorter sentences and much more mundane circum-
stances. Perhaps the bear never gets a ride from a director;
perhaps the ride is only from a script girl, or an assistant
editor. Or maybe he finds his own way to Hollywood after
many travails, after working on oil rigs in Texas, fruit picking in the Salinas Valley, coal mining in Wales, or any other
physical labor that sounds good in star bios. The possibility
of truth becomes the delightful empty core of Hollywood, the
probability of mythification: who cares whether or not Lana
Turner was really discovered, in her tight tight sweater and
sheath skirt, blond hair falling provocatively over one teen-
aged eye, mouth wrapped around a cherry straw, on a barstool
in Schwab's? *Sic semper urso:* you either take or leave the bear

story, as the bear cruises through the nightmare hills of the Southwest, the orange stone mountains like fingers gripping a sandy, perilous cliff, the sudden, strange-shaped protuberances rising like fantastical creatures out of the flat desert landscape, the eerie glow of moonlight on the silver granules and crystals, on the gleaming quartz, pale pink and white, on the fools' gold, on the squat plants blooming with rosettes that look like small reptiles and amphibians, pulpy, membranous flowers certain to induce unique hallucinations. Striations spring into the existence of the bear void, caused when he rolls over and exposes more or less of his hooded eyes to the rays of the moon, now on his back with his legs hanging limp in all directions, the void pale pearl gray, now curled up with his head against his belly, the void like midnight, like the insides of sea caves, like the hearts of murderers. Exhausted from waiting for rides, from looking with vain hope in his blank bear eyes at every passing vehicle, he might sleep all the way to Hollywood barring any unforeseen loud noises or changes in the tenor of the director's story, the ideal way to enter that Emerald City, as if borne upon the tip of a twister, set down ready for action at one end of the yellow brick road.

As often happens in Hollywood novels, the unforeseen does occur: the bear awakens with a start when "Gimme Shelter" suddenly blasts from the car radio, turned up to siren pitch by the enthusiastic director. The director sings along, "Love, children, is just a kiss away, a kiss away," and the bear jolts upright, as if he's been given a mainline shot of rock and roll, the purest speed, in his hairy arm.

"You dig music?" the director asks as he sees the alert ears sticking up into his rearview mirror.

"Do I dig music," the bear muses, never having thought of it in those terms: music being a way of life, a necessity, a buzzing in his otherwise deathly silent bear brain, the life fluid of the Dance, much as gorgeous-colored molds looking as if they belong in carnival in Rio grow virulently in agar, as peacocks dine on sumptuous African grasses. The bear hears music and then dances, no choice involved, no pervading feeling of pleasantness invading his muscles: the Dance comes upon him, more spine-tingling than nice, and he must dance as he must continue breathing, an action of reflex which nonetheless makes him heady, high, light-footed, brain and body full of lighter-than-air gases, floating fumes, a bear zeppelin with twinkling toes. "Yes," the bear says. "How about you?"

"Sure. I love the Stones, grew up on the Stones. I'm not as old as I look and I grew up late," the director says, then stops as a thought comes upon him as blatantly and unsubtly as a mallet hitting him over the head. "You ever done any acting? I might be able to use you."

"I don't act," the bear says. "I dance."

"What d'ya mean, you dance? Everyone in Hollywood dances. You got a great face, a real gimmick. I'm going out there to save a turkey movie from the trashpile, maybe what it needs is you. It's just a feeling, y'know, but in Hollywood you learn to listen to your feelings, to stay loose."

"I dance. I've played gigs everywhere as a dancer, a professional. I suppose I could act, though," the bear says, "if it would get me to Hollywood. California sounds good to me right now." California exists in the bear's head as a pink cloud or as a flock of silvery-golden butterflies, images of beautiful nebulousness flitting across the darkened movie screen of his mind and fogging it briefly with their ethereal glint; California has already become his end point in the depths of the confused bear brain, a future in the sense of irrevocability, in the sense that the bear knows that's where this dark blue Jensen is headed. The perfect hippie: blowing with the wind, going with the flow, moving wherever the ride takes him, the bear lies back in the soft redolent leather once more, though he can't control his four-four jiving toes which continue dancing to whatever song comes on the radio even after "Gimme Shelter" plays out. Luxury makes listening to the man in the front seat easier, even for an animal as eager to lie down in a bush as on a tufted sofa, and the bear becomes aware of how effortlessly his body sinks down into the back seat, of how the leather caresses his fur, cradles his head as lovingly as any bear mama, and the car actually (oh, cliché) purrs, a small, deep throaty sound like a lion having an ear gloriously scratched might make as he tilts his head into the scratcher to get it deeper, deeper, to tickle the absolute heart and soul of the ear.

"Baby, you got a ride with the right guy. I'm the Movie Doctor," the director says, tapping on his chest with all four fingers of his left hand as his right holds the steering wheel, as if the bear might confuse him with his car, might wonder which instrument was doing the talking: the middle finger of the tapping hand wears a huge diamond set in gold, the fourth finger a sky-blue star sapphire, points gleaming like the planet Venus in the summer sky, set in silver. "When directors have nervous breakdowns, when stars get put into private hospital rooms for exhaustion, when they get to the post-production and find out all their shots went wrong, that there's nothing worth putting together into ninety minutes of schlock, that's when they call me in. I drive in from Aspen, ask for huge fees to compensate for my lack of fame and for never seeing my name up on the silver screen, shoot a few key minutes or work magic on the movieola, and go home with a new car. When I was a kid, they said I showed more promise than anyone since Welles."

"What happened?" the bear asks politely; having learned through experience the tonalities of human speech, the rising and falling and the retorts these variations demand, the bear realizes that the tone of poignancy of the ultimate sentence needs a question to balance, to frame it much as Rembrandt's dark brooding sidelit wonders need massive wood and gilt frames to attract the errant, unschooled eye.

"I've got a colored past," the director says in a tone which indicates to the bear that a punchline is upcoming: he keeps his eyes glued to the back of the director's head, unbreathing, waiting, though he hardly ever gets a joke. "I was branded Red and blacklisted. The fifties, that's what happened. I got out of this country quick, and didn't come back until I could do it in style." The Movie Doctor spent a decade in Spain and in Italy directing improbable westerns and worrying about his tax attorney back in Los Angeles while the whole country tried to decide whether or not men and women of a certain evil political affiliation were convincing the youth of the land, through movies these errant artists wrote and directed, that making lots of money was bad. These evil men and women all made lots of money before the question arose; during the decade in which the paradoxical doubting began, many of them stopped making money because the bosses became afraid, and they had to give up their big houses in Beverly Hills and their diamond necklaces and their polo ponies and their Lamborghinis. Though the bear listens with interest, head cocked to one side, ears uplifted and round, the picture of cute stuffed animalness, he understands nothing of politics; when M.D. looks into the rearview mirror to confirm the fascination of his listener, he sees in the shape much the same as a single frame of film a frozen bear in an attitude of total concentration, and ascertains that here he has found an ally.

"You wait, kid," the director says. "I'll make you a star."

"Thanks," the bear says, knowing all about stars, having watched the heavens quite a bit recently, communicated with some major constellations.

"And you can stay with me, I've got plenty of room, till you make it big," M.D. says. "Just see you don't forget who gave you your start. If you should ever need a Movie Doctor." The director begins to hum along with the next song, an early Lou Reed number when he was still with the Velvet Underground, and the bear shimmies his shoulders against the leather, nods his head, even wiggles his ears a little as his toes dance away, his massive body ducking in and out of the director's rearview mirror as the music blares from the radio. "Hey, you got some good moves there. Bet you can really do it when you're let loose on the floor. Could be real cinematic. Let me tell you about this last picture I worked on, this real dog." But the bear already inhabits Danceland, his consciousness floating in deepest outer space, his eyes wound up in his

head like an OD'd junkie's, his arms feather light and shaking, his legs molten Jello; the director can talk all the way to
Hollywood as long as he keeps the radio blasting, certain of a
quiet, attentive audience in a semiconscious state, the best
state for listening to fascinating stories someone tells others
about himself.

"Can you take over for a while?" the director asks after
many hours of talking and driving. "I'm afraid I'm going to
conk out any minute, and I'd hate to dent this machine."
Dawn nears, the sky changing from navy blue to pale pink
with a strip of gray in between to mark the transition. The
bear rouses himself from half-sleep with this request, considers it, the unique combination of syllables which he's never
heard before, runs it through his tape-recorder brain over and
over hoping to detect, cryptographically, some clue to its
meaning. Finally, there can be only one answer.

"No," the bear says, "I don't think I can."

"That's pretty ungrateful of you, kiddo," the director
says. "You sit there in the back seat like a maharajah and I'm
your chauffeur for hours and hours, and when I want a little
shut-eye you go haughty on me. You afraid of driving my
car? It's insured. I'd rather you banged it up than me, much
easier to take."

"I can't," the bear says, considering his own words with
care equal to that which he used to decipher the Movie
Doctor's meaning. "I can't drive." The director studies the
bear's face in the rearview mirror as if the glass were a lie
detector able to reveal falsehood at a glance, but the bear's
blank earnestness shines through and he believes him with a
smirk indicating that nothing can be put over on him, no
artifice unrecognized by this creator of artifice.

"You really can't drive, huh," the Movie Doctor says, in
a flat tone like a television newscaster's, relating the newest
disaster, plane crash, typhoon, right before the weather and
sports.

"That's right," the bear says, holding up his huge front
paws to confirm that he's no Emerson Fitipaldi: claws curling

around the toes, fingers hardly worthy of the name, hair everywhere, definitely a parody of Lon Chaney's hands in *The Wolfman* when the full moon is cut into the action and the look of terror creeps across Larry Talbot's (Chaney's) face because he knows he's about to grow wolf (bear) claws. The director reaches into one of the myriad pockets of his denim jacket and brings out a tiny, shining silver case with a latticework top as fine as the mesh of windowscreens, holds it to his ear as if listening to the song of a captive cricket, shakes it lightly, then pulls the car over to the grim, dark shoulder of the road.

"See what you're forcing me to do?" M.D. asks without turning his head toward the bear, addressing the heavens, the interior of his car, the windshield, the radio disc jockey, absolving himself of all guilt as he pops a couple of small white pills, smiles, then returns the cricket container to its warm pocket. The next few hours of the ride, punctuated by pullovers to roadsides so the director can once again listen to the insect-whir of his pillbox, M.D. speaks and drives faster as his skin turns grayer, and the bear finds himself lulled to near sleep, despite the rock and roll of the radio, by the electric hum that seems to be coming from the human body in the front seat rather than from any of the magical appurtenances, cigarette lighters, window closers and openers, lamps and lights, of the car.

Los Angeles doesn't appear majestically from behind a hill, glimpsed around a bend or from the midst of a parting curtain of foliage; instead a collection of glittering lights, white and yellow and red, of streaking cars like moving neon in the black. Even if the bear had been awake when the dark blue Jensen finally arrived, he would've missed the moment because there is no moment: suddenly you realize you're in L.A., and that you've been in it for miles, that it's stretching as far out behind you as you can see, and as far ahead, the whole world L.A. The bear languorously rotates his head, blinks, and realizes he's in the city just as the car slows and pulls into a parking lot surrounded by the semi-trees which mark the Los Angeles landscape, the low shrubbery, the white lines of carefully drawn parking spaces to fit small and medium and large cars.

"Scenic tour time, kiddo," M.D. says, "only now it's not guided. A self-tour, very hip. While I run across the street to my bank and turn this little card into some hard cash, you cruise the park. This here's Hancock Park, there's the Los Angeles County Museum of Art, there's the famous La Brea Tar Pits, be careful you don't slip in and become a fossil. Meet me back here in ten minutes."

The moon shines yellow, a perfect banana crescent, above Los Angeles, and the bear steps out of the dark blue car, stretches by arching his back into a shape in which the moon could fit and reaching his solid arms out as far as they can go, claws extended in feline parody, looking like no dancer but instead like some prehistoric bear about to hunt for tender prey. Then he bends over until his arms drag on the concrete, a simian bear, his back hunched up, his chest forming a cave or trap, perhaps for small animals to wander into in the dark, his forehead, flat above his eyes and rather Neanderthal, sitting down upon the parking lot surface, flowing into the blacktop. By the time this ritual finishes the director has disappeared, and the bear looks around dolefully, not liking to be alone in strange territory. Nothing to do but explore or stay by the car, a clear-cut choice, and even though bears find choices nearly as distressing as being alone, without conscious thought the bear sets out upon the closest path, concrete as the parking lot, through the meager Los Angeles foliage to find who knows what.

There in the moonlight he stands stock-still, the fur on the back of his neck prickling and rising, his legs rigid, as other creatures do the same. Spectral bunnies aware of a nonhuman, noncanine presence, their forest incarnations aroused though they have generations of park-bred bunnies behind them; still in the moonlight, their ears gleaming with yellow auras and near-transparent, their silvery fine pelts shining too, white as with some ghostly phosphorescence, herds of them, fleets of them, all with their backs to the bear in bunny solipsism, the moonlight upon their little tails and shoulders, an ear twitching in one sector, a tail in another, a small leg moving involuntarily to scratch a head. Bunnies as anomalous as ostriches in amid the many-storied buildings, as anomalous as a bear at midnight in Hancock Park, all standing still as the statues of prehistoric mammals. The bear steps forward with hesitance, with trepidation in every silenced breath, and as he moves the bunnies too begin to move, not anything as blatant as steps but muscles clenching in powerful legs, ears lowering for flight, chests expanding with deepening, preparatory breathing. What does he want from them? His bear-ness surfaces, real, a hunter in the dark of Los Angeles, muncher of rabbits, throttler of smooth bunny necks, perhaps? Or a kinship, a knowledge of the oddity of the situation, of the unlikelihood of all their existences here among concrete, the concrete of parking lot and building and of statues of giant sloths and mastodons, the bunnies and the bear really as dinosauric as the former, as out of place? Who will ever know, because as he takes his first mincing, careful steps the bunnies leap together, a corps de ballet leap right out of the *Nutcracker* snowflake scene, and disappear into bushes, trees, shadows of street lamps like smaller, nearer moons (perhaps it's the lamps shedding the unearthly glow upon the rabbits after all and not the yellow bear tooth of a moon, though this doesn't occur to the bear), and a disappointment of large proportions swells in the bear heart, in the lungs, and escapes as a sigh; his body aching from the enforced stillness, he slumps into four-footed posture and hunkers back to the car to wait for M.D., safer in the world of machines because it is a world without disappointment, a world of functioning mechanisms, of perfection, or at least of fixability.

Leaning on the car, his skin still prickling from his run-in with rabbits, he hears a rustling in the shrubs and realizes that a Los Angeles park at midnight abounds in dangerous wildlife, that an urban forest far exceeds a sylvan one in fright potential.

"Looky here," a black kid says, tall and lean and with a skinny-brimmed hat on his head, shades on his eyes, sixteen or seventeen, and with a buddy being borne out of the shrubs right after him who must be about the same age only chunkier, just as invisible in the dark. "It's one a those giant three-toed sloths. I seen the statue right over there. Dig this, man."

"Nah, it's just a reg'lar bear, man, don't you know nothin' 'bout animal life," the second says, walking right up to the bear's chest and staring into his beady, bland eyes.

"No, man, I was raised in the ghet-to, the reason I never did good on those I.Q. tests, never knowed nothin' 'bout no animals but my papa," the first says. "You figure this three-toed sloth dude got any bread or dope on him?"

"No, man, don't you know nothin'? Bears don't carry no money or dope 'cause they ain't got no pockets to put it in. Look at this dude. You see any pockets, any purse, any brief-case or shit? Course you don't." Now they're both up close to the bear, he stands with his back glued to the dark blue paint job of the Jensen, his arms back against the cool of the car windows, his head straight forward, as if he doesn't see these surrounding thugs at all, as if he stares at some great phantom bunny in the distance, wistfully and expressionlessly. The chunkier kid fingers the bear's chin while the thin one tickles his armpits.

"What we gonna do with this three-toed sloth, you figure?" the thin one, obviously not the brains of the outfit, asks while looking right into the bear's eyes, as if asking this of the bear himself rather than his hefty companion. "Take him home to mama?"

"Le's jus' meditate 'pon this a second," the fat boy says. "See where this bear's standing? By this here fancy car, too fancy a car for any bear to be driving if you ast me I say he's got himself a accomplice, and that if we wait around like smart niggers we'll see some real bread soon."

"How come you grew up so smart and I grew up so

stupid," the thin one asks, the question man. "We both come from the same socioeconomic background."

"It's genes, man. My mama and papa smarter than your mama and papa, you dig," he says; then, "Shhh," as they both see the director crossing the street and walking toward the parking lot. "I bet this mus' be our bear's rich boy coming." The bear doesn't have the understanding of this situation necessary to panic, so he continues to stand still and observe until, like a light bulb being born out of his forehead, the idea that he and the director are in danger comes upon him full grown and armed, that these kids are interested in far more than the essence of bear-ness as opposed to the essence of three-toed sloth-ness. He hears the rappings of the director's high-heeled boots coming closer, closer, unconcerned and light, shuts his eyes so he can judge better when they're nearly upon the group of which the bear finds himself a reluctant member.

The kids crouch down around the bear's legs so they can remain invisible beside and behind the car until the last moment, planning to spring out and surprise their rich prey, counting on the bear's continued silence. A mistake. Calm and clearheaded (in the face of danger from two black kids: if the attackers were lions, tigers, rival bear factions, or any other branch of natural disaster, the bear's heart would be pumping double time, his muscles tense, his eyes clouded with fear, scared to near death), he waits until the footsteps are nearly upon him (though no conscious plan has been hatched for this: he merely knows what to do, animal prescience much better in certain situations than human forethought, intuition beating knowledge), then leaps into the air with a bone-chilling "Whoooooo" the likes of which the two kids from the ghetto have never heard, even when their mamas come after them with screams of disbelief at their boys' antics. The bear spins as he leaps, legs flashing like brown furry knives, body twisting in midair like a ballet dancer's, feet scissoring a mini-entrechat. The boys yell out wordless calls to each other to return to the bushes, fall away from the powerful legs, and scramble back into darkness just as the director comes upon the scene, the bear dancing in the air as two black kids first kneel at his feet as if they were praying to some hairy idol, then rush away tripping and calling and swearing, realizing something is very funny here, that the situation, appearing to be comic to the just arrived, is probably more than serious, probably dangerous since bears new to Los Angeles don't acquire entourages with such rapidity unless they're heavyweight champions of the world.

"What gives?" the Movie Doctor asks as the bear falls to his knees from his protracted flight, crouches for a moment on all fours as if preparing to take off after the two scramming kids, then stands and brushes himself off with extreme, near-human dignity before he answers.

"They were going to rip you off," he says. "They knew I didn't have any money, but they thought you would."

"Damn," M.D. says, impressed by the bear's perspicacious handling of such a real world situation. "If you don't make it in the movies, you can always have a job as my bodyguard. I'd scare hell out of producers if I came into their offices with you trailing behind me. Maybe we'll do that anyway on this job we're here for, see what happens. Okay with you?"

"Sure," the bear says, thinking that he's never met anyone who talks in so many words that don't compute, words that seem to mean nothing, the complete collection of syllables sounding like nonsense scat singing to the overworked bear brain, and all he can do is agree to everything.

"All right," the director says, obviously pleased with the situation he feels he's created, the director of real life. A new star, a bodyguard, a bear after his own heart: all three discovered in the course of a trip from Colorado to Hollywood, quite out of the ordinary; usually M.D. discovers some hitchhiking young women with mundane offerings, sometimes he discovers unique venereal diseases. This magnificent bear makes all those sufferings worthwhile, even exalts them since, at this stage, they seem to have been sufferings for art, for the creation of something bigger than any social disease, more important than any number of hitchhiking beauties. The director's chest visibly swells, his forehead blushes a proud, ripe pink, and he holds the back door of the Jensen open for the bear to climb in.

"We'll be home in a few minutes," he says to the bear lounging in the back seat, already used to luxury. "We'll get a good night's sleep, then talk business tomorrow."

"Great," the bear says, aware that his stock has risen, his image (an important Hollywood concept) has improved, but not sure how: perhaps crescent moonlight becomes him. They cruise down Wilshire Boulevard in silence, the director thinking about the coup he's about to create, the columns he's about to make, after introducing the bear to moviedom; the bear's head empty as the outer reaches of space, as the insides of a black hole, his small eyes hypnotized by the succession of streetlights and traffic lights and regularly placed bus stop benches and mailboxes, lulled, this urban bear, by every sign telling him he's back in the city again.

In Hollywood, following a strictly laid-out plan formulated by the Movie Doctor, the bear is seen dancing at all the right parties. This makes a small, elite sensation. Then he is whispered about over lunches at Chasen's and the Bistro. At dinner parties with studio heads and producers in attendance (and attended, also, by M.D.), it is mentioned that his Dance is sublime and unique, and finally he is spoken about at a meeting called to discuss the fate of several proposed films (everything done in the passive voice in Hollywood, the nonexistent town itself being a kind of massive magnetic ear collecting every murmured thought and opinion, every sleeper's dream in which he whispers a name, each instantly generated bit of gossip breeding in the air like a virus waiting for a warm, damp throat in which to nap, or carried on the wind like a spore). By this time the bear has become a phenomenon, and one day the phone rings at the director's rented house where the bear lives in a cabana by the pool and the director comes to the cabana's door saying, "It's for you," and winking one eye, a tic that the bear, in his amazement at getting his first phone call in a lifetime in show biz, completely overlooks.

The cabana's the most luxurious temporary home the bear's ever lived in, a palace amid his vague memories of other short-term and makeshift housing, amid motel rooms in which he slept curled up in a corner on the floor while people slept in twin beds, double beds, king-size beds, and water beds, amid vans and buses, barns he shared with cows and fleas and which inspired in him a hatred for anything bucolic and a love for a half-imagined rich life, which appears to him in a vision of a long-haired Persian cat, legs invisible beneath silky fur and plump body, curled up on a satin tasseled pillow (in this vision, more sensuous than most the bear has, he can almost smell the sandalwood incense and perfumed shampoo, the closest vision the bear has to a human romantic fantasy involving more than one of the senses, involving tingling skin and tickled nose and not simply closed eyes), and campsites, which equally repel him for he can feel there the presence of his wild relatives in his prickling skin, his twitching ears, in the invisible dreams of pursuit and kill which he has nightly (quite distinct from the bear void, for in these dreams he has a body in his sleep; his legs move as if running, his lips curl back from his teeth, and small moaning noises come from his throat and chest) while sleeping out under the stars with humans wrapped securely in giant quilted plastic bags and dreaming, with the aid of miscellaneous organic hallucinogens, of a groovy and unified cosmos circling around and above their heads.

The floor of the one small room of the cabana is covered with large cushions made of Indian fabrics, deep-hued paisleys, stylized and muted florals, and pretzeled interpretations of men and women together looking not unlike the enigmatic goddess with the many balletic limbs, making them seem like a primitive comic strip artist's attempt at portraying the idea of motion to his audience or cartoon-literate children. The walls of the cabana show the bear to himself, resplendent amid Oriental luxury, a pasha among bears, a reclining hirsute sultan, a bear created in the image of Saks Fifth Avenue interior design ads: the walls (and the ceiling, a phenomenon which mystifies the bear in his innocence and lack of awareness of Hollywood clichés) are mirrored, perfect jewellike mirrors with no cheapness or distortion, sheets of glass like the clearest mountain waters flowing from unsullied snow, diamond mirrors Windexed daily by a diminutive and taciturn maid who, the bear perceives, inhabits some other mysterious portion of the director's house and fears the bear living in her backyard: when the pool man comes on Wednesdays, she stands like a sentinel behind the vast sliding glass doors of the den, making sure he doesn't get gobbled up by the monster languishing in poolside opulence at the whim of her nutty employer.

When the bear holds the phone to his ear, anticipating wonders he can't imagine, not even sure what will happen and unable to speak a single word, a continuing stream of words comes to him and causes the fur on the back of his neck to bristle as at the sight of a crazed wild boar in the forest.

"Freitag," the voice says, "this is Freitag. I hear you dance. I don't care what your shtick is, bear, no bear, but we have a part for you, can't promise you anything, lots of others want this part and it's only because I hear you dance that I'm calling. Lots of others say they dance, but then you get them on location and turns out they need a masseuse and a trainer and a dancemaster and Capezio legwarmers and already you're over budget. Get M.D. to bring you down to the lot tomorrow at nine, to my office, you have an appointment already written down so no need to confirm and reconfirm like those others do as if calling all those times is some kind of magic charm, as if the telephone memorizes their insignificant names and whispers them to me while I doze here at my desk in the sunny afternoons. Little do they know I never sleep, and I never answer my telephone. I have twenty girls to do that, little girls with long red fingernails needing constant polishing, the outer office smells like a manicurist's parlor but at least they answer the telephone. Do you understand what I'm saying to you?"

"Of course," the bear says, his look bland and saintly, while the director stands at the door of the cabana watching the progress of the phone call.

"Then good-by," the voice says, and a crackle and a slam like thunder and lightning signal the end. The bear stares at M.D. with the inscrutable bear expression still on his face but with a tilt to his ears, a cute angling of the head, which M D., an ardent student of bear-ness by this time, fascinated since the bear moved into his cabana, understands to be quizzicality.

"He was a child star in the old days. Under a different name. We've all had two or three names here," the director says. The bear nods, a gesture he's unknowingly picked up from human companions, because, as a nameless beast, he's suffered the plague of changing appellations until most recently he's escaped names altogether, goes by his generic title, which at least fits him, which indicates that the bearer is a large brown hairy fellow associated with hugs, with a certain kind of sweet roll, with fire prevention and children's cartoons. The Movie Doctor has entirely lost track of his own real name and has become identified with his trade, with what he's better at than anyone else in the biz, no one calling him an affectionate name ending in "y" or "ie," no one even calling him baby or boobie or darling or any of the other common endearments you'd associate with living in Hollywood; he's simply M.D., the Movie Doctor. Who knows what incarnations Freitag has been through in his rise or fall from child star to studio head?

"What time does he want you, kiddo?" M.D. asks.

"Nine tomorrow morning," the bear says, then notices the cleaning woman spying through the kitchen window, no doubt ready to rush the cabana area with a meat cleaver or butcher's knife should the bear raise a clawed hand in the direction of her foolhardy employer.

"I'll be glad to go with you, and watch out for your best interests since you don't seem to have much of a head for that kind of stuff, no offense, baby," M.D. says, "but don't expect too much help from me. Freitag scares hell out of me. He's been known to dictate eight different memos simultaneously, sign contracts ambidextrously, and screw you so you don't know what hit you until nine months later when all you can do is claim immaculate conception. As a kid, could he tap dance."

That night, by the light of an ethereal Los Angeles moon shining as silvery as a giant klieg light, the bear swims in the director's shadowy pool, then hunkers out and shakes the magnetized water from his oily, thick coat. Falling asleep in the cabana, a pack of wolves crosses his movie-screen consciousness, the most ambitious of animals, their yellow keen eyes glittering as the moon, their mouths open in slavering smiles. At the sight of a pack of wolves, bears climb into their winter caves and pull their metaphysical blankets up to their chins, abandoning whatever recent prey they've caught and prepared to eat; but the bear, being a civilized dancing bear having done no time in Yosemite or Yellowstone, doesn't know this, and soon falls, weightless and struggling, into a troubled void of bear sleep.

No guards in ersatz cop clothes stand sentrylike outside the studio, in fact, nothing glitters or shines or croons love songs to Pico Boulevard to indicate the presence of magic going on inside, of the cosmic prestidigitation that puts twelve-foot-tall dancing and singing beauties of both sexes upon huge white walls in the dark.

M.D. parks in a painted-in spot numbered ninety-two with expensive European oil marks on it, years of Jaguars and Ferraris hungry for tune-ups sitting waiting for revved-up owners in high-powered meetings. The bear hesitates before getting out of the car. Should he have worn his basketball jersey? Brought his tambourines? Told M.D. to lead him into

Freitag's office on a leash? Amble in on all fours, do a somersault, applaud himself, then sit with his mouth open, his eyes dull, waiting to be tossed a small shiny fish or some other edible token of appreciation? Walking in nude, in just his bear fur, and on two feet, seems paradoxical, an unwise impression to give for contract signing, for commerce: either animal or human, but not both, either a bear or a man in a bear suit instead of this creature in between.

"This is your big break, buddy," M.D. says as he holds the car door open for the bear. "Just be cool. Do you want to live in my cabana for the rest of your life?"

The bear considers this, because the cabana's the best living arrangement he's ever had, private and warm and well-upholstered. Obviously, M.D. thinks he should have higher aspirations, M.D. thinks you either live in Bel Air, Aspen, or Spain, eat paté or caviar, and always have the pool cleaned once a week. The bear half knows, theoretically, the emptiness of all this high life, but almost thinks, for a moment, that sometimes art is rewarded, that the Dance bringing him fortune could not be misconstrued as grubby capitalism; this thought, wrapped in golden symbols, comes to him as small, dainty Dall sheep picking their way up an impossible cliff, tiny pink hooves stepping on glacial straightaways, fuzzy ears twitching, until they reach the pinnacle and look down on all the clumsy wolves and bears and moose down below, on all the earthbound mammals devoid of keen sense, of the ability to climb to the top of the world with nary a misstep. The bear gets out of the car, shimmies his shoulders, and winds his hips around in a sinuous motion while his hands snake through the air, feels that he still has It, and follows M.D. through many light green hallways to Freitag's office.

Freitag's office awakens in the bear a tiny, hidden-away genetic memory of a forest fire, and as soon as M.D. closes the door behind them, he plasters himself to the nearest wall, his back straight against the cool blue paint so conducive to typing and phone answering, his weight balanced on his toes to make sudden flight, if necessary, easier. The bear feels the air-conditioned breeze of anarchy tickling his nostrils and ears, and he doesn't like it. Young women stream before him in seemingly unconnected attitudes, looking like the continuous cels of animation drawing before they jell into a cartoon: women drop and pick up papers, women run from desk to desk to answer momentarily unguarded phones, women type and reach for erasers and type and reach for erasers, women open file drawers and slam file drawers. A syncopation, a complicated Jamaican percussive rhythm emerges from all this to comfort the bear, who begins to shuffle his feet in a Samba on the floor to the clicking of high heels, the tapping of long red fingernails, the exclamatory ringing of telephones; his heels begin a Mashed Potato, his hands start to tap the wall in time and his neck strains upward, his eyes closing, his mouth opening slightly.

"Come on, baby," M.D. says. "Save that shtick for Freitag if you want bigger bucks. Maybe he'll even give you your own parking space."

The bear quiets his body in what appears to be an elaborate nervous tic, a shudder into stillness resembling movie death throes, as M.D. announces their arrival to a golden-haired secretary sitting nearest a huge natural wood door, a sculpted door with many terraces like some rich Vietnamese rice farmer's paddy, a door with the built-up good karma of many noble redwoods, a door exuding power.

"Tell Mr. Freitag we're here," the director says, looking uneasily at the hairy ursine monolith beside him and trying to be polite with the introductions. The girl, who has a slooping Myrna Loy nose, piquant Jean Harlow eyes, and a wide Gina Lollobrigida mouth set onto a face of smooth white powder, looks at her perfect fingernails and cuticles without examining the new callers.

"What name, please?" she asks in a voice imitative of the ideal cadence of the universal Time Lady on the telephone, the comforting three-in-the-morning voice always in control because it knows the exact and correct time.

A woman driving a flock of fluttering white papers like

doves toward a file cabinet strides by the bear, and he cowers and wishes for a cave with three covered sides to protect him from the elements. The Movie Doctor says, "Tell him his bear is here. We have an appointment."

"It will be just a moment," the girl says, "why don't you have a seat. Your bear too." She breathes inaudible words into an intercom as M.D and the bear find seats as near her desk and away from the swirling maelstrom of the outer office as possible.

The bear's toes dance an intricate ballet as he sits, inspired by the dissonant music of the office. M.D. stares at the sculpted door with a lost-in-space look, the ability of humans to travel through the void at the most inopportune and unusual moments, leaving their vulnerable bodies exposed to the horrors of reality, in this case a horde of maenads with all the weapons of modern office technology.

"You may go in now," the golden-haired girl says, tilting the top of her head toward the ominous door while her hands, red-nailed and parodying prayer, stay in front of her face.

Freitag stands, with a phone in each hand held a discreet distance from each ear, behind a gigantic rosewood desk: a robust man, large and memorable, with the beginnings of wrinkles around his eyes and mouth, the thinning hair, the thickening stomach much regarded by masseuses and tennis pros. People speak of him constantly in the studio halls, his name a litany, a broken record, an overused piece of teenage slang picked up by *Time* magazine, the name of the deity or the President in an election year. People say of him: "How handsome he must have been when he was young" (since all he achieves in advancing middle age is "a fine figure of a man," not bad for a studio executive but certainly not superstar material). Nothing could be further from the truth (a word Freitag abhors, along with art, beauty, conscience, and budget): as a child, executing exhausting tap dances in single takes for awed directors and grips and script girls, they whispered, "Give him ten years, won't he be breaking hearts." As

an adolescent too lanky of leg and arm, his face a trifle lop-
sided with teenage dismay, the overlong nose, one eye higher
than the other by the slightest fraction of a man-made measurement but still discomfiting to conversation, the mouth
hanging open a moment too long after forming a tortured
word, they said, "He's at that awkward stage, just wait until
he fills out, he'll be the biggest thing to hit the screen since
Valentino." Beauty of the face and body have clearly eluded
him through an asymmetry of rhythm, a man out of sync with
his true potential, and beauty of the spirit doesn't interest
him; his vicious staccato tap dancing became the rapid-fire
insistence of his speech, and he wears the finest hand-tailored
suits and shirts, and silk ties in the deepest colors, to perpetuate the myth of his youthful Adonis-self because of the
general Hollywood sympathy for aging and lost charms.

The Movie Doctor closes the sculptured door after himself and the bear (noting that on Freitag's side it is Danish
modern, blond and flat), relegating the office noises to the
twilight zone of nonsoundproofed peasantry. Freitag looks at
the bear with his eyes half closed, the look you get when your
nose is over a fine glass of wine just proffered by an anxious
wine steward, a look seeing through the walls of the restaurant
and across oceans to gently sloping hills in France covered with
bright green tangled vines as they might have been painted
by Van Gogh, to clichéd rural vineyards with buxom maidens,
their skirts hitched up, their toes purple, their hair in vaguely
suggestive disarray; Freitag falls in love with the bear, or
more probably, with the possibilities the bear instantly pre-
sents to his tap dancing brain for making vast amounts of
money for the studio. Freitag slams both phones down, smiles,
and sits behind his gleaming maroon desk, gesturing at the
same time that the bear and M.D. should also sit.

"You do the best bear I've ever seen," Freitag says. "The
walk. The stupid face. It's hard to believe. I'd heard you were
good, but what do they know, between three in the morning
and noon anything looks good to them. We had a small part
for a bear. We'd even seen two or three clumsy imitations,

oh, the zippers down the backs, the noses sewed on or made of shiny plastic. But now, I'll get the rewrite started right away, you're going to make this picture. I hear you dance. It's not asking too much to see a sample before we draw up the contracts, don't worry, I'll be more than generous with you, as an unknown bear you won't get a better deal anywhere in the city, I guarantee it. Dance."

The bear stands up and shakes his body as if shedding clinging drops of water after a quick swim in a river; with his mind clear and his feet ready, the music begins as it always does, sounding far away at first like a weak radio signal, the dial just leaving the all-news station and approaching the glorious top-forty-with-a-little-progressive-stuff rock and roll number, closer, closer, and the sounds, the beat, begin to swirl like opium smoke in his bear brain, permeating and sweet and ineffable: slightly sinister and desirous, it's Them singing "Gloria," G-L-O-R-I-A, Van Morrison when he still wailed, and the bear's knees begin to rise and fall, not straight up and down but with a slow-motion grace, articulation in his feet showing as the toes, then the ball pads of his furry tootsies, then his bear arches, then his heels touch the soft shag carpeting on the floor of Freitag's office and then in reverse motion lift up again. The sexuality of the song demands a protracted Jerk, and the bear raises fisted paws into the air and circles in a sports-car turning radius while jutting his short-tailed behind out, sinking lower, lower, his knees turning to rubber, his thighs meeting his heels, until he swoops and swerves out of his crouch in a movement usually reserved for champion ice skaters not bound to hard land but skimming the glassy magic surface of their dazzling water mirrors, making twists and turns and pirouettes seem as smooth as the invisible liquid that flows through all windowpanes. The bear comes out of the swoop and into a Boogaloo, rotating his hips and shimmying his shoulders, his neck a flower stalk in the wind, his head an overlarge, overripe blossom heavy with red red petals, his hands feather-light sparrows in the air. A brief dance, a dance for security and profit, though even so the bear's art transcends capitalism and wins an ovation from Freitag as the bear stoops into a bow and then resumes his seat, hardly winded, eyes unshining, unpatinaed as ever, expressionless.

"Wonderful. I'll give you a thousand a week, you're just an unknown you must remember, and you'll have to do publicity appearances for us, the regular stuff, talk shows, the opening of shopping malls, maybe eventually an autobiography, ghostwritten of course. You'll get a small percentage of the first picture, and the percentage will be renegotiable after that, to both of our advantages, I'm sure you can see the point. I'll have our legal department draw up the contract if you agree. You can come back sometime next week to sign and so we can work out the details of your first picture, your image will be very important from now on, in fact will be the property of this studio, not to be abused or desecrated, much as if you'd borrowed somebody's vintage Rolls-Royce to drive around in for a while. It's settled then."

The bear looks at M.D. to see whether or not the offer is as it should be, but the Movie Doctor's gaze wafts out Freitag's window like smoke, focusing on the tops of buildings, the clouds skimming them like marshmallows floating on hot chocolate, the gentle filmy air outside the window that gives everything in Los Angeles a tarnished golden glow. In the courtyard outside of Freitag's office, two men in bear suits and pink tulle tutus get into a car parked near M.D.'s looking disheartened and rumpled.

"All right," the bear says to Freitag. "It sounds fair to me. Probably the best gig I've ever had."

"A marvelous voice," Freitag says, eyes half shut and glazed, tilted a little heavenward, "perfect for the movies, for the leading man, just a little diction coaching to remove some of that roughness around the edges, perhaps you ought to learn some French to help with that. There's just one other thing. A name. What is your name? Can we use it? Will it look magnetic up on marquees? We must take all this into consideration, you know, even today with all the funny names actors insist on keeping. Your films will be middle of the road, family pictures. Most families aren't too bright. You need a name they can remember."

"He does need a name," M.D. says dreamily, as if talking in his sleep.

"I don't have a name," the bear says, sounding slightly riled, "and I don't want one. I've gotten along all this time without a name, and no one's minded."

"Hold on, mister, just hold on. Our imagination department will think up a name for you, and you'll like it. What are we supposed to bill you as, a big question mark up on marquees, a big blank space? That doesn't sell tickets in the Midwest, Mister Bear, that doesn't bring smiles to children's faces when they say it, doesn't make mothers' eyes light up. Do you understand what I'm saying to you? Do you?"

The bear shrugs, a gesture designed to communicate his easy acceptance, after all, of any ridiculous human contrivance, his basic docility, his alternative to a sheepish smile and nod (but given the reality of bear flesh and its rolling, tumbling nature, the acrobatic fat just under the fur, a shrug becomes a hilarious earthquake); Freitag's face shines with victory and happiness, such is his delight with his new discovery, such is the love he feels for this bear with the shimmering blue aura of dollar signs all around him and with the invisible zipper in his suit.

"Mister Bear," Freitag says again, "you'll like it here in Hollywood. I sense the kind of fellow you are from your dance. A fellow dancing to a different drummer, excuse the expression (Hollywood was built on clichés, you know, there's money in clichés), a fellow longing for the better days of the past when everything was simpler, sex, money, I suppose even love. You'll fit right in here if you don't look too closely. But then, you're an artist, you know the value of artifice. All of those chumps out there who tear the days off their desk models each midnight, they think false eyelashes are a sin. I don't care if you're a bear or not a bear, if you get my meaning. Do we have a deal?"

"Sure," the bear says; his head feels full of tap dancing images, almost as if he's lain in soft fall leaves for a nap only to find out later they've been ant-infested, and that the busy insects have invaded his ears, his eyes, his nose, and are trying to carry away bits of his brain for a picnic. With no corresponding bear vision for superstardom, the bear finds his head to be ice clear once M.D. steers his hot car back onto the straight roads outside, and has no difficulty taking a little snooze during the trip home. Not cut out for the world of business, the bear finds himself exhausted, his heavy body like a medicine ball let loose in a crooked-floored gymnasium, his eyes befogged as if by a most pernicious night. So he sleeps, when men would be toting up the figures in their heads, adding and subtracting, buying Porsches in their minds. The bear speeds into bear dreamlessness in the back seat of the Movie Doctor's Jensen Interceptor with no fear, no camera-shyness, no tax attorney, no alimony payments, no Cannes Film Festival passes, no wide-lapelled tuxedo, no guest spots on the *Tonight Show*, no experience in commercials: the last of the Great Hollywood Discoveries, leaving Freitag blushing with love like a schoolboy seeing for the first time the dark brown top of his young English teacher's nylon stocking.

Here's what we've got in mind, you let me know what you think, whether you okay the project or don't okay the project," Freitag says to the bear as the bear sits across the giant rosewood desk from him, alone with the tap dancing mogul in his blond-doored office for the first time, a solo meeting required by Freitag, to the bear's confusion and bewilderment. "We've got this western, a pedestrian project, with a part for a bear, nothing special or big, just a mundane bear part. Then you came along, and everything fell into place, and instead of giving this picture to some kid from NYU we'll give it to M.D., if you okay it, and write you a much bigger part, nothing starring, you understand, just a good strong secondary part which could only get you a best supporting actor nomination, or maybe the Academy will have to invent a whole new category for you, give you some special deal like they did for Shirley Temple. So what do you say, Mister Bear? As a supporting player, you should be aware that you're getting quite a plum when I ask you to okay the director. If you say okay to M.D., then it's M D. If you say no, it's no to M.D. That's quite a plum for a bear new to the scene."

The bear looks over each of his shoulders, right first, then tilts his head to give him that look of near-human intelligence, positions both hands on his thighs in an attitude indicative of decision making (all this obvious to the ardent bear observer; the bear commits these actions thoughtlessly as part of the answer rather than as a procedure of anguishing over a choice). First of all, he has no idea whatsoever what a western is. West means the direction California was from where he used to be: no geography major, this much he learned from fellow hitchhikers sharing their own meager notions of the reality of the road, the notion that it always leads to the place you want to go. A movie about California? That sounds fine to him. Then there's the question of M.D. Why would this man ask him to refuse his friend a job? This mystifies the bear, who of course would like to have M.D. as the director of the film he will appear in (what is a director?). He carefully lets these thoughts flit past the great white blank of his awake consciousness, vacant as an unused sound stage, as the void of space, again in the form of butterflies that fly by too quickly really to observe, just a flash of gold like pure butter, a totality of wings, then nothing. "Sure," the bear says in his slow voice, "M.D.'s fine with me. I appreciate your concern."

"Wonderful, looks like we've got ourselves a project. I'll get a script to you within the week, don't worry about how small your part is, we're working on that already. And a script to M.D., let him think he's deciding to work on this, going back to feature-film directing at his own wish. With you in the film, he'll do it, I have no doubt. So—" and Freitag looks at the bear coyly, with much feeling which the bear can't understand (the bear who would never understand when someone was making a metaphysical pass at him), "you want to shake on it?" Freitag reaches out a shy hand across his mammoth desk as the bear watches, then instinctively responds like a good trained dog with his own hairy paw stuck out to meet Freitag halfway. They shake, the bear doing his best imitation of a human handshake, though his claws, the basic physiology of his fingers, don't permit a real strongman grasp. Freitag shakes with amazing gentleness, as if he were meeting for the first time the hand of his infant son; an ecstatic look lights up his eyes for a moment, gives them an opalescent glow, then leaves quickly, no sign of weakness to be shown this bear love; after all, business is business.

"Listen," Freitag says, trembling little tears sitting at the inside corner of each eye as his fondness for the bear's money-making potential spills out, "you're comfortable where you are, you're happy at M.D.'s? Because you're a man of property now, I could arrange for you to have your own apartment, even your own home, a two-car garage full of two cars of your choice, a live-in Spanish-speaking maid, whatever you want, name it. What do you say?" Freitag holds on to the bear's hand as if it were a life preserver with TITANIC written across it; the bear relaxes his claws, the pads of his foot, until a limp bear paw is clasped by a much more fervent human one.

"Life is fine at M.D.'s," the bear says. "It's the best living gig I've ever had." The bear tries to wonder what more there could be to life, what Freitag seems to be suggesting to him, but no picture conjures up in his empty movie-screen consciousness, the whiteness and blankness looking like a photo negative of a moonless, starless sky. His ears straight up and quizzical, he asks: "What more should I want?"

"All I want is for you to be happy, to have no complaints, to not come to me with stories of broken romances, of not being able to meet extravagant bills, of nervous breakdowns, of plastic surgery, of anything that needs to be kept out of the columns and out of people's mouths when they're having lunch in Beverly Hills and need something to talk about. That's all I want, Mister Bear, for you to be happy and for me to be happy, not such a difficult combination to achieve as long as you like where you're living. You've got a swimming pool?"

"I live right next to a pool," the bear answers, rather smug for an animal (of course animals can be smug: ever see a poodle dressed up in a brand-new pale pink sweater with matching ear bows?).

"Fine," Freitag says, his concern vanishing as he lets go of the bear's fatigued hand, satisfied that his prodigy is living a clean and fruitful life, about to make lots of money. "Wonderful. I'll have my car take you home; have a swim, sit out in the sun, enjoy life, soon you'll be a real star and you won't even be able to lie out by the pool in solitude, photographers and interviewers and writers for *People* magazine and the general public will be hounding you for pieces of yourself that you can't spare, and then you'll thank me for taking such good care of your early career."

"Thank you," the bear says, guessing from the intonations that thanks are called for, though he understood little of this speech.

"Don't thank me," Freitag says, holding up both hands, palms out, in a gesture of refusing a last drink from an alcohol-pushing party host. Traces of limpid adoration are still stored in liquid form in his eyes, and he must resist an impulse to hug the bear, something undignified, not fitting for a man in his position. Why has he never felt this way before about his big money earners (because they weren't six feet of fur, roly-poly and blank-eyed?)? "No need to thank me. Your natural talents, cultivated over years and years of work, have brought you here to me, I'm just the vessel of your success. I haven't made you, created you, any of those other clichés. You came to me fully grown, and I was just smart enough to develop you for the studio."

"All right," the bear says. "Good-by," and he retires to the luxury he's become so used to these days, a bear leading a cushy life full of soft pillows, deep leather car seats, sweet smells in the air, a pool heated to exactly eighty-two degrees on every day of the year. He sprawls across the back seat of Freitag's limo, most undignified; the walkers and bus waiters on the street try to get a glimpse of the luminary riding in the big car, but it just looks like a bearskin rug stretched across the back seat to them, and they figure James is on his way to pick up some blue-haired oil millionaire's widow who has to keep her thin old knees warm on the drive home to Bel Air. Some of the younger ones shout vegetarian and antihunting epithets, shaking their fists in the air, as the giant car rolls by, the driver unperturbed by the human street life, more wary about what he's driving home, though it seems quite docile, even sleepy, and looks well fed.

At home the bear dives, without thought, into the deep end of the oval pool in the Movie Doctor's backyard, swims back and forth once, then steps out to shake, twisting his body in complete three-sixties so that the water flying from him looks like the sputtering, flaming gases of the sun as they spray into the universe and the wet pattern left on the concrete resembles the beginning stages of the creation of the cosmos, random and starlike and incipient before the bear walks through it, leaving dark footprints over some of the most delicate tracings. He eats a couple of huge raw fish which the taciturn, resentful maid tosses daily through the door of the cabana, delicious dinners adding to the girth of his chest and waist, making him an even more delightful dancer because of the also-dancing flesh, then goes to sleep to dream of nothing, no eyes upon him, no guilty conscience, no memories, all the things that create dreams in humans, the cabana reflecting a collection of five bears, on each of the walls and on the ceiling, a menagerie of sleeping bears in various angles of repose.

In the morning the bear awakens to find five M.D.s staring at him, though this doesn't startle him; in fact, he wakes up as slowly as usual, stretching each part of his body as if it were something foreign to himself and waiting to be tried out, the way a baseball player might approach a brand-new bat. First one arm, the next, a leg, another leg, his neck bent in all directions, his stomach puffed out, then sucked in, his back contorted into various geometric shapes like textbook illustrations of all the theorems; M.D., the ardent bear fancier, watches quietly, astounded, memorizing the ritual for a secret bear diary he's begun keeping, noting every cute thing the bear does in hope of one day writing a bear novel or bear screenplay, bringing all this wonderfulness to the world which little appreciates bear-ness, which shoots at bears in national parks, enslaves them in zoos, mocks their corpulence in cartoons. M.D. understands bears, he's sure, and can discern the truths about the species from this one specimen that talks and dances and wins roles in movies after hitchhiking across the country.

"Good morning," the Movie Doctor says, pleased with the whole operation he's just witnessed. "The studio wants to see you later this afternoon. They've got something for you."

"They told me it would be a week before they had a script," the bear repeats faithfully, having memorized all of Freitag's speeches, a difficult task for the bear brain, but he wants to study their staccato rhythm, their unusual blend of indecipherable syllables, has intended all along to discuss them with the much more sympathetic M.D.

"I don't think this is a script," M.D. says. "Something else, very secret sounding, one of Freitag's gimmicks, I think. I'll go with you to the studio if you want, kiddo, make sure he doesn't walk on you."

"Yes, I'd like that," the bear says, finally awake and wondering what this human being is doing looking at him so curiously. In Hollywood, everyone seems to have an expression of warmth and amazement in his eyes for the bear, not the hard look of professional sizing up that might be expected. All except for the maid, who grew up in Iowa and was told zoo horror stories (kids being eaten, mauled, turned into lifetime bedwetters) in her childhood, an atypical Hollywood resident, actually she commutes from Glendale to go to work when M.D. isn't in town and demanding her continual services, such as feeding the visiting bear.

"Get ready, baby, and we'll cruise by the studio and see what the man's cooked up for you," M.D. says, running his hands through his thick curly hair as if to straighten it with a touch. "I'll be damned if he doesn't have unnatural feelings for you, that Freitag. Watch out, kiddo, or you might end up in the columns after all." He walks back through his sliding

glass doors which reflect, right around noon, the blue rippling
water of the pool, making them look like companion pools
ready to be dived into, as if giving the bear time to apply
makeup, shave, comb his hair, or dress. The bear sits on his
round bear butt on his sumptuous pillows in the cabana, examining the bear who stares back at him: looks all right,
the same as always, hair bleaching a little lighter from the
chlorine in the pool, waistline a little larger, but all in all the
same old bear and ready as always to hit the road. He continues sitting for a few minutes, trying to stay inside the cabana for the time a human being might think a bear needs
to compose himself for the public, an impossible feat since,
as soon as M.D. leaves, his toes start to itch and jive, his
shoulders want to wind and shimmy; the stillness, the Zen
clear-mindedness he's trying to perpetuate in his head only
gives way to the omnipresent rock and roll background that
always plays there, and his body wants to dance. He heaves
his heavy body up, does a quick fancy strut just to appease his
muscles, then trots off to the blue, swirling, sliding glass doors
to find M.D. and get going, find out what portentous secrets
Freitag has in store for him.

As they pull into M.D.'s usual spot in the studio parking
lot, the bear becomes aware of an itching between the pads
of his feet, the little hairs there tingling with tension, with
knowledge of their own existence, though he hardly acknowl-
edges this feeling until it strikes next, as he gets out of the
car, in his stomach. Gurglings, wrenchings, all the feelings
of having another living being in there, like the gremlins who
sit on the wings of airplanes, pushing and pulling and creating
all the mischief they can. The bear leans up against the car as
if ready to fight off the original midnight parking lot assailants, but all he can do is grab his own belly and make low
noises in his throat; no visions well up behind his eyes (and
perhaps even a man would not have recognized this series of
physiological happenings as a premonition, so used to heart-
burn, to indigestion, to migraine headaches), but he feels,
quite irrationally he knows, as if a pack of snarling wolves

were about to fall upon him for dinner, as if he were about to be trapped in front of a sheer rock cliff, tied up and shot full of tranquilizers, then shipped off to a zoo in one of the more depressing Midwestern cities.

"What's wrong?" M.D. asks as he watches avidly the bear first clutching at the dark blue Jensen with his mammoth claws, then doing the same at his own stomach, his eyes rolling, his mouth open with tongue hanging out one side and jumping about like a trained cobra dancing to well-known flute music.

"I don't know," the bear coughs out before a sudden calm comes over him like a cooling summer shower obliterating the merciless sun; his insides relax, his eyes sink back into his skull, his tongue snaps to attention and doesn't seem enlarged anymore, fits neatly behind his long yellow teeth. "I had a funny feeling."

"Well, don't tell Freitag about these funny feelings, babe. If he finds out you're uninsurable, you're out of the biz."

The bear nods, knowing this never happened before, that he's no epileptic, no wheezing hypochondriac, and also knowing, without consciously coming to any conclusion, that something is about to happen, that he must gird his bear loins, prepare for whatever Freitag has cooked up; his head spins with residual dizziness as he walks into the studio office building, following a few paces behind M.D. as if he were the director's trained bear. They traverse the gauntlet of Freitag's outer office, the bear, weakened by his parking lot malaise, walking hunch-shouldered and shaken through the Mongol hordes of secretaries, right up to the golden-haired woman who guards the mogul's door, the outside of which is as chiseled as her face.

"Oh, he's waiting for you," she says when she sees the Movie Doctor and his bear (the way she perceives this strange duo: bears do not have free run of the streets of Beverly Hills and Hollywood, they accompany owners on errands, much as poodles or Yorkshire terriers might). "Just let me buzz him to let him know," and she presses an unknown and mysterious code combination of buttons on the phone console as large as a stereo, coos into the telephone with an enigmatic, pleased look on her face as if she herself had brought in the bear, then motions to the door with her gloriously fingernailed hand, the nails done in dark violet today, long and graceful and Oriental in gesture.

The director walks through Freitag's monolithic door, stops, takes a deep breath, barring the bear from getting a peek of what's waiting for him, but he's patient as always, knowing that sooner or later, more likely sooner, he'll see. "Come in," he hears Freitag's staccato voice saying, "bring in our Mister Bear," and the director walks in, all the way to the far wall where the window looks out over the courtyard, until he's facing the bear who still lingers outside the door-way, knowing that his parking lot premonition is about to bear fruit, that the butterflies of prophecy are what's making that horribly whirring noise just inside his ears. He bats at his head with his paws, hoping to dislodge whatever ma-chinery drives him batty with its humming, then walks in too, stationing himself by the large rosewood desk before he follows Freitag's and M.D.'s gazes to a magnetic portion of the room.

There she is, a gorgeous female brown bear, nearly as tall as he, dressed in a pink spangled tutu and a delicate rhine-stone collar and leash which attach her neck to a small man in cossack clothes standing three-quarters behind her so as not to destroy the illusion that she exists autonomously, a bear on her own, separate from the world of human bondage. Her fur stands out in all directions, feathery and trimmed and poofed out by hairdressers, and she primps in a near-human manner, hands to her ears, then to her hips, then to her nose in mock-modesty (the bear can't see the cossack nudging one, two, then three fingers in her back to prompt her, making gentle tugs on the leash to indicate how she should incline her head), no cigarette burns or other marks of cruelty upon her, a perfect bear with the same bland, expressionless eyes (though on her they look now coy, now flirtatious, probably the way the glittering Los Angeles light from the large window strikes them, the way they water in the smog) as he has; their eyes lock, his arms stuck to his sides, his head straight forward, and the men in the room imagine bear lightning bolts being exchanged, smoldering rays being shot out, everything you find in romantic novels where the heroine's an orphaned governess and the hero's a Byronic brooder about to inherit a vast and spooky mansion. This goes on for seconds, minutes, and then the cossack pulls the leash around to her back and moves his fist cleverly in her neck, and like a clockwork ballerina she begins to dance.

A foot elevated in a kick, a rising on the toes, a subtle spin done within the restraints of the leash and the cossack's short reach, her arms stretched up to the ceiling, then down in a compliant attitude to her knees; her legs, thick and without inspiration, look like twin tree trunks, oak trees trying to plié, as they obey the commands of the fist in her neck, and though she points her clawed toes in parody of the best ballet style, she cannot escape her bear-ness, even if her arms flow as smoothly as snakes through the golden, shimmering air, even if her head tilts at piquant angles as it's pushed by the cossack's fist; her ears stand on her head at a diagonal, pointing to the wall in back of her rather than at the ceiling, indicating intense concentration, discomfort, effort, all the things the bear forgets when he begins his dance, all the binding things rather than the liberating ones, and he feels sick, his head full of the moths of distress once more with wings beating feverishly just inside his ears; his stomach once more grinds into the other organs like an on-the-loose bumper car in an amusement park, his knees buckle like molten rubber. The Movie Doctor watches, fascinated; Freitag smiles serenely, certain that it's love at first sight. Meanwhile the bear perceives that he's about to die from this aesthetic affront, all his insides churning blood through them, his extremities empty of liquid, mere collections of throbbing nerve endings; his feet feel leaden, rooted, his body sways above them like a flagpole in the wind, his eyes flutter in his head like sparrow wings as the dance continues, the galumphing girl bear now leaping into the air, toes pointing downward, and landing with a crunch on the reverberating, soundproofed, untested floor of Freitag's office.

"She's here with the Brazilian circus, but if you like her we'll buy her in a minute, nothing's too good for you, I even have visions of putting your offspring in pictures too," Freitag whispers as if at a virtuoso cello performance, but the bear hears only every third word, the others getting mixed up with the whirring, the humming, the batting inside his head, and suddenly there are bells and stars like some patriotic Fourth of July fireworks display surrounding the bear ballerina and popping inside the bear's eyes; she falls to the floor in a mock-dramatic bow, forehead touching the shag carpeting, arms outstretched toward him, legs in an unlikely split having just scissored twice in the air after the cossack yanked up sharply on the rhinestone leash. Prone, her tutu like overripe tulip petals around her bulky body, she lies there waiting for the signal to rise, but before it can be given the bear faints dead away in front of her, falling like slow-motion moving pictures of buildings being demolished, of bridges collapsing into waterways, of all types of destruction made graceful through the magic of movies.

"Catch him!" Freitag yells though neither of the other men moves, and the female bear still lies prone in her bow waiting for the okay; M.D. watches aghast at this new bit of bear lore, the Story of the Fainting Bear, watches the scene play out, the bear sink to the floor with ten times more grace than the whole dance of the female bear, Freitag's scream of concern, the cossack's bland indifference to animal disturbance. Nobody catches the bear who knocks his head on no furniture, crumples neatly breaking nothing. Then, as if acting out a scene from a movie, the Movie Doctor lifts the pitcher from Freitag's desk, levitates it through the air to over the bear's head, and spills its contents into the bear's nose and eyes, making a great wet spot in the shag carpeting, a darkening stain, and causing the bear to cough and wheeze and sputter like a cold car starting up on an icy morning.

A sense of drowning in unknown waters until the bear's black-as-the-bottom-of-the-Atlantic consciousness conjures up an image of the director's pool, the bear sees himself getting out of the pool, shaking off his hulking body, and he rises still in a trance, in his fainting stupor, and shakes his body and head in parody of his sinuous Twist, letting his mouth loll open in a look of intense stupidity, letting his tongue flail at his muzzle, finally shaking his eyes open so he can return to memory, to the scene that he unwittingly left. He opens his eyes just as the cossack yanks on the sparkling rhinestone leash attached to the delicate jeweled collar, which pulls the female bear up with one sharp jerk to a standing posture, her eyes dim with unrealization, no knowledge of the bondage she's in. The bear feels his eyes fill with fluid, become limpid with regret, with sadness, with inability to change the world (all this in a Promethean vision of caged zoo bears waiting for the long-anticipated daily meal, in slavering torment), and he shakes his head once more and sends those few teardrops flying around the room.

"I don't understand," the bear says, rubbing his eyes with his mitts, and the female dives back, crouches behind the cossack, stares at the bear with snarling teeth, with ears flat back against her head, sure some black magic joke's being played upon her: one of her fellow creatures speaking in a man's voice! The cossack pulls a small whip out of his black leather belt and strikes her about the head with it, on her cringing ears, on her snout, and she makes noises of fear and sorrow in her throat, high noises sounding as if they should be coming from a small kitten rather than a full-grown female brown bear, and she reluctantly returns to her spot in front of the cossack and stands once more in her demure posture, trying to control her grimacing mouth.

"You expect me to feel something for her?" the bear asks in desperation, his voice coming out high and low at the same

time, his ability to speak seeming to diminish in direct proportion to the growing disbelief of the female bear, "you
expect me to . . ." and the bear searches for some word he
does not know, some vague concept which appears in his
movie-screen consciousness as a mother bear cuddling and
playing with two young cubs, though he can't imagine where
this picture comes from since he can remember no mother
caressing him, can only remember his recent existence, life
in the Movie Doctor's poolside cabana. He rubs his eyes
some more as the female stands at attention, her body stiff
with fear of the bear though her larger fear of the cossack
keeps her from cowering and shaking and moaning. Freitag's
face changes from hopeful expectation and parental gladness
to the face of a disappointed old man, he wrings his hands
with anxiety and with a sudden uneasiness which he's caught
from the two large animals in the room, the one emanating
fear, the other bewildered grief, while M.D. still watches
in amazement, taking mental notes on the vicissitudes of bear
behavior.

"You don't want her?" the cossack asks Freitag in an in-
determinate accent sounding like Russian, French, Spanish,
and Italian blended together into a thick milkshake of deformed vowels and consonants; he's the only one who's re-
tained his composure, his voice even, his face as expressionless as the bears', the misdeeds of animals being everyday for
him, the whip a necessity, the leash a given. The bear looks
at Freitag in breathless anticipation, his near-human understanding disappeared in the shock, wondering what Freitag
will say, whether he will be forced to accept as a companion
this awkward bear female without grace, without percep-
tions, belonging completely to the one world that is only a
little more than half of the bear's being; his eyes meet Freitag's
in pre-answer trepidation as Freitag strives to know what the
correct answer might be, for in his mind he still has visions
of dollar signs, of a blessed union between these two would-be
movie stars, of somehow training this graceless female to talk
since the evidence demonstrates that bears can be taught

speech and grace, of a major coup for the studio with stock rising ten points overnight with the release of the bears' first picture together, a western with human roles subservient to the animal stars, a breakthrough in conception. But the very blankness of the bear's eyes frightens him, their wild expressionlessness, and he hasn't the heart, the will, to press this further, though through all this his love for the bear has diminished remarkably as he's seen the money-making possibilities cut in half, loves him only half as much.

"I guess not," Freitag says, the shortest sentence he's uttered since he was eight years old and already a virtuoso tap dancer.

"Thank you very much," the cossack says, making a curt bow, fingering his whip, yanking on the rhinestone leash to guide the female bear out of the office which seems to double in size when the burly animal and her trainer have disappeared out the blond door. The bear slumps into one of the chairs surrounding Freitag's desk, a chair that crumples and strains under his weight, bending like a pipe cleaner.

"Thank you," the bear says, everyone thanking Freitag for doing nothing. He stretches his legs straight out, lets his arms hang loose over the sides of the chair, leans his head on a shoulder as if all his body parts were disconnected, dislocated, or put together with only the most tenuous wiring keeping them a group but unable to make them sturdy and upright. Already the vision of the female bear dancing her heavy-footed dance fades from his head, turns to butterfly wings and then to dust, to melting snowflakes, to the ethereal petals of a blown-upon dandelion. His body aches all over as if from going ten rounds with Muhammad Ali, the whirring in his brain continues though he's gotten used to it as if it were the white noise from an office machine, and the presence of Freitag and the director hardly matters to him: he's alone in his thoughtlessness, in his stupor, recovering as if from a serious illness though all he's encountered, not viruses, not bacteria, not infectious spores carried on the wind, is a dose of unaesthetic behavior huge enough to knock him for a loop.

"He didn't like her," the Movie Doctor says, amazed, moving his fingers mysteriously as if writing invisibly in an invisible notebook in invisible ink, this inexplicable bear behavior cleaning his clock too. Only Freitag remains clear-headed enough to feel indignant.

"I do my best for you," he begins, starting slowly and gaining speed with every word as if tapping at a furious, increasing double time, "I write you in a big part, I take pity on your lonely situation in life, I find you a gorgeous female, this big girl who not only obeys over twenty commands but can dance, and with a thank you you faint dead away on me and I end up with the circus mad at me for wasting its time and its star bear on a philistine. People would think you don't appreciate me, me your friend and your mentor, your sponsor in this evil town, your benefactor. Life isn't so simple when you're six feet tall and covered with thick brown hair, people will be waiting to take advantage of you, to give you bum steers, but not me, and it's me you step on in your climb to the top; I should have known better than to get involved."

"But look at him," M.D. says, dreamy, not looking at the bear at all but at some extremely lucid point on the far wall, a revelatory point worthy of inspection, a clear spot revealing the wisdom of the ages, the secrets of the universe, the truth about bears, "he's no ordinary circus bear. I've been watching him for weeks now. I'm going to write a book about him. He's special, an artist." The bear looks at the director with awe in his blank eyes: that's the most intelligent thing a human's ever said about him, and it sounds too pat to be true, too good to be real, and the bear shakes his head once more to stop the leftover whir for a moment and make sure he heard right. The air remains cool, aluminum with the smell and feel of air conditioning, with M.D.'s words hanging on it as if they were written on a steel razor edge.

"I'm no ordinary bear," he says, paraphrasing the director since it sounded so good, although he's not exactly certain what it means, and mouths the syllables carefully, to be sure he's an accurate mimic.

"All right, all right, maybe my real talents have never been in the field of matchmaking, I was only trying to do Mister Bear a favor, get him some action, that's what Hollywood is famous for, and if the studio made a little bit of money from all this that would have been okay too, but I know when I'm beaten," Freitag says, sitting down and putting his face in both his hands, a gesture that makes him look young, even childlike. "So you're no ordinary bear, Mister Bear. An artist. Well, you'll get your chance to show what you can do soon enough, your script is nearing completion and M.D. has agreed to direct, so the package is almost put together. I thought we had a female supporting player lined up to act opposite you, too, but I guess not; we'll have to do more looking for that, but that's what we're here for, to arrange things so they'll be pleasant for our stars, we're actually just glorified baby-sitters and social secretaries. How I long for the old days; I bet Thalberg never tried to pimp for a bear."

"You're blowing all this way out of proportion, babe," M.D. says to Freitag, his eyes still looking like he's just smoked a joint of the best Colombian marijuana, his face flushed. "You've got this beautiful bear here, this first-class performer, this dancing machine, this hot hot property, this secret weapon, and you're bitching? I can't believe my ears. Just because he didn't go for the big klutz of a woman you set him up with: I thought we were all professionals here, babe, all real world all-stars." The bear holds the chair arms as if he's in a plane about to take off, splays his feet on the floor to give himself a solid base from which to swoon. Once more he hears human beings taking charge of his future and he's powerless, worse than ever because his sensitive animal nature can't seem to assimilate the events of the past few minutes, seems dangerously out to lunch because of them.

"Whoooooo," he moans softly, a quarter-strength moan unlike his usual bellows, a moan without body, without verve, with none of the sterling qualities of depth and impressive loudness. Both men suspend their conversation to watch his mouth open in a large o, widen, then close halfway, shaping the moan as it emerges like a potter molding his clay on the wheel, like a bear mother giving birth to a mouth-born baby-moan until it's all the way out and seems to linger on the steely air-conditioned air for an instant as a tangible thing before it finds its way to all corners of the soundproofed office only to disappear into the spongy walls.

"We've hurt his feelings," the director says, and Freitag looks alarmed. "He's touchy, you can't talk about him like he's not there, like he's some animal. I've been watching him for weeks and I never heard him make a sound like that before."

"I'm sorry," Freitag says, genuinely upset, sincere in his apology. "Don't worry, everything's the same as before, the script's coming soon, the Imagination Department's working on your new name, you'll be a star in no time. Don't cry," he says, anthropomorphizing to a certain degree because the bear's cry sounds more like a baby in distress, a baby with a deep voice, than like an animal in psychic or physical pain, though no tears come from his eyes this time, "we're still friends. I'm still mad about you."

"Whoooooo," the bear calls, louder this time, and he holds his hands out in a supplicating posture; the Movie Doctor moves in closer, eyes sparkling, front row center for this new development in bear behavior: as far as he can tell, the bear wants something, this bear who's never demonstrated any imagined wants before, who's been happy in his cabana next to the swimming pool, with his fish tossed to him twice a day, who refused female flesh of his own species on some vague aesthetic grounds understood by no man, this bear wants. Fascinated, in a faith healer's gesture, he reaches out one of his own hands and touches it to the bear's outstretched digits, waiting for sparks which don't flash out, not a major disappointment, and he withdraws his hand.

"Ice cream," the bear cries, remembering the only thing that's made him happy in the past, needing in this sad weak moment to experience again his life's happiness though he can't really remember what it was, just the words come to mind from the extreme unpleasantness of the situation, and he knows he must have it, and also knows that the Movie Doctor is sucker enough to get him whatever he wants: animals knowing the soft touches in the human world, the ones who can't resist big brown eyes. "Whoooooo," he moans balefully, impressing even Freitag with the enormity and seriousness of his desire.

"He wants ice cream," M.D. repeats to Freitag as if translating, and Freitag shakes his head in understanding.

"Right down Pico, take him immediately, I insist, we can talk business some other time, this poor fellow's suffering, can't have my favorite bear suffer," Freitag says, standing again behind his desk and gesturing with his upper body, leaning, as if half showing guests out the door.

"Right," M.D. says, grabs the howling bear by one front leg, and leads him out through the office and the halls where even jaded Hollywood secretaries, the ones who'd claim to the young men who take them out on dates that they'd seen and heard everything, stare in amazement, walk a little closer to the walls to avoid the bear's spitty cries, finger the buttons on their blouses as if their precious hearts might be exposed to the venomous assault of the beast. Finally they're at the car, the bear's wailing subsides when he sees the comforting bullet shape of the Jensen, its soothing midnight color, its leather interior, its ability to speed him toward the ice cream of his dreams, and the director holds the back door open for the tormented creature, gently guides his bulky body onto the creamy leather seat, then climbs in front like an overpaid, overtrained chauffeur to drive the car as quickly as possible to its important destination with a seriousness that could only denote to an unseen observer that state secrets shrunken to microdot size must be hidden on the bear's person (if an animal has a person: on his creature, perhaps a better idiomatic expression), and that said bear's person must be trailed by spies, by assailants and assassins and in need of the most capable, strenuous guarding. The bear enjoys this illusion he's half aware has been created, lounges in the back seat letting out an occasional plaintive sigh or half-moan just in case the director should falter at a yellow traffic light. A mission of the utmost seriousness and importance is being carried out, and the bear won't let M.D. forget it.

"Whooooooo," the bear calls out, plants his face and both hands against the brilliant diamond-glass of the car window when they nearly pass by a store with ice cream cones painted all over the front of it, huge, cubist, abstract cones looking like other utilitarian items, light bulbs, clubs, but the bear, tuned in to ice cream-ness, knows their essence, and the director, taking this cue, turns into the small parking lot, just four lined spaces, in front of the store. The store appears to be empty of customers, not much business in the middle of a weekday until the kids get off school and come in to try to steal things, sneak out without paying, smoke dope in the tiny makeshift bathroom, and throw food at each other. Two attendants stand leaning on the counter, gazing out their huge plate-glass window at the cars passing by, almost unaware that a customer has pulled into the lot until the more alert one nudges the other in the ribs and they both get out sponges and cloths and start polishing and cleaning in an effort at looking professional, as if the prospective ice cream buyer demands as much attention and artifice as one looking for a new car. One of them throws a switch that lights up the sign surrounded by the grotesque, painted, red, green, and brown ice cream cones.

"Thirty-one flavors," M.D. murmurs reverently, reading the sign as it sparkles neon in the field of phallic clubs. The car's engine ceases, M.D. pulls out the keys, leans to the door, then turns and asks the bear, "What flavor do you want?" as an afterthought, moving as if sleepwalking, as if lulled by this image of modern availability of desired goods, a capitalist dream of ice cream. This question stuns the bear: what possibilities in thirty-one flavors, what unimaginable delicacies, what delicious colors to tickle and cool his strained bear throat. The idea of going into the store himself, of looking at all the cardboard vats full of the stuff and choosing the colors, the flavors, without aid, never even occurs to him since he knows the rules and regulations of animal existence in the big city and elsewhere; he knows the Movie Doctor must select for him, that ultimately his ice cream cone will be dependent upon the man's good or bad taste, and he's resigned to this, even rather enjoying the fatalism of it, the ice cream cone to come floating back to him though he's put in no thinking time, no anguish, no dimes and nickels of his own. The bear cocks his head, one ear up, one down as his blank bear brain attempts to consider the possibilities offered here, the combinations inherent mathematically in the number thirty-one when it's applied to double- and triple-decker ice cream cones, but he comes up with nothing until he turns and looks once more at the front of the store and immediately he starts to salivate when he sees the red, green, and brown four-foot-tall ice cream cones tilting at piquant angles all over the building.

"Red and green and brown," he says, and the Movie Doctor shakes his head like a waitress at this instance of life imitating art, then gets out of the car.

"You stay here," he says to the bear, "we don't want to make any trouble, do we, kiddo. Besides, you're Freitag's secret weapon. We can't reveal you to the clamoring public too early, babe. That would be negative hype, poor PR, which is as lousy as bad karma."

The bear watches the director walk through the squeaking, ringing door of the ice cream shop, watches, hypnotized, as he walks to the counter and speaks to both employees, sets each one scurrying and digging into various cardboard vats of claylike, globby, gooey substances, and then he becomes too excited. He can't help himself: he's never wanted anything so much as he wants this ice cream (at least he can't remember ever wanting anything so much, the intensity of the experience helped along by the short span of his memory), and he slyly opens the car door and lets his feet hang out into the air. The glass of the store window has signs pasted on it advertising specials, ICE CREAM CAKE ROLL—$2.99, TAKE

HOME A QUART, SEE OUR CUSTOM BIRTHDAY CAKES, and for a moment the director disappears behind one of these large signs, obscuring the bear's view of his ice cream cone. Steam boils out his ears, his mouth opens in a silent roar, and he stands up outside the car, crouching so he won't be visible to passersby and driversby but so he can see that the Movie Doctor is having an ice cream cone put into each of his hands, receiving one from each of the attendants, and the bear's head starts to reel in anticipation, spit to dribble out onto his chest, the female bear forgotten, blotted out, in his desire. He sees M.D. reach into his pants pocket and pull out a handful of change, an intricate maneuver demanding his holding both cones in one hand, and the bear fears for the safety of his cone, wishes to levitate it to himself immediately (as house dogs sit and stare at dinner steaks defrosting on sinks, as cats concentrate their whole attention on goldfish swimming lazily in round bowls, animals all seek the power of telekinesis, the ability to bring desired objects, mostly food, floating and shimmering on the air to their waiting mouths, a trick they haven't yet worked out or the whole world could be in bad trouble).

The intensity of the moment can't be contained by his crouching, coiled-spring body, and he sticks one back leg out straight and goes into a whirling spin, arms folded on his chest in false nonchalance, face clenched in concentration belying the chaos bubbling inside the stifling confines of the bear brain. No music plays but the chant "Ice cream, ice cream," and his grounded foot lifts his hefty body to this tempo, turning, turning, until he faces the street in his dervish course and stops, stunned, each hair on his body standing erect. His neck prickles with a feverish, chilly excitement he's never known, and he stands still, one foot frozen in the air, not a wriggle in the toes, not a tremor in the supporting calf.

There, across the street, two lank people walk, the woman's wispy, oily hair blowing in the California breeze, the man stiff-legged, jerky, moving like a marionette controlled by an untrained puppeteer. The bear perceives many plantlike stalks sprouting from their hands, with flowerlike growths adorning the other ends of the stalks, trailing on the sidewalk. Actually, Joy and Ray walk a troupe of dogs in tutus, tiny, mangy Chihuahuas with bodies like well-stuffed pork sausages and legs like gnarled bonsai tree trunks, old Chihuahuas well past their back-flipping dog-tricking prime, with tutus like wilted tulips. Ray and Joy have perhaps a dozen of them, so progress in walking becomes tortuous with one or two of the Chihuahuas stopping at a time to scratch behind a frayed ear, attack a flea on a hairless butt. Or the leashes become entangled, causing the enmeshed canines to walk gimpily, fretfully, their bug eyes watering in concern and discomfort until Joy unwinds the leashes, freeing them.

"This is ridiculous," Ray says looking at his red, throbbing fingers encircled and entwined in leather Chihuahua leashes. "That dude who sold these little fellas to us should've warned us that we were getting an unruly mob instead of an animal act. The more I walk behind these guys, the more their bodies start to look like nice, fat footballs, and the more my toes itch to start kicking."

"They only bite you because you tease them," Joy says, sighing. She knows that he'll never understand animals and wonders why he's chosen to spend his life with them. "How much did we take in today? Enough to stop at a store and buy some dog yummies, or some rawhide chews?"

"Look over there!" Ray says, making an involuntary pointing gesture which momentarily strangles a few Chihuahuas, twisting their little necks into hunchback positions and bringing them to standing postures approximating those of a corps of spastic ballerinas.

The bear, dim eyes straining as his neck twitches in near recognition, sees the man pointing something at him (a hand? a stick? a rifle?), hits the ground, and assumes a sprinter's crouch, readying himself for the unknown onslaught. When Joy looks over in the direction Ray's pointing, she sees a backboneless hunk of brown fur hiding behind a dark blue Jensen Interceptor.

"Man, for a minute I thought it was our bear," Ray says. "What a meal ticket that big fella was." Ray's face, as near beatific as setting concrete can become, glows yellow in the late afternoon sunlight for a fraction of a second as memory softens the events of the real past.

"Our bear was bigger. Don't you remember? And our bear was so graceful. Like really big people are sometimes graceful," Joy says, brushing her hair out of her eyes as if she will be able better to view the past that way.

A jogger, a serious runner with all the protruding parts of his body sweatbanded, cruises by at top speed with the requisite jogging dog, a tall lean Irish setter, and all the Chihuahuas start barking and yipping, a Chihuahua orchestra performing a contemporary symphony, earsplitting cacophony, and the big dog gets pissed off, all these runts acting tough with him while they're wearing those sissy getups, and he comes over with his lip lifted and sneering and revealing huge yellow teeth. Joy and Ray scoop scads of Chihuahuas up into their arms and quickly turn the corner to hurry to the orange van parked down the block.

The bear crouches down lower as another car pulls into the small ice cream shop parking lot. The car's a '72 Buick convertible outfitted with huge tires, racing stripes, and an outlandish, large stereo with bulging speakers, driven by a high-school kid with his girl friend nuzzled up close to him. Before they can switch off their blasting radio like a loudspeaker system, the bear hears a few rumbling bars of the Rolling Stones singing "I Can't Get No Satisfaction," one of his old favorites, its sinuous, snaky riffs perfect for his outdated dances, made for hip shaking and head rolling and the suggestion of rubber in your joints, not a bone in your body. Within the space of a moment the radio blares and shuts off, the kids get out of the car to buy some ice cream, and M.D. opens the door to return to the bear carrying in his hands one mundane single-scoop vanilla cone and one glorious, huge, unbelievable, tricolored monster of an ice cream cone which, together with the Rolling Stones and the brush

with memory and all the desire in his poor bear brain, sets
the bear to dancing to the continuation of "Satisfaction" playing like a tape deck in his head.

He Boogalooes with shoulders strutting up around his
ears, holding first one arm out in front of him, limp, bouncing
to the music no one else hears, then the other until the arms
decide to come to life and begin climbing imaginary vines
with ideal grace while the bear feet continue to weave; his
head hangs back, forehead to the sky, eyes closed, tender neck
exposed to the Movie Doctor, his whole body dancing an ice
cream cone dance. As if he's reached the top of the palm tree
he's been climbing, he changes into a Twist as if sliding down,
his whole body Twisting the night away with abandon, lewd
and ludicrous, hips swirling, arms rotating, shoulders spiraling, everything about him moving in perfect circles like those
which diagrams of space shots show, the perfection no human
being can achieve. Lower, lower he Twists to the floor, then
bends backward and fans his knees as if parading under a low
stick, and he rises on the other side of the invisible stick trium-
phant and works right into a Locomotion, body loose again,
arms choo-chooing like pistons, feet shuffling. With the approach of the Movie Doctor, the imminence of ice cream, he
does a Chuck Berry Duck Walk, holding an imaginary cigar to
his lips and brushing off imaginary coattails, and the Movie
Doctor stops cold, stands still and amazed, awed at this display,
so that the bear Duck Walks right up to him, leaps into the air
scissoring his legs once, twice, three times, lands in a split
with back arched, head set free from the confines of neck,
then rises and grabs the ice cream cone which he swallows
in two large gulps. And, oh, the ice cream feels so good rushing down the short bear throat, makes his long yellow teeth
tingle all the way up to his eyes from the coldness of the big
bites, and his eyes close, in heaven, and his once graceful
body goes clumsy in flaccidity, in satiety, as the Movie Doctor
watches his bear star, the bear he could watch forever, the
bear deserving books to be written about him.

A Note on the Type

The text of this book was set on the Linotype in a type face called Baskerville. The face is a facsimile reproduction of types cast from molds made for John Baskerville (1706–75) from his designs. The punches for the revived Linotype Baskerville were cut under the supervision of the English printer George W. Jones.

John Baskerville's original face was one of the forerunners of the type style known as "modern face" to printers—a "modern" of the period A.D. 1800.

Composed by Fuller Typesetting of Lancaster, Pennsylvania and printed and bound by The Haddon Craftsmen, Inc., Scranton, Pennsylvania. Typography and binding design by Virginia Tan.